THE LION'S DEN

THE FIRST BOOK IN THE LION'S DEN SERIES

EOIN DEMPSEY

Go to eoindempseybooks.com to join my mailing list.

This book is for my brother Conor.

PROLOGUE

September 1932, outside the city of Akron, Ohio.

The sun was setting now. The horizon flashed hot orange and pink, the clouds morphing to match the backdrop. Seamus took a few seconds to and peer across at the skyline. Beauty seemed out of place here. No one was talking. The only sound was of shovels plunging into the dirt and wheelbarrows being filled. His hands were stiff, and he balled his fingers into a fist, pushed them out, then did it again. His gloves were almost worn through. His spine ached. He leaned back to stretch it out and produced an audible crack. The foreman was a hundred yards away, talking to one of the other company men, but Seamus knew he wouldn't do well to be caught slacking, even at this time of day. He pushed his shoulders back and got back to work. The ditches on either side of the road went back as far as the eye could see, but the road seemed to stretch out forever. How far he'd fallen. How far. He glanced at his watch. It was almost five-thirty, almost quitting time. The trucks would be here to take them back to the camp soon. It had been a good day today, not too hot and no rain. The worst days were when the rains came, and the ground turned into a muddy abscess, sucking at the shovels as they drove them in. Those days everyone came back covered, the whites of their eyes the only thing to differentiate them from the mud. This had been a good day.

The whistles to signal the end of the workday came. No one celebrated. Each man just took his shovel, pickaxe, wheelbarrow, or whatever he'd been working with and loaded them back onto the trucks. Seamus lined up, aware of the talking going on around him but not wanting to join in. He pulled a pack of cigarettes out of his pocket and lit one. The smoke filled his lungs and billowed out his nostrils as he exhaled. They'd have dinner to look forward to, perhaps a stew with a little meat in it and some vegetables, when they got back to camp. Then the drinking would begin. The same as every night. Each man had his reasons for drinking. What were his? Why did he wake up every morning with a hammer pounding inside his head and a tongue dry as desert sand? Why was he going to do it again tonight? He took another drag of his cigarette and reached into his pocket for his wallet. He took a few steps away from the group as he pulled out the faded black and white picture of his family. His old life in his hand. He was in the middle of the frame, dressed in a smart gray suit, with a look on his face befitting a man of stature. The children were seated on either side of him, except Conor, who was in his mother's arms. He remembered the day the photograph was taken, in a photography studio in Manhattan, on a cold winter's day back in '26. Maureen was ten, Michael was eight, Fiona, five, and Conor not even two. Marie wore a look deep content on her face. She was beautiful. It was the only photograph he had of them all together. Before the collapse. Before the consumption took his wife.

The trucks arrived, and Seamus climbed up and sat down

beside a man he didn't know. The man introduced himself, but Seamus didn't feel like talking. The stranger didn't take the hint. His name was Larry Proctor. He was a few years younger, about thirty. He had a thin face and a nose that pointed at the end. He was skinny and tall, and his clothes worn and ragged.

"And in case you're thinking I'm heir to the soap company, I can assure you if I were, I wouldn't be here. Can I get one of those?" Seamus reached into his pocket and drew out a cigarette for the man. "You been here long?" Larry said.

"Six months."

"Where you from?"

"You always ask this many questions, Larry?"

"Only when I'm getting to know somebody."

Seamus let out a laugh and took another drag on his cigarette. The trucks were moving now. The barren landscape on either side dragged into a blur as they picked up speed.

"I'm from New York."

"Oh, a city boy, eh? I bet you'd never done a hard day's work before the crash, did you?"

Seamus glared at him. "What do you know?"

"I see you is all. You've got that soft complexion, not like some of these guys who've been out in the sun their whole lives. What did you do before ... all this?"

"Before the world came crashing down? I was in banking."

"So, this is all your fault is it?"

"The crash? You're not the first person to accuse me of that."

Larry seemed to know better than to keep up that line of questioning. "You got a family back in New York?"

"Where are you from, Larry?" Seamus said.

"From Salem, Massachusetts. And no, before you ask, I ain't ever burned any witches."

"I wasn't going to ask that."

Seamus turned to look out at the landscape flashing past. Thankfully, one of the other men sitting across from them was from a town near Salem and released Seamus from the bondage of conversation.

They arrived at the camp ten minutes later. Dozens of men jumped down off the trucks. The camp consisted of twenty or so tents of various sizes. Luxuries like hot showers were a memory and the men had to travel to the barber in town to shave, but most wore a full beard anyway. Seamus said hello to several workers he knew, promising to see them later. He made his way back to the tent he shared with two other men. George Ellison and Sam Blake were there already, lying on their bunks. George had owned a chain of drug stores in North Carolina before the crash. He was about forty, with a shaggy black beard and a scar across his neck no one asked about. He had a wife and six kids to feed back home, and wore a look of desperation most days. Sam was much younger, maybe twenty. He was from Cincinnati, and had been riding the rails for a while before arriving here three months ago. He was a handsome kid with blue eyes, a shock of blond hair and stubble to match. Seamus said hello and sat down on his bunk. He reached under his bunk for a half-full bottle of moonshine and took a swig out of it. One of the local bootleggers was making a fortune off the working men in the camp. He came around every night selling his bathtub gin. Gin was the easiest booze to make, and mixed with soda pop or fruit juices was just about drinkable.

"Taking the edge off?" George said.

"Whatever it takes," Seamus replied. "Where were you guys today?"

"Digging ditches for water mains outside the city," Sam said.

"Same job, just different dirt," George said.

Seamus didn't answer. He took a key from around his neck and reached under his bunk for a small leather-bound chest. The key opened the lock. He reached in and pulled out a stack of letters, leaving the small bundle of banknotes behind. He locked the chest again and pulled the top letter off the pile. It was from Conor, dated three weeks before. There was barely any point in reading it—he could recite it word for word. But seeing the letters and words his son had written lit the darkness inside him. Conor was playing baseball and was on the same team as his best friend from next door. Was seeing his seven-year-old son playing baseball so much to ask? He looked at the last letters from the other three children for a few minutes, poring over the lines they'd written as if they held the key to his entire existence. No men cried here. It wasn't fitting for a grown man to show emotion like that. He put the letters back in the chest and slipped the banknotes into his pocket, making sure Sam and George didn't see what he was doing. The others didn't move as he walked out into the evening air. He strolled through the camp, greeting several men as he went. Several huge pots cooking over fires signified that dinner would be ready soon. Even with the substantial meals here, he was still slimmer than he'd been since he was in the army. The days were hard. It was difficult to get enough food to sustain his body. How much longer would he need to spend here? What was there to go back to? He moved past the last tents and left the camp behind, treading with care as he entered the woods—the only place he knew prying eyes weren't watching. When he was confident he was alone, he counted out his money. It was less than what he'd sent last time. Had he spent that much on moonshine? He made his way back through the shadows toward the light of the camp. He went back to the now empty tent and deposited the money back in the chest. He slipped it under the bed, grabbed the bottle of moonshine, and left for dinner.

George and Sam were around a fire they'd set with logs from the woods. Seamus took a seat on a wooden stump beside them. He finished his meal in seconds and went back for more. He got a few pieces of bread this time, dipping the ends in the stew. Seamus was able to savor his food now that the great hunger that had been gripping him was largely satiated. He took swigs from the bottle of moonshine by his side between mouthfuls. The bottle was almost empty within minutes. The men talked about the job, and the upcoming presidential election. Roosevelt seemed like a shoo-in with the economy like it was. A figure emerged from the dark behind them. Seamus almost cursed out loud when Larry took a seat on the stump beside him. He introduced himself to each of the men and settled down to eat. His silence only lasted as long as his food. He started asking questions again. He asked each man where he was from and what they thought of the job. George and Sam didn't seem bothered and answered his questions as he asked them.

Several hours passed. Seamus bought another bottle of moonshine from the bootlegger making the rounds. It was a little more expensive than the speakeasy in town, but that was to be expected. He returned to the fire where Larry was still sitting with the other men. They hushed as he came back.

"What are you talking about?" Seamus said.

Larry looked around. When he seemed sure no one else could hear what their conversation, he continued. "How long you planning on staying here, digging dirt?"

Seamus threw a stick into the fire. "As little time as possible. I just don't know how long that is yet."

"But if you could get out of here tomorrow, you would, right?" Larry said.

"Where you going with this?" Seamus asked.

"I was talking to the boys here," he said, gesturing toward Sam and George. Both men nodded in almost perfect unison. Whatever Larry was selling, they seemed to be buying it. "I have a proposition for you."

"For all of us?" Seamus asked.

"For whoever wants in. I could use three men."

"You could use three men? For what?"

"I heard something from a girl I met a few nights ago."

"What'd she say? 'Get your damn hands off me?'" Seamus asked.

The other men laughed. Larry smiled and took a sip from his moonshine bottle. "No, she didn't. I'd say the opposite actually. She works as a maid for some rich prick in town. He could be one of the guys benefitting from our hard work out here. She says he's got thousands in a safe in his house. Many thousands." He emphasized each word. "She got the combination."

"Why are you telling me this?"

"I could use a few reliable men to get the job done. I spoke to George last week. He said you and Sam were the smartest guys here."

Sam patted George on the shoulder. "Oh, stop, I'll get a big head," he said.

"I've never done anything like this before. Why are you asking me?" Seamus said.

"Because most of these guys 'round here couldn't find their head with both hands. I've done jobs like this before. The most important thing is to have a smart crew who ain't gonna panic as soon as something goes wrong." Larry took another sip from the bottle in his hand. The reflection of the fire was burning in his eyes as he spoke. "She told me all about the house." He pulled a piece of paper from his pocket. "Got a floor plan. Thousands, she said. Enough to get us all out of here."

"What's in it for her?"

"Thirty percent for her, same for me, the rest split between you three."

"Thirteen and one third percent each," Seamus said.

"Of thousands of dollars," George said. "If there's ten grand in there ...."

"We'd get thirteen hundred and thirty each," Seamus said. "I'm not doing it. Too risky."

"What risk?" Larry said. "There's no security there, just the old man and his wife. The security is the gate and the safe. My girl's gonna leave a key for us by the back door and the safe's downstairs. We'll have the key to the gate and the combination to the safe. We'll be in and out before anyone knows it. They'll sleep through the whole thing."

"This is your chance to get out of here," Sam said. "But if you want to stay here shoveling dirt for the rest of your life, fine. More for us."

"You're sure there's no security?"

"My girl's been working there for years. She needs the money to go see her sick mother in California or something. If you don't want in, there'll be plenty others to take your place. It's gonna be hard to find someone here as smart as you, though."

Seamus rubbed his eyes. Who was he now? He was contemplating doing this. Even a few hundred dollars would mean he could return to his family. The dearth of them in his life was almost too much to take. He knew they were safe, and the money he sent home meant they were fed, but what prospect had he of going back to them? He could be here for years. They'd be grown and gone by the time he made it back. He heard his wife's voice in his mind, imploring him to walk away from Larry and his job. Another swig from the moonshine bottle banished her. He barely used to drink when she was alive.

"Show me those plans for the house." Larry handed him a pencil drawing of the outline of the house. It was huge. The safe was marked in a room labeled as the downstairs family room. "Why four?"

"One to wait in the car. One to do security at the door. One to go into the family room with me and cover me while I open the safe."

"And he sleeps through the night?"

"According to the maid they sleep like babies."

"What? They wake up every few hours and cry?" Sam said.

The men laughed. Seamus remembered his children as babies. The mistakes they'd made with Maureen, and how bad he'd felt at leaving Marie to go to that godforsaken war in '18 when she was pregnant with Michael.

"Where are you getting the car from?" Seamus asked.

"The maid. Cora's her name. She said she'd lend it to us for the night."

"Where the hell did she get a car from?" Sam said.

"I don't know. I didn't ask. She's got a car—that's all you need to know."

"And no one gets hurt?" Seamus said. "I'm not going along to the goddamn OK Corral."

"What do you think I am?" Larry said, feigning insult taken.

"I have no idea. I don't know you."

"The OK Corral? How we gonna shoot anybody when we ain't gonna be carrying guns?" Larry said. "We're getting in and out. That's it."

Seamus had no idea who this person was and if anything coming out of his mouth was real or some vague fantasy he'd cooked up. Larry seemed to have absolute faith in his plan. There was some comfort to be drawn from that. Maybe this was the miracle Seamus had been waiting for, or maybe it was his chance to spend the next ten years behind bars. He hadn't seen his children in two years. That thought kept bobbing up to the surface of his mind like a cork in water.

"Why us?" Seamus said. "Don't you have other friends here at the camp?"

"I know other men here, sure, but no one I can trust."

"And you trust us?" Seamus said.

"You men are different than most of the workers here. My father had his own business. I was set to inherit it when the crash happened. You men are the same as me. I don't have kids, but I want better than this. One job and we're golden."

"We get to go home to our families," George said.

Seamus lit a cigarette, offering one to the others. All three took one. Would the man he was before all this even recognize him now? Would getting back to his family change him into someone he didn't want to be? He dragged on the cigarette before taking more moonshine. The dream of having enough to support his family, to be what they once were, drifted across his consciousness again. They'd never be the same again—not without Marie. They stood forever changed, but surely there was some way back. Was it this job? Would that rich old man miss the money? Was stealing to support your family wrong? There were no answers, only a decision to be made.

"OK, I'll do it," he said. The other men clapped their hands together with bright smiles on their faces. "Why do you care so much if I come?"

"You're the smartest guy here," Larry said.

"Dumb enough to say yes to you, though," Seamus answered.

The men laughed, even though he wasn't joking. He finished his cigarette and threw the butt into the fire.

"So, what's the plan?" he said.

Larry reached for the plans to the house, and the men gathered around.

~

Sunday was the day of rest at the camp. It was a time to write home, to sleep in, to prepare for the rigors of the week ahead. Seamus, George, and Sam spent the day in their tent, going over what they were going to do later on that night. None of them had any experience in anything like this and Seamus doubted Larry had either, despite what he said. Seamus suggested they not return to the camp after the job. The other men agreed that they'd make their way to the train station in the city and get the first train out the next morning. It didn't matter where. The three men packed up the few possessions they cared about. The letters from Seamus's children bulged in his pocket. His savings were in a money belt around his middle.

The hours in the day seemed to go far too quickly. Before they knew it, it was time, and Seamus and the other three men were waiting by the side of the road. The darkness seemed to envelop them. The only light was from the moon in a cloudless sky. Seamus looked at his watch. It was almost eleven-fifteen. Cora was late, and the men were questioning their decisions.

"Calm down. You'll be rich in a few hours," Larry said.

No one answered him. Seamus looked back toward the dirt track that led back to the camp. He could go back to the tent and forget about Larry and his plans. A car appeared in the distance, its headlights scything through the dark in front of it.

"Told you she'd be along," Larry said.

The car slowed to a halt in front of them. Cora, the maid, reached across the front seat and opened the door. She was young, probably not more than twenty-two or three. She was pretty, and her red hair fell over her forehead in charming ringlets. She was wearing a black dress and looked like she'd been to church that day. The four scruffy men climbed inside. Larry sat in the front. Seamus had made sure to shower that day. For some reason, it seemed important. Maybe because he knew he'd be in a car with a lady. The icy cold showers in the camp didn't encourage use, but he'd braved them that day.

"So, who do we have here?" Cora asked once all the men were in the car.

Larry turned around and was just about to introduce them when Seamus cut him off.

"No need to tell our names."

A smile spread across Larry's face. "That's why I brought you along." He turned to Cora. "These are the men who're gonna help us get rich—that's all you need to know."

"Suit yourselves," she said and lit a cigarette. The smoke whirled inside the car as she started the engine, and they set off.

"It's about a twenty-minute ride to my house," Cora said. "You men of mystery can drop me off. The old man's house is only a mile from mine—Larry knows where."

"And there's no security?" Seamus said.

"I told you that already," Larry said.

"No harm in checking," Seamus said.

"No, it's just the old man and his wife," Cora said.

"Any guns in the house?"

"Not that I know of, and I've cleaned every inch of that place." Cora rolled down her window and flicked the cigarette into the darkness. "It's gonna be an easy job. In and out."

Seamus bit his tongue. No use arguing. The car fell silent. Sam was shaking beside him. George was staring out the window. It didn't feel like they were going to be rich soon. They drove on.

Twenty minutes of near-silence passed before they pulled up at the corner of a suburban street. Cora turned around to the men in the back. "Don't mess this up. It'll be easy."

"In and out. We get it," Seamus said.

Cora glared at him for a few seconds.

"Don't worry about a thing," Larry said.

"The house is that way." She pointed to her left. "Here's the keys." She presented two keys to Larry. He took them with glee. She opened the door and stepped onto the sidewalk without another word. Larry got out and said a few words to her before bidding her goodnight. She disappeared down the dark street.

Larry took his place in the driver's seat, with Sam beside him up front.

"Let's go over the plan one more time," Larry said. He lit up a cigarette. The flame on the match danced in his trembling fingers. "OK. Sam—you're the driver. You wait outside with the engine running. We shouldn't be more than five minutes. Me and Seamus will open the safe, and, George, you wait by the front door to see if the cops come. You're the lookout."

"Got it," George said.

Larry put both hands on the steering wheel, took a deep breath, and started the car. Seamus looked out the back window. Cora was gone. There were no other cars on the road, no people on the street. Aside from the lights in a few windows, there was no sign of life. The car pulled to a halt at the top of a steep hill, about fifty yards from the house. Larry put the handbrake on. The house was just how he had described it. It was two stories, built with gray brick. Large windows stood on either side of what appeared to be an oak front door. If Cora was true to her word, her boss, Mr. Francis Sharp, a local rubber magnate, was asleep upstairs with his wife, June. Their three kids were grown and probably living in their own mansions now. Black metal fencing surrounded the house, but Cora had given them a key to the gate also. The men got out of the car. Sam took his place in the driver's seat and gave the men a nod.

The three men edged up to the gate. There was no sound anywhere. Absolutely nothing. Seamus looked at his watch. It was almost midnight. He reached into his pocket, took out a handkerchief, and tied it around his face.

"You planning on robbing the stage coach after this?" Larry whispered.

"You can't be too careful," Seamus answered.

A small servants' door sat to the left of the main gate. Larry took the keys from his pocket and slid one into the lock. He cursed under his breath as the key didn't work. He tried the other. This time the handle turned, and Larry pushed the door open. The driveway was lined with gravel, so the men kept to the grass. George shook his head as he beheld the two new cars sitting in the driveway. The three men stopped at the front door as Larry fumbled for the keys again. The door opened with almost no sound. The only light was from the moon and stars shining through the windows. Larry smiled as he led the other two inside. He held a finger to his lips as he motioned for George to stay at the front door to keep an eye out for neighbors or cops. Large oil paintings of landscapes hung on the wall on either side of them. A telephone rested on a small mahogany table. Thick shag carpeting cushioned their feet, and it was just possible to make out the twinkle of a chandelier at the bottom of the stairs.

Seamus remembered from the plans of the house that the family room was to the right. The safe was behind a portrait of Ulysses S. Grant above the fireplace. Larry tapped Seamus on the chest, and the two men walked toward it. Seamus took the painting off the wall and placed it against the couch. There was enough light in the room to make out the numbers on the dial on the safe. Seamus touched Larry on the shoulder, urging him to pause, to listen. Larry shrugged him off. He reached into his pocket for the piece of paper Cora had given him, squinting to make out the combination. A floorboard creaked upstairs. Seamus put a hand on the other man's arm, signaling him to stop. They both stood still a few seconds before Larry turned to the safe again. He whirled to the first number, twisting the dial on the safe, then, twisting it in the opposite direction, entered the second number. He entered the last number, looked at Seamus, and pulled the handle to open the safe. Nothing happened. He pulled on the handle again—still nothing.

"What the hell?" he whispered.

Seamus heard another floorboard creaking upstairs. "We gotta go," he said.

"You can't be serious," Larry said. He turned back toward the safe and entered the numbers again. Another noise from upstairs. What would they be forced to do if the old man came down? Seamus and the other two men had all agreed no one was to be harmed. Larry had never addressed the issue, had dodged the question when they asked him. Seamus felt like he was being squeezed in a vise. Larry pulled the handle again. Nothing.

"Cora got the wrong combination," Seamus said. "Time to go. I think the old man's awake."

"I'll deal with him if he comes down," Larry said and lifted his shirt to reveal a revolver.

"We said no guns."

"Relax. Just a few seconds. Let me try this one more time."

After trying the combination a third time, Larry pulled the handle and the safe opened. A huge smile spread across his face. The safe was packed with cash. He reached in and picked out a wad of banknotes.

"It's the goddamned jackpot," Larry said. They were all hundreds. He handed Seamus the money in his hand, pulled a bag out of his pocket, and began stuffing stacks of bills into it. Another noise came from upstairs. Where the hell is George? Larry was filling the bag, seemingly oblivious. Seamus was just about to tell him to hurry up when the lights went on. They both turned around and saw Francis Sharp standing in the doorway holding a double-barrel shotgun.

"What the hell do you think you're doing?" The old man roared. He was about five-foot-six, with a manicured white beard. He had a spare box of shells in the pocket of his dressing-gown.

"Now, just hold on a minute," Seamus said and slipped the cash in his hand into his pocket.

Larry turned around and set the bag of cash down. "We can talk this out," he said.

"Save it for the cops," Sharp said.

"I think we all need to take a deep breath," Larry said and reached for the gun in his pants. He drew it, but Sharp was too fast, and his shotgun thundered. Larry caught the full brunt of the blast in his torso, and his body flew back against the wall in a bloody mess. Sharp turned the gun toward Seamus. He went to say something but saw that the old man's mind was already made up. The shotgun bellowed again, but Seamus had thrown himself to the ground. The pellets tore the siding on the wall to shreds, splintering wood and plaster all over Seamus. Sharp reached into his pocket to get more shells. Seamus looked over at Larry's mangled body. HIs gun was a few feet away. Sharp would be reloaded in seconds and wouldn't miss again. There was only one way out, and that was past the old man. He was standing in front of the only door. Seamus reached for Larry's pistol, took it in his hand, and fired before Sharp could level the shotgun at him again. The bullet shattered the window and Seamus ran for it. He had the split-second thought of the money he was leaving behind but dismissed it as he jumped through. Better to be alive and poor. The sound of another shotgun blast rang through his ears as he landed on the lawn outside. The gun was gone. He'd dropped it somewhere. George should have been standing by the front door, but was nowhere to be seen. Seamus bolted for the servants' gate. He was through the gate by the time the front door opened. The car was still parked at the top of the hill. He could make out Sam behind the wheel. The kid turned around as Seamus ran toward him.

Seamus opened the door and jumped into the passenger seat.

"Where are the others?" Sam asked.

"Larry's dead. George is gone. Drive!"

Sam turned around to put the car in gear. A blast hit the back window, shattering it. Sam lurched forward, gasping in pain as the car stalled. Blood appeared on his neck and face. He was still breathing. The old man was walking toward them. He fired again. This time the blast hit the back of the car. Sam couldn't drive, but was in the driver's seat. There wasn't time to move him. Sharp was reloading his shotgun. He wouldn't stop until they were all dead. Seamus reached over the young man and took off the handbrake. The car began to roll down the hill. The shotgun sounded again, hitting the back of the vehicle as it began to pick up speed. Sam was in a daze, his eyes half-closed. It was hard to tell how badly wounded he was. Seamus looked back. Sharp was fading into the background as the car picked up speed. The car was careening toward the curb, and Seamus leaned over to take the wheel. He righted the vehicle momentarily, but the steering was too stiff, and they ran off the road and through a bush. The car came to a halt on the front lawn of a small house.

Sharp was gone, but the cops would be coming soon. Seamus leaped out of the car and ran around the driver's side. He opened the door. Sam almost fell out.

"C'mon kid. We've gotta get out of here." He pulled him out and stood him up, taking his arm over his shoulders. Sam was able to walk some but moaned in pain with each step. A light came on in the house. Seamus had no idea what to do. The kid needed a doctor, and fast. He went to the door and knocked. A man in his forties came to the window with a baseball bat, screaming at them to get lost. Seamus pulled out the wad of bills Larry had given him. There must have been almost three thousand dollars in his hand. He waved it at the man in the window. He stuffed the money back in his pocket and used his free hand to pull down the handkerchief covering his face. This man had to think he could trust him.

"I'll give you five hundred dollars to let us in the house," he said.

The man wavered for a few seconds. Seamus held up the money again. The man at the window nodded and went to the door, letting the two men stumble through. The kid was getting weaker, and Seamus had to take almost all his weight. The man led them into the kitchen and flicked on a light.

"Anyone else here?" Seamus said.

"Yeah, my wife and two daughters are still asleep upstairs somehow."

"What's your name?"

"Arnold."

"We need your help, Arnold. We won't do you or your family any harm."

Arnold helped set the kid down on a kitchen chair. Sam slumped over the table. He had lacerations on his neck and shoulders and an ugly wound on his right shoulder blade.

Seamus took the money out of his pocket. "Another five hundred if you get us to a doctor."

"You'll have to take him to the hospital. It's across town."

"No hospitals. I need to take him to a doctor to fix him up and then get him out of here. Think. There must be someone."

"I don't know, I mean, my friend is a vet."

"Where does this friend live?"

"A few minutes' drive."

"Let's go."

Maybe they still had a few minutes before the cops came. It was worth the risk. He'd be damned if this kid was going to die because of Larry and his idiotic scheme. And Cora ... how could she have missed the shotgun?

Arnold helped him carry Sam out to the car, and they laid him on the back seat. Seamus backed the car out onto the street, the wind fresh through the blown-out rear window. They pulled out. He expected to hear sirens, but they were gone by the time he heard a faint wail behind them. They drove a few minutes before turning down a dirt road to a wooden house. Arnold jumped out of the car and ran to the door, pounding on it. A minute passed before a bleary-eyed man with an impressive twirling mustache answered the door in a nightdress. Seamus got out of the car, waving the money again.

"I'll give you a thousand dollars to fix my friend up."

He just hoped he had enough. He'd already given Arnold his thousand dollars and hadn't had the chance to count what he had left. The vet agreed and went back inside to get changed. The two men carried Sam around the side of the house to an outside kitchen where he supposed they made sauce or the like. They laid him down on the wooden table. Seamus had time to count the money at last. He had thirteen hundred dollars left. A thousand for the vet would leave him and Sam with just about enough to escape with, but their dreams of getting rich would have to wait.

The vet came in, dressed as if he were about to birth a horse, with long black gloves and a stained apron. He was handsome, with slicked back black hair and sallow skin.

"What happened to this man?" he said.

"Shotgun blast. Through glass."

The vet examined his wounds for a minute or two. "It's not awful. If we can get the shot out of him and stop the bleeding, he should make it."

"Should?"

"I don't have painkillers for him, not ones that won't kill him, anyway. Put this is in his mouth, and I'll need both of you to hold him down." The vet handed Seamus a smooth, rounded piece of wood.

"Everything's going to be OK, kid," Seamus said to Sam before he put the wood into his mouth. The other man took his left arm while Seamus held down his right. The vet picked up a scalpel and began.

. . .

The process of taking the shot out of Sam's back and shoulder took about an hour. The vet stopped the bleeding and patched him up. Seamus handed over the money. Arnold left to walk home, Sam's blood on his clothes and Sharp's money in his pockets.

"He'll need to rest for at least twenty-four hours," the vet said. "But not here."

"I don't think we can do that, Doc. And don't worry, we have a train to catch in about three hours. We'll be out of here by then."

The police would be around in the morning, and it wouldn't be hard to find the skid marks leading onto Arnold's lawn. They had to get out of Akron.

"Just be careful with him, and make sure he has plenty of fluids," the vet said.

"Thanks."

"I'll leave you men here. You can be assured of my discretion. I'll trust you to let yourselves out."

Seamus nodded and handed over the money. The vet went back inside the main house. How could they have been dumb enough to trust Larry? The cops would trace Larry back to the work camp, and it wouldn't be long before they realized who he'd been talking to and who'd been missing during the night. He just hoped George hadn't gone back, for his sake.

"George ran for the hills pretty quickly, didn't he?" he said to the sleeping figure of Sam. "Smart guy. He knew better than to mess around once he heard the shotgun go off."

He let Sam sleep an hour past the dawn. The young man was groggy and in considerable pain as Seamus helped him out to the car. They drove to the train station in the car Cora had given them. The back window was smashed, and the rear was full of holes where the shot had hit. A few early morning drivers gave them surprised looks, but they didn't run into any cops. He dumped the car in the lot and helped a semi-conscious Sam into the station. Seamus figured Cora could get the car back later. It would be easy to say it was stolen. The first train was to Cleveland, but that didn't matter. It could have been to hell itself. Seamus paid for the tickets and managed to get the kid onto the train. They found seats at the back, far from the prying eyes of the early morning commuters. Seamus sat on the outside with the kid asleep by the window. The train moved off as the sun emerged from behind the clouds, bathing the early morning in golden light.

~

The journey to Cleveland took about an hour. Seamus let the morning commuters get off first, waiting for the train to empty before putting his arm across the kid's shoulders to take his weight. Sam opened his eyes for a few seconds, mumbling a few words about the camp before falling silent again. Seamus helped him off the train. The conductor glared at them as they stepped down onto the platform.

"My brother had a few too many last night. I gotta get him home to his mother before she has me for breakfast."

"We've all been there," the conductor said with a smile.

The two men stumbled on. Seamus flagged down a taxi outside the station, and they got in.

"Any decent hotels around here?"

The taxi driver turned around with a quizzical look on his face. Seamus knew what he was thinking—a man in his late thirties with a younger, unconscious man, looking for a hotel at eight in the morning. It was almost humorous.

"He's my brother," Seamus said. "He needs some sleep. We had a rough night."

"Sure thing, pal," the driver said. "I got somewhere for you."

"Nothing too seedy."

The driver nodded and drove on. Five minutes later, they pulled up outside what seemed like a respectable hotel. Seamus paid the driver, who sneered at him one last time before speeding off. He led the kid into the hotel lobby and sat him down on a couch in the corner. He went to the desk and got a room. The clerk didn't seem to notice the younger man or didn't care. After the same conversation with the elevator operator about drinking the night before, they made it to the third floor and then the room. They struggled through the narrow doorway before Sam fell on the nearest of the twin beds and was asleep before Seamus removed his boots.

The bathroom was down the hallway. Another man was standing at the mirror as Seamus walked in. Seamus returned his greeting and went to the other sink. He washed his hands, stretched out his aching back. The water felt good on his face. The whites of his eyes were flecked with red blood vessels. His short brown hair was knotted and uneven. Several days stubble lay rough on his face. He saw Marie's face in the mirror. He'd blocked out her dissenting voice for too long. He'd done too much she wouldn't have approved of. She'd made him a better man, made him a good husband and a responsible father. What was he without her? Was he the type of man who broke into rich men's houses in the dead of night, or was he a man Marie would have been proud of? It was time to choose. He went back to the room, too tired to do more.

The kid didn't stir as he opened the door. The bed was more comfortable than he thought possible. His children appeared as he closed his eyes, and he vowed he'd never leave them again. He needed them as much as they needed him.

~

It was lunchtime when Seamus flicked his eyes open. A few seconds of confusion about where he was ended when he saw Sam in the twin bed beside his. He put a hand up to his forehead as he remembered Larry's body flying back against the wall. George was probably on the way back to his six kids in North Carolina. The cops would likely be looking for them by now. Sharp was the kind of man who had friends on the force, the kind of man who the police would want to please. The story would be in the newspaper tomorrow, which gave them another day or so before they had to get out of Ohio. But would Sam be able to leave? Did he even have anywhere to go? He didn't seem to have moved in the night, but he was definitely breathing, and that was good enough for now.

Seamus got out of bed. He'd slept in his clothes and left a dirty residue on the white sheets. The money belt was still secure around his middle. He left it alone and recounted the cash in his pockets—Sharp's cash. They had three-hundred-eleven dollars. More than enough to escape. He checked for the children's letters. They were still in the inside pocket of his jacket, tied up with a piece of string. He took a few seconds to read one from Michael, his fourteen-year-old son, before putting it back in the pile. The rumble in his stomach drove him to his feet. He put his shoes on, went to the bathroom, washed up, and then took the stairs to the lobby. Cleveland wasn't a city he knew, but anywhere is welcoming when you've got money in your pocket. He walked for a few minutes before he found a restaurant and sat down for steak and onions. He ordered a sandwich to go and went back to the hotel room. Sam was still asleep, so he left the sandwich on the counter and headed back out.

The feeling of walking along the street, albeit alone, and in a city he didn't know, was liberating. He'd spent the last six

months digging ditches and laying pipe, and the previous eighteen wandering around looking for any work that paid. He'd
done it all—laborer, farmhand, carpenter's assistant, bookkeeper, fruit picker, and even a stint in a carnival helping set up
the attractions. The time in Akron was the longest he'd spent in
one place, and the job he knew he'd define his time away from
home by in his memories. But enough was enough. He was
missing his children growing up. Letters weren't sufficient.
Perhaps things had improved back home now, and there was
some work for men like him with degrees in finance. He
remembered turning down jobs five years ago. Everything was
different now.

His clothes were worn, and no amount of washing would
restore them now. He couldn't go home looking like this. He
walked until he found a haberdashery and had them fit him for
a new suit with a crisp white shirt and a hat to match. He
bought the same for Sam, guessing his size. He was a few
inches shorter, maybe five eight to Seamus's six foot one, but
they were both slim and wiry from months of digging in the
dirt. He asked the man behind the counter to dispose of his old
clothes and walked out into the afternoon air. The barbershop
was his next stop, where he got a trim and the best shave he'd
had in years. He almost felt whole again.

It was after four in the afternoon when he arrived back at
the hotel room. Sam was still asleep. Seamus put down the
brown paper package of clothes he was carrying, took off his
hat, and sat down on Sam's bed.

"Hey kid, wake up."

The young man stirred and then opened his eyes. The pain
hit him right away. His eyes shut tight, and he groaned.

"I got you some pills for the pain," Seamus said. He had
filled a glass of water already and handed it to Sam, who
downed it in one. He went to the bathroom again, filled the

glass, and came back. This time he swallowed the pills with the water.

"How're you feeling?"

"Like some crazy old man shot me in the back with shotgun."

"We have to get out of here tonight."

"Leave? Why?"

"Our descriptions are going to be in the paper tomorrow. We have to get as far away from here as possible."

"But they didn't see us, you had the handkerchief over your face, and I was in the car."

"They'll trace Larry back to the work camp, and it won't take Sherlock Holmes to figure out that we're missing and we were in cahoots with him."

Sam tried to sit up in the bed but stopped short and grimaced in pain. "I don't think I'm in shape to go anywhere."

"You're going to have to be. We can't stay here. I'd bet dollars to donuts the taxi driver that brought us here from the station this morning recognizes us in tomorrow's papers."

"You think we'll make the papers?"

"Rich men like Sharp don't like poor men taking their money. He won't rest until we're behind bars. It wouldn't look good in front of the other guys at the country club if we got away."

Sam didn't answer, just took a few seconds to digest what Seamus had said.

"You hungry?" Seamus said. He got up and brought the sandwich over.

Sam managed to sit up to eat. He was almost finished when he asked the question. "Why'd you do all this for me?"

"All what?"

Sam almost spat out his food. "All what? Bringing me to the vet to fix me up last night, bringing me here. Spending most of the money on me."

"You think I'd just leave you there?"

"I mean, we knew each other at the camp, but we were never close. We talked, but I don't know much about you, or vice versa."

Seamus stood up and walked to the window. "I couldn't leave you there, and I realized it was better to do something good with that dirty money, rather than keep it for myself, or even for my family."

"Thanks."

"No problem."

"No, I mean it. I owe you."

"We all owe somebody, kid."

Sam took a few seconds to finish the sandwich, and then the bottle of soda pop Seamus had gotten him too.

"I don't know if I can travel tonight."

"You can, and you will. No use saving you and then seeing you rot in the joint for the next ten years. We leave tonight. You can rest another three hours or so, but then you need to be ready."

"Where are we going?"

That was the question Seamus didn't have an answer to. Would it be safe to go the kids? Would they trace him back to his sister's house in Newark?

"You think you can go home?" Seamus asked.

"Back to Cincinnati?" He threw the paper plate across the room. "No. No way. I wouldn't go back if I could, and besides they'd never have me. Let's just say we didn't part on the best of terms. You see this?" Sam said and rolled back his shirt sleeve to reveal a dozen or so burn marks. "My old man didn't like using the ash tray so much."

Seamus sat down, unsure of what to say. He thought back to conversations they'd had at the camp and realized the kid was right. They'd never talked much about anything other than money and the job. He didn't know anything about him.

"How old are you, kid?"

"Eighteen."

"And you've been riding the rails how long?"

"Two years. Same as you."

"And you left because of ..." He pointed to the burns on his arm.

"And some other things."

"You got brothers and sisters still stuck there?"

"Got a little sister, age fifteen and a little brother a year younger. I been sending money back to a neighbor to give to them, cos I knew my Dad would drink it all."

"D'you reckon they get the same treatment as you did?"

He nodded. His lips were tight as a scar on his face.

Seamus stood up and went to the window. He spent forty-five dollars on the suits and another five on everything else. They had about two hundred and sixty dollars of Sharp's money left. The savings in his money belt were for his children, and no one else.

"You got much money?"

"Maybe two hundred bucks," Sam answered. "It wasn't so easy saving money in the camp."

"Tell me about it," Seamus said and sat down on the bed. "Get some rest. We're leaving in three hours." Sam laid down again and was asleep in a minute or two. Seamus stared up at the ceiling. He lit up a cigarette, contemplating the possibility of going home. 'Home' was the phrase he used in his mind, but it didn't have the same meaning it once did. The house he'd bought back in '21 with Marie was gone—repossessed by the bank. 'Home' was where his kids were, and that was with his sister, Maeve, her husband Frank, and their two daughters. They'd been living there since he'd gone. How could he go home now, with a few hundred dollars in his pocket and no job? What if the cops tracked him down? He took a deep drag on the cigarette and peered out the window. Answers didn't come easy.

~

The orange light of the setting sun was bathing the room when he woke Sam. The younger man grimaced in pain again as he opened his eyes. Seamus had the pain pills ready, and Sam took the glass of water beside his bed to down them in one. He got out of the bed like an old man and yelped in pain as he tried to lift his right arm. Seamus took his old shirt and tore it into strips to make a simple sling. He'd need to get into his new clothes before he could use it.

"I bought you a new suit," Seamus said and picked up the package at the end of the bed. He tore it open and placed the shirt, blazer, and slacks on the bed. Sam looked at him for a few seconds. "What is it, kid?"

"Thanks."

"Getting it on you isn't going to be easy."

It wasn't. Even with Seamus's help, the pain of putting on the new shirt and blazer caused Sam to cry out in pain several times. Five minutes later, he was dressed, sweat still beaded on his brow, with his arm now secure in the sling Seamus had fashioned for him. They were ready.

"You look good in that suit," Seamus said.

"Thanks. I'll need to make a good first impression wherever I end up."

They left the hotel room together and made their way out to the street where Seamus hailed a taxi. Streetlights were flickering to life as darkness fell. The newspapers would be going to print soon with reports of the robbery. Their life of anonymity would come to a temporary end. Time to go. It was hard not to think about money. Seamus had counted the notes in his money belt as Sam slept. He had one-hundred-and-thirteen dollars. After splitting the remainder of Sharp's cash, he'd be going home with about two-hundred-and-fifty. It would be enough to keep the children fed for a while. Maybe they could rent somewhere for a few months, but if he couldn't find a job, it would be all for nothing. The kids would end up back at Maeve's house, sharing a room with him. Frustration at not being able to fulfill his most basic task as a father surged through him. What would they think of him?

The thought to go somewhere else grew in his mind like a weed. The men in the work camp always spoke of California as if there were more jobs there than could ever be filled and the living was easy. Year-round sunshine and rolling surf. Somehow, he doubted the fantastic stories the men spread around the campfire, yet many of them upped and left for the west coast once they'd saved up enough money. Perhaps there was something behind it. He looked at Sam. He was leaning up against the window of the taxi, staring out into the night. It was apparent that he was still in severe pain. What was he to do now? What were his brother and sister to do?

The taxi pulled up outside the train station. Seamus gave Sam his half of Sharp's money and paid the driver. He still had no idea what he would do as he helped his friend out of the car. They walked in silence, stopping after a few paces to check out the departing trains' schedule. The next train was to Cincinnati in five minutes, the one after to New York, and then ten minutes later to Los Angeles. They could go almost anywhere, but Seamus didn't feel free. He knew the kid didn't either.

"Decision time," Seamus said. "Where's it going to be?"

He took a few seconds to answer. "I've been mulling this over, searching my mind. There's probably a job, and maybe a future for me in California, but I can't stop thinking about my kid brother and sister. I can't just leave 'em there any longer. That's why I did that stupid job with Larry—to get enough money to get them out of there."

Seamus shook his head, incredulous at what he was about to do. "I know I'm gonna regret this" He reached into his pocket and pulled out his share of Sharp's money. "Take it," he said.

Sam looked at him as if he was insane. "What?"

"Just take it before I change my mind." The younger man shook his head. "Yes, take it," Seamus said. Sam put his hand on the money. "Just promise me one thing."

"Of course."

"Go home to Cincinnati, get your brother and sister out of that house, and be on the next train to California."

"I promise," Sam said. "I'll get them and we'll leave together."

"You should have enough to get you out there and get somewhere to stay."

"What about your family? Don't you need the money for them?"

"Let me worry about them. Just do as I ask, OK?"

"You have my word. What are you going to do?"

"Go to New York and make my way to Newark. I'll make it work somehow." The conductor whistled from the platform below. The train to Cincinnati was leaving. "That's your cue, kid."

"I don't know how to thank you," he said.

"Just get your brother and sister to California. That's all the thanks I need."

"Thank you, Seamus," he said and turned to walk away. He was gone a few steps when he turned around. "I just realized, I don't even know your last name."

"It's Ritter. Seamus Ritter. My dad was German, my mom was Irish. Long story."

"For another time. I won't forget what you did for me today, Seamus Ritter."

Sam turned and hurried down the stairs to the train. Two minutes later, the whistle sounded again, and the train set off.

Seamus was alone again and sat on a bench on the platform, reading the letters from his kids. They hadn't written in a few weeks, but what did that matter when he was going to see them tomorrow? A warm feeling of hope spread inside him. He didn't have enough money to move out now. He was going to have to squeeze into that single room with the four of them or sleep on the couch downstairs, but for some reason, he knew everything was going to be all right. It was unusual to feel optimism these days. It was unreasonable, yet he felt it. He was going to make this work. He'd been hiding from life for too long.

The train to New York was leaving, and he took a seat by the window. He'd be gone before the morning newspapers hit the newsstands, and Francis Sharp would have to content himself with killing just one of the burglars who tried to steal his money. The train pulled out of the station and into the night beyond. The excitement he felt at seeing the children again surged through him, and a broad smile spread across his face.

1

New York City, September 1932

Seamus Ritter stepped onto the platform at Penn Station. This wasn't the triumphant return he'd imagined. He let the crowd envelop him before walking in the direction of the stairs. He didn't have any of the original clothes he left with, or even a suitcase. The bulge of his children's letters in his pocket lent him a few seconds of comfort: The only contact he had with them in the two years he was away.

Two years. And what did he have to show for it? Was the sacrifice, pain, and deep longing he felt all this time worth a couple of hundred dollars in his pocket and a new suit? The money would only keep them going for a few months. Not nearly enough to move the children out of his sister's house, let alone to buy a place of their own. There was no dressing it up— he had failed. He was returning to his children a failure.

Seamus felt cheated. Men were walking around in suits with briefcases by their sides. Men like him. He was one of

them before the bank went under and they lost the house.
Before the children lost their mother.

The crowd dissipated and he made his way to a newsstand
on the platform. He flipped the newsie a coin and picked up a
paper, scanning for any sign of his own name. It was ridiculous
—no way the police in New York would be looking for him, no
way the papers would print his description. But he flicked
through the first five pages, poring over each headline.

Stories of the upcoming election dominated, as well as the
New Deal promised by Franklin Roosevelt. Mahatma Gandhi
was beginning a hunger strike in India, and an upstart called
Adolf Hitler called for parliament in Germany to be dissolved.
He scanned the next few pages until he found the article,
tucked at the bottom of page seven. His hands shook as he read
the words on the page.

AKRON, OHIO

BUSINESSMAN THWARTS ROBBERY

AT LEAST THREE MEN WERE INTERRUPTED DURING AN
ATTEMPTED ROBBERY AT THE HOUSE OF LOCAL BUSINESSMAN
FRANCIS SHARP ON SUNDAY NIGHT. ONE ROBBER, LARRY PROC-
TOR, WAS PRONOUNCED DEAD AT THE SCENE. AT LEAST TWO
OTHERS ESCAPED AND ARE WANTED FOR QUESTIONING BY LOCAL
POLICE.

That was all. No description of him or Sam, the kid he escaped
with. Hopefully Sam was on his way to California by now with
the money Seamus gave him. George, the other man Larry
roped into his madcap scheme, seemed to have gotten away
without anyone even noticing he was ever there. The police
would have gone back to the camp and noticed that he, George,
and Sam had disappeared, but he didn't have a record and
doubted the other two did either. If the vet Seamus paid to fix

up Sam's wounds kept his mouth shut, they were home free. They wouldn't be searching for him in New York or New Jersey.

A palpable sense of relief flooded through him and he skipped to the sports section at the back to try to distract himself from the thoughts flooding his head. The Cubs just clinched the pennant. He loved baseball once—when there was time for such things. Before leaving to find work to support his children. Before he became a stranger to them.

Memories of what he ran from crept into his subconscious like poison gas, and he saw Larry's body, torn and bloody, on the ground beside him. *How could I have been so stupid?* Desperation can turn the wisest of men into fools. He folded the newspaper.

"You ok, pal?" the newsie said. He was a boy of about fourteen—around the same age as his son Michael. "You don't look so hot."

Seamus tucked the newspaper under his arm. "Just a little tired, bud. You wouldn't believe the week I've had."

"Try me."

"Maybe next time." Seamus tried to smile but the newsie only looked more puzzled.

He wasn't going to waste any more time trying to impress this kid. He made for the stairs. The knowledge that the police weren't at the top of the steps calmed him. *No need to look over my shoulder here.* New York City cops wouldn't be erecting any barricades for a robbery in Ohio two nights before. He was going to get away with this. He was inching his head out of the alligator's jaws. He needed a drink, but arriving at his sister's house to see his children unannounced—after two years away and smelling of booze—wasn't a good idea.

He settled for a cigarette instead and lit one up. He took a few seconds to inhale the rich smoke into his lungs, closing his eyes as he breathed it out.

The sounds and bustle of people around him brought him

back into the moment. He slalomed through the crowd until he reached the board where the trains to Newark, and home, were displayed. The next one was leaving in seven minutes: A train home—or to his sister's house, at least—which was the closest thing his children had to a home in this world. The joy that lit his heart at the prospect of seeing them again was instantly doused by how he'd failed them. He brought back little more than he left with, and even fewer opportunities than he had on the worksite in Ohio. All this time he dreamed of coming home in a new car with enough money to buy a house where he could live with his children and be a father. It was all he wanted. It didn't seem like too much to ask.

He had that a few years ago, and a wife also. But the house was gone, and so was she—cold in the New Jersey ground. He wanted to talk to her, to beg her forgiveness for his failures as a father, for not being there for their kids, but he long since stopped trying. What was the point when she never answered? Talking to her did little more than underscore the stark fact that she was gone forever.

Seamus sat down on a bench. What should he do when he saw them? They'd probably be in school for another hour or so. Should he call ahead? His sister didn't have a phone, but her neighbor did. It might be better if he could beat the kids to the house. His sister would be there and he could sit and talk with her. That might dull the shock the children might experience upon seeing him—if he were sitting at the kitchen table when they arrived home from school. Perhaps it might seem more normal, more planned—as if it were something he cooked up with their aunt to surprise them.

He doubted that, or that he'd even get there in time. But fooling himself into believing those things helped to calm the raging sea of his nerves. It was hard to know who to be more afraid of—the police or his own children. The reunion of his dreams involved hugs and smiles, an outpouring of emotion, and the cessation of the terrible longing he felt all this time away, but he knew it wasn't guaranteed. He was confident about the three younger children, but Maureen made him unsure. A sixteen-year-old girl has enough to worry about without her father leaving. Maureen didn't explicitly say anything in her letters, but the anger between the lines was clear to see.

He strode to the ticket booth. Buying the ticket made his return seem official. He took it, put it in his pocket, and stepped out onto the platform.

The train was about to leave, and Seamus squeezed into a seat beside a lady in her seventies who was knitting a baby's hat. He pulled a photograph of his family out of his pocket, taken back in '26. He remembered the icy wind that day and how Marie wrapped up the children to take them out. They wanted to make a day out of it, but it was too cold, so they took a cab to a restaurant straight from the photography studio.

He held up the photo to catch the light. Maureen was ten then, Michael was eight, Fiona, five, and Conor not even two. It had been so hard, and the strained look on his own face told of the stresses of getting Conor and Fiona to look at the camera. They had to take a dozen photos or more, and his smile soon cracked. Yet Marie's face showed deep contentment, and not an ounce of the frustration he knew she must have felt. She was beautiful. It was the only photograph he had of them all together.

"Is that your family?" the lady beside him asked.

"Yes," he said. "It's from a few years ago. The kids are older now."

"You'll wake up one day and wonder where the last 30 years have gone. Cherish every moment with them while they're young."

Her words hit him like bullets. He missed so much. The lady smiled at him and went back to her knitting, apparently unaware of the effect her words had on him. Seamus pulled the pile of letters out of the pocket of his new suit and peeled off one he knew to be from Maureen. He felt a little strange reading something so intimate beside a stranger, but the woman had no interest in what he was doing, only putting down her knitting to glance out the window at the marshes and wetlands alongside the track. The letter was dated March 1932, six months ago. The children's letters had started out once a week, but dwindled over time to once a month. It had felt like they were forgetting him, moving on with life without either their mother or father. Orphans with one parent still alive.

A few months after he left to make something of his life once more—and after ending up digging ditches—it became obvious he was failing them. Ensconced in the day-to-day labor, he realized the act of providing for them meant he couldn't be with them.

He could fool them in his letters, and even himself. But he left when so many others stayed, deserting his family when they needed him most and burdening his sister with the responsibilities he couldn't face. Now he was coming home two years later, almost broke...without even a suitcase.

It was impossible to tell them the truth, so he'd lie to them again, along with everyone else. How could he tell them he returned because of a botched robbery, or even explain why he participated? Keeping quiet seemed like his last best chance to appear a winner.

He opened the letter, though there was really little need to read it. He almost knew it by heart. Maureen wrote about the other children, explaining how they were doing in school and how brave they were, never complaining of sharing one small room in their aunt's house. She said little about herself—her friends, her hopes, her dreams, or the strain of living in someone else's house. Maeve had her own two daughters to care for, and her husband Frank worked long hours and didn't seem to spend much of his free time in the house.

Seamus wondered what would actually change upon his arrival home. *How will my being there improve things? Where will I sleep? How can I help with the children if I'm gone all day working? Assuming I'll find a job at all.* Things hadn't improved since he left, and Roosevelt's promise of a New Deal for American workers was no more than a political slogan.

Seamus put the letter back into the pile and pulled out one Fiona and Conor had written the year before when they were ten and seven. They mentioned little other than friends and school, toys, and a dog they saw the previous day. Seamus glanced at his watch. It would be around three o'clock when he arrived back at the house, so the kids would be there.

The lady beside him stood up as the train stopped and he rose to let her out. He smiled and wished her well, slipping the letters back into his jacket pocket. Newark was next.

The train was emptying out, and no one else sat beside him. Seamus stared out the window for the few minutes it took to reach Newark Broad Street Station. He stood up, went to the door, and stepped onto the platform. A stray flare of paranoia reared up as his shoes hit the concrete. He controlled it, thinking of it as an animal to be hushed. It wasn't wholly unreasonable—he was likely a wanted man in Ohio. Not that he'd ever go there again. But it was likely over. The rich old man they tried to rob would content himself with the fact that he killed one of the thieves, and the local police would let it go.

Seamus had more pressing matters to deal with. The house was 25 minutes' walk from the station, which was the perfect amount of time to gather his thoughts. He reached into his pocket for a cigarette and lit it. He stopped to inhale the smoke for a few seconds before continuing out of the station and onto the street.

Smoking, he walked past the still-shuttered bank that folded two and a half years before. Someone had daubed the word *Thieves!* in red paint across the door where he used to work. Seamus threw down his cigarette, remembering the last day. The manager, Jim O'Grady, broke the bad news. No one was surprised, but some still cried. Seamus could still recall the look on O'Grady's face: The genuine sorrow at having to tell his staff of twenty-five that there would be no jobs for them anymore. Afterward, the old man took Seamus aside to tell him how awful he felt for him, what with being newly widowed and having four children. A few months later, Seamus's house was gone, and then so was he.

His college degree was no good anymore. The only thing he seemed to have to offer was his physical strength and willingness to do anything to support his family. He spent the last six months digging ditches and laying pipe, and the previous eighteen wandering around looking for any work that paid. And he did it all—laborer, farmhand, carpenter's assistant, bookkeeper, fruit picker, and even a stint in a carnival helping set up the attractions. He looked down at his hands, callused and worn. The dirt seemed to be ingrained under his fingernails so that no matter how much he washed, he could never get it out.

The atmosphere was different in the city than it had been a few years before. The bright sun was in stark contrast to the gray below. Many businesses were shuttered off, boarded up, the doors padlocked. A homeless man sat outside the façade of a hardware store Seamus frequented many times in the past. The man's face was covered in dirt and a heavy beard, but Seamus recognized his eyes. Billy had been the bravest man in his battalion. He saved five men's lives one day in '18 and got nominated for the big one, but had to settle for the Citation Star. A crippling sadness overtook Seamus as he beheld Billy now—little more than skin and bone, and his lips were covered in ugly lesions. He wanted to ask him what happened. Where was his family? How could a country treat men who served like this? What was gallantry worth? But he knew he couldn't. He'd only met him a few times since the war, in speakeasies mostly.

"Billy Tyler?" Seamus said. "Is that you?"

Billy pulled an almost-empty bottle to his lips and mumbled something incomprehensible. Seamus left him a dollar and walked on.

Maeve's house was five minutes away. He spent the time trying to remember each of the children as babies. Some sparse memories emerged from darkened corners of his mind, but it was hard to pinpoint any routine he had with them then. He saw them when he came home from the office and held them on most days, but all the changing, feeding, nurturing was Marie's work. *So much wasted time.*

What he said in the first exchanges with his sister and his children was vital. It had to seem like this was part of his plan, that there was a captain to his ship. They had to trust him, so he'd make it appear like coming home as a surprise was a part of some grand scheme with an unknown happy ending. Letting them think that might be the only way of actually getting there. He'd say he missed home too much, and then the job ended… not mentioning where and what the job was. Just that it was over and he couldn't stand to be away any longer.

It was true. The pain of being away from them drove him to agree to the ridiculous plan to rob that rich old man's house. The idiot who came up with the plan was now dead. Seamus barely escaped with his own life, and almost all the money was gone—spent on getting away and keeping the kid who agreed to drive the getaway car alive. Seamus imagined him sitting on a train, his shoulder bandaged up by the vet they paid off.

Frank's parents' house came into view as he rounded the corner. They worked their whole lives to afford it after moving from Ireland, and now it was Frank's. Several children played on the street, but none were his. He kept walking, only a few paces from the steps leading up to the porch. A child's bike sat on the lawn, toys strewn around it. The youngsters on the street started whispering as he listened at the bottom of the stairs.

Voices bled through the screen door, but it was hard to make out who.

Should I knock, or walk straight in?

He rapped on the wooden door. Nerves rose like corks bobbing up in water, and he put his hands in his pockets to hide their shaking. Footsteps approached and his sister's face appeared behind the screen door.

"Hello, Maeve."

The blood drained from her face and she had to remove her hand from across her mouth to speak. "Seamus! What are you doing here? You never wrote."

She pulled the screen door back with a creaking sound.

"I'm sorry. I thought it'd be a nice surprise for the kids."

"They'll be surprised, all right."

The spike of vitriol in her tone was nothing he hadn't expected. He stepped through the door and embraced her, but she withdrew quickly.

"Where are the kids?" he asked, but he could hear their voices now, speaking German, just as his parents insisted when they were growing up. Maeve had clearly carried on the tradition.

"They're in the kitchen having a snack. They just got home from school."

Maeve looked him up and down. "Where's your suitcase?"

"I don't have one."

"And a new suit?"

"We can talk later. I'm going to see the kids now."

He took his hat in his hand and walked on. The sunlight from the window flooded the kitchen in white light as he stopped in the doorway. Maureen was standing at the sideboard making sandwiches for the children. Seamus's heart stopped as he watched them sitting at the table with their cousins, eating peanut butter and jelly sandwiches with the crusts cut off. He stepped inside. Michael stood up, drenched in shock.

"Father?" he said and ran to him, throwing his arms around his torso. Fiona and Conor soon followed their brother, and all three of them were hugging his waist now.

Maureen hadn't moved, other than turning around to face him. She was a young lady now, as beautiful as her mother had been, still holding a knife thick with peanut butter. Maeve's girls, ten-year-old Patricia and eight-year-old Jennifer, still sat at the table and looked at him with bewildered eyes.

Seamus ruffled Michael's hair as the fourteen-year-old boy stepped back. He had to forcibly separate eleven-year-old Fiona and little Conor, who would be eight in six weeks, from him.

"All right, that's enough," Seamus said in English.

"Where were you?" Conor said.

"Are you going to stay?" Fiona said.

"Are you going to live here with us?" Michael said.

"No, silly. He's brought back lots of money and he's going to buy us our own house. Are we going back to our old house, Father?"

Seamus crouched so he was at eye level with Conor and Fiona. "I came back because I missed you all so much. I'm going to try to find a job here and stay with you."

"There's no room in the house," Conor blurted out.

Seamus stood up. Maureen put down the knife. The tears in her eyes didn't mask the strain of irritation in her face. It was easy to understand why she felt that way. She stepped forward as the younger children gave their father space to move toward her. She put her arms around him. The feeling of her hair under his chin brought an errant tear to his eye. He rapidly brushed it away. He had to be strong in front of the children—that was a father's role.

"We had no idea you were coming back," she said.

"I couldn't stay away any longer. I had to be here with you."

"Are you going to stay here with us?"

Seamus turned to look at his sister standing in the doorway. "I was hoping I could."

Maeve's lips tightened, but she nodded. The children cheered and wrapped their arms around his waist again. Joy cascaded through him, tempered only by the sight of Maureen standing back with her arms crossed. Her eyes seemed to bore into him like drill bits.

2

There was no bed for him. Maeve's two girls shared a room now after Patricia gave up her room to his kids. Conor took his father by the hand and brought him up the stairs. He was so much bigger now—tall, just as Seamus was at his age. Seamus took a breath, trying not to focus on all that he missed. Conor led him down the hallway to an open door.

"This is our room," he said.

He'd known this house, and this room, before he left, but it never looked like this. Two sets of bunk beds stood against the wall on either side, with a small table under the window between them. It was about the size of a jail cell. The beds were made with perfect one-inch folds, but that was where the tidiness ended. Toys and stuffed animals were strewn all over the floor. He imagined the chaos of readying the children for school every morning—getting them dressed and their lunches packed, making sure they had everything they needed. Maeve had her hands full with her own children, and he doubted Frank helped much. His eldest daughter was a remarkable person. Her mother would have been proud of who she'd become.

Michael appeared at the door behind them. "What do you think?" he asked.

"It's great."

His son paused, as if trying to evaluate whether he was telling the truth or not. He was no fool. "How much longer are we going to have to live here?"

Seamus looked at his son, the feeling of helplessness returning. "I'm going to get a job. A good one, like I used to have."

"When Mother was alive?"

"Yeah, just like back then. I'll track down work and we'll find somewhere to live. Just us."

"When?"

"I don't know, kid. I wish I could say. It's a hard time right now. All I can tell you is that I'll do my best, and I don't ever want to leave you or the other kids again. Is that good enough for today?"

Michael looked up at him for a few seconds before nodding. Seamus went to the window to look out. The boys followed him. They told him the names of the kids they played with on the street, though Seamus remembered some of them anyway.

"Do you want to go out and play?"

Neither boy spoke until Conor broke the silence. "No. We want to stay here with you."

They stood at the window in silence for a few more seconds before Seamus turned to them.

"I'm not going to leave you again. Do you understand?"

The boys nodded and Seamus led them back downstairs, where Maeve was standing in the foyer. Seamus suggested they go to the park. It seemed a fitting way to spend the afternoon and mark his arrival home. Maeve insisted that Seamus wait on the porch as she and Maureen got the children ready to leave. He was smoking a cigarette as they came outside. The children watched him stub it out before he joined them. Conor grasped his hand as they descended the stairs. Maeve walked beside them, her girls and the three other kids a few feet behind. Maureen still hadn't said more than the few words she exchanged with him in the kitchen. Time would come later to work on her. The children ran ahead, leaving Seamus and his sister behind.

"How are they doing in school?"

"Well. Very well. Their grades are excellent."

"I knew that much from their letters."

"I've spoken to each of their teachers. You can rest assured they're doing great."

"They're good kids, and they're lucky to have you to look after them. I want to thank you for being a mother to them all this time."

"Thank Maureen. She's been their mother these last couple of years. She does everything for them. Gets them up in the morning, makes them breakfast, packs their lunches. She's there when they have nightmares or problems at school. It's her not me."

Seamus knew his sister wanted him to answer, but finding the words was difficult. They caught in his throat like thorns. He had stolen Maureen's youth, thrusting the role of mother to her siblings on her. A deep shame settled over him. She never mentioned mothering the other kids in her letters, but it made sense. Maeve had enough to deal with already, so Maureen had to be the one to make up for his shortcomings.

"I'm proud of who she's become," he said after a few seconds.

"Tell her that. She needs to hear it from you. She's not a little girl anymore. Did you know she has a boyfriend now?"

"No. Who?"

"Leo Bernsen. He's in school with her. His father has a store on Washington."

"Is it serious?"

"They probably think so. He's come to the house a few times."

Seamus rubbed his eyes with thumb and forefinger. He couldn't think about Leo Bernsen right now. There were too many other things to deal with. They reached the park and the kids ran to the playground. Maureen went with Conor, even though he likely didn't need her.

"Did she talk about me much when I was gone?"

Maeve stood beside him watching the children play. "Maureen? Less as time went on. She settled into a pattern."

"Out of sight, out of mind?"

"Maybe. When you first left, you were all the kids could talk about. There were tears at bedtime most nights for weeks. They felt like they lost both parents."

"I had no choice."

"Didn't you?"

Maeve's words hit him like a fist. "There was nothing here."

"Plenty others stayed. I don't know many other single parents who left their four children with their sister."

"There was no work here. I had to support them."

"I understand that, but most of their friends' fathers stayed. Even the ones who lost their jobs. They found a way to survive. Why did you really leave? Was it for them, or for yourself?"

"I'm sorry, I—"

"I know what you went through. We all loved Marie, but leaving wasn't the answer."

"I did what I thought was best at the time. I never thought I'd be gone so long."

Maureen was helping a little girl, perhaps three or four, onto a swing. Seamus watched her for a few seconds before speaking again.

"Does she understand that I left for them?"

"I don't think I do," Maeve said. "You need to tell them the truth: You couldn't handle being here after Marie died. It's ok to show them that." She put a hand on her brother's shoulder. "It's time to make up for the mistakes of the past. She needs you. She's growing old before her time, looking after the kids day and night."

"She's just like her mother—better than I could ever hope to be."

"She needs a father." Maeve reached into her bag for a cigarette. She lit up and continued talking. "Do you have any prospects? What are you planning to do to get your children out of my house? We don't have room for all of you."

The thought to tell Maeve the full truth entered his mind, but left just as quickly. He would settle for the truth of the situation he found himself in right now, rather than what had driven him home.

"I'm going to see my old boss, Jim O'Grady, and see if he has any contacts, or knows of anything. If I could get a job like I had—"

"As an investment advisor? No one has any money to invest. Why don't you write to Uncle Helmut—I've been in touch with him—and see if he has a job for you in the factory?"

"In Berlin? I can't leave the kids again. I won't do that. Not for any job."

"Bring the kids with you. Maybe just for a while...until you get back on your feet."

"I'll see what's available here first, but I can promise you one thing: I won't rest until I get them out of your house. All I want is the life we had before everything went to hell. A place of our own, and my children with me."

She glared at him for a second as if she were evaluating his words. "You can stay with us until then."

She went to her children and left him standing alone.

The vise seemed to be tightening, as he knew he couldn't stay more than a few weeks with Maeve. He had a little money, enough to put down on a deposit on an apartment, but how would he pay the rent? He wondered if he knew the children at all anymore. Were the letters an accurate reflection of their experiences, of what they were becoming, or were they the distilled thoughts they thought he wanted to read? They were all so lighthearted, displaying none of the real challenges they must have faced with an absent father and a dead mother. What hand had his sister in the content of those letters?

Michael was playing football with a few other neighborhood boys, and Fiona and Conor were on the swings with their cousins. Maureen stood alone at the edge of the playground. Her green eyes flicked up at her father as he approached. Her wavy dark-blond hair fell free around her pale, angular face, which reminded him so much of her mother. It was like her ghost was standing there among them. He stopped beside her in silence for a few seconds, watching the children play.

"I didn't realize you all had to sleep in one room."

"You know the house. Where else were we meant to sleep? On the street?"

Seamus bit down on his lip. He longed to reach out, to hug her, but stayed still. Something inside held him back. He wasn't sure how his affection would be received. He reached into his pocket for a cigarette. The brief thought to offer her one flashed across his mind before he dismissed it. He put it back in the pack without lighting it up.

"I didn't know all that you did for your brothers and sister while I was gone."

"Someone had to look after them."

"I'm so sorry for putting you in that position."

"I remember what you said when you left. You told us you'd be back in a few months—six at the most—and when you did, you'd have enough money to get us our own place. Maybe even buy us a house. When are we moving out, Father?"

He fumbled for the right answer in her icy-cold eyes.

"I don't know."

"You were gone two years and you don't know? You came back with a new suit, but no suitcase of clothes. Do you have money for a place of our own?"

"Not right now. Things didn't work out the way—"

Tears welled in her eyes. "But that was why you left. Mother died and you left. You said you were going to come back and everything would be better. Well?"

He couldn't answer. He could have told her that there were no jobs, that he tried everything he could and sent most of the money he earned home, but what good were excuses now?

"You should have stayed with us!" She was almost shouting now. "You left us for all that time, but nothing changed. Mother is still gone. We're still living with Aunt Maeve."

Fiona was pushing Conor on the swing. Conor called out to him, waving. Seamus waved back.

He was empty inside, crushed by the weight of humiliation. He'd always been someone to be respected. Someone his children could look up to. Were those days gone forever?

He closed his eyes and threw down the cigarette. "Maureen, I want to tell you that... It's just ..." *Where are the words when I need them? This was so much easier on those nights alone in my cot at that worksite, or on the train on the way back here.*

She turned to him, staring at him with those green eyes. The sadness in them was almost more than he could bear.

"I'm sorry I let you down. I know I failed you. I have some ideas about getting a good job—like the one I used to have when you were growing up. I'm going to see my old boss, and Maeve suggested I write to Uncle Helmut in Germany and see if he has anything."

"You're going to leave us again?" White-hot rage burned in her eyes. "No! You're not going!"

"I'm not leaving. Listen to me." He tried to take her hands, but she shrugged him off. He continued nonetheless. "You have my word of honor on that. You won't have to be a single parent ever again. Give me the chance to prove myself to you. I won't let you down."

"How can I believe a word you say?"

"I'm going to make this better, for all of us." Maeve was standing on the other side of the playground, staring at them. The other kids didn't seem to notice.

"I should have stayed. Leaving was selfish and it was wrong, and I'm sorry. At fourteen you should have been out playing with your friends and studying in school, not looking after three children. I won't put you through that again. We'll stay together, no matter what."

"I want that too," she said.

He needed to calm things down, to get their conversation back to some sense of normalcy before it spun out of control. Pivoting to school seemed like the natural route to take. Talking about something more ordered, more formal, gave him space to breathe. The pressure building in his chest eased.

They stood talking for a few more minutes. She parroted what she expressed in her letters: School was going well. It was hard to find time for homework sometimes, and then she had to stay up late, but she invariably managed to get it done. Helping Fiona and Conor with their work took up a lot of the time she needed to do her own. They'd developed a system and it seemed to be working...

He thought to ask her about the boy Maeve mentioned. She never mentioned him. She was the age he'd been when he met her mother, but that could wait for another day.

"We'd better get the children home," she said after a few

more minutes. "We need to start on our homework before I make dinner."

He wanted to say no, that they could stay a little longer on his first day back—they should celebrate. But then he realized that she was right, and it was her decision to make. She was the head of the Ritter household now, the heir to her mother's role.

She had done his job long enough. It was his duty to take that responsibility back, to let her live her life and find her own way, and erode the cliffs of anger inside her. The only way to gain her trust was to keep his word, and the only way to keep his word was to stay, provide for the family, and not break them up again. Circumstance had made liars of better men than he.

Maureen called the children back. Michael, in the middle of a game, was the only one who grumbled. Maureen didn't shout, but the tone of her voice carried an implicit threat. Michael threw down the ball and said goodbye to his friends.

"They'll all be going home soon enough anyway," she said as her brother arrived.

"Not Tommy and Ralph. They'll stay out as long as they want."

"And do you really want to be like Tommy Radisone and Ralph Martin? Their parents wouldn't care if they never came home again."

"At least they don't have their sister bossing them around."

"Don't talk to Maureen like that," Seamus said. "Come here." He grabbed at Michael's shoulders. "Every kid needs someone to boss them around, but I think I'll take the job now."

Maureen nodded and pushed her brother toward the park gates. Fiona ran ahead with her cousins and Conor grabbed Seamus's hand again, looking up at him with adoring eyes.

⁓

Frank came in the door as they were sitting down to dinner, wearing a flat cap and carrying a grocery bag full of meat. At thirty-five, he was a couple of years younger than Seamus. His red face and skin shone in the light as he took off his hat to reveal his prematurely balding head. He dropped the grocery bag as Seamus stood up to greet him.

"Look who's back," he said. Seamus stood up to greet him and the two men shook hands. "When'd you get into town?"

"This afternoon."

"This calls for a celebration," Frank said with a smile. "You finished dinner?"

"I should stay here with the kids—my first night back, you know?"

Maeve stood up. The children at the table stopped shoveling their food into their mouths for a few seconds, sensing something was coming. "You had dinner yet, Frank?"

"I got something on the way home. I have some people I want to introduce your brother to. You're looking for a job?"

"Whatever I can get."

"I just left them. They're still there, a few minutes away. Could be a good opportunity—you can't let anything pass these days. Things haven't improved much since you left."

"You should go, Father," Maureen said. "I'll get the kids off to bed."

"Ok. Let me clear off my plate."

"No, the women will do that. That's not for us. Come on," Frank said.

Maeve glared at them a few seconds before reaching down to pick up a piece of food Conor dropped. "You'd best go then."

"We won't be late, will we?" Seamus said.

"Depends," Frank said. He said goodbye to his wife and children and walked out the door. Seamus told the children he'd be back to tuck them into bed before following his brother-in-law out the door. *Did I just lie to my kids? Should I go back inside?*

Frank was already halfway down the block. Seamus hurried after him.

"I didn't think you were ever coming back," Frank said as Seamus caught up to him.

"Why d'you say that?"

"Because I don't think I would have," he said with a smile. "My girls have loved having their cousins around, and Maureen and the kids are great, but the house is getting a little cramped."

"I know. Thanks for putting up with them all this time."

"You have money to move out?"

"Not enough."

Frank blew out a breath. "How did I know you were going to say that?"

Seamus felt a hot stream of embarrassment. What kind of a man couldn't support his own children? It didn't used to be like this. He had been the one with the good job, the house. Once he was a man to be envied. Now he was to be pitied.

"How's life working on the docks?" Seamus said.

"I wouldn't know. I got laid off a few weeks after you left."

"Maeve never mentioned—"

"She doesn't know. I didn't want to trouble her with that. She had enough to deal with."

"So what are you doing? Where are we going?"

"I'm glad you see the connection there, but let's not spoil the surprise."

They walked across town for 20 minutes as the sun disappeared and darkness came. Frank led him down toward some warehouses that seemed deserted. No trucks sat in the lot outside and all the doors were closed. The only light was from the moon above.

"What's going on, Frank?"

His brother-in-law didn't answer, instead gesturing for him

to follow as he made his way around the side of the last warehouse. Seamus stopped walking, wary of what he was getting into. Frank turned around and curled a finger in his direction. He could trust him—he was a little loose sometimes, but he was family. Seamus shook his head and traipsed after him. Frank knocked on a metal door, and a few seconds later the peephole opened up.

"It's me. I've got a good man here."

"Who?" came the voice from behind the door.

"My brother-in-law. I've known him for 12 years—he's a trustworthy guy." Frank turned around and winked at Seamus.

The door opened and the two men stepped inside, where a large truck was parked in front of them. Several men were loading wooden boxes inside the open back. The man who answered the door, a middle-aged man in a flat cap and overalls, looked Seamus up and down before turning to Frank. "What are you doing back here?"

"I wanted to introduce Seamus around. He just got back in town and needs work."

Some surprise—typical Frank. The police are looking for me in Ohio and I come home to this? But what if it's the only way to make ends meet? What if doing this will be the difference between being a father and having to leave again?

Prohibition was on the way out. People were sick of abiding by the laws of the puritanical class, and the politicians were sick of hearing about it. It had been a disaster, so places like this were on borrowed time now.

"Good to meet you," the man said. "The name's Ted."

Seamus shook his hand and introduced himself. Ted excused himself and got back to loading the truck with the other men. Seamus turned to his brother-in-law and shook his head.

"So, this is where you come every day when my sister thinks you're at the docks?"

"The work's easier, the hours are shorter, and the pay's a lot better."

Seamus nodded, watching the five men working in silence. The idiocy in Ohio was his first brush with crime, and he swore since it'd be his last. Could he do this for a while? He'd have to see what his other options were first. There were a lot of questions to be answered before joining the men working here.

Frank approached the shelves that lined the walls of the warehouse. He used a crowbar to pry one of the wooden boxes open, pulling out a bottle with clear liquid inside.

"Rum. All the way from sunny Cuba." He handed the bottle to Seamus.

"You'll pay for that out of your wages," Ted called.

"Ted runs a tight ship, but he's got a heart of gold underneath that rough exterior." Frank waved over to the man Seamus assumed was running the place.

"Can I sample the supply?" Seamus said.

"Sure. Let's celebrate."

A single table surrounded by some wooden chairs sat on the other side of the truck. Frank fetched some glasses from a cabinet on the wall and set them on the table. The two men sat down, and a few seconds later were sipping the rum.

Seamus watched the men working for a few seconds, and when he was sure they weren't listening in, leaned forward to ask a question. "Who runs this place?"

"Ted's the guy giving the orders tonight, but it varies."

"No, Frank, who's running this place?"

Frank sat back and took a swig of rum. He smiled before answering. "Does it matter? The work's good and we're giving the people what they want. Sounds like a perfect business to me."

"Do I have to repeat the question?"

"The big boss is 'Lucky' Luciano, but he doesn't exactly come down to help load up the trucks too often."

"What do you do here?"

"Load the trucks, deliver the booze, collect the money, and deposit it back here. Easy."

"Easy if you don't get pinched."

"Losses happen, but the cops know the story. They don't bother us. As long as the right wheels get enough grease, the whole system keeps flowing. We're a staging point between the city, Atlantic City, and the rest of south Jersey. The booze moves through and we send it on its way, all while we get our own slice of the pie. No one gets hurt."

Seamus downed the rum in his glass. He'd seen plenty get hurt in the newspapers—bodies strewn in bloody messes on the streets—but he didn't think it best to mention it. Frank poured him another glass.

"You think they'd take me on?" He couldn't believe he was entertaining the idea, but what was better—selling out his integrity or losing his family? It didn't seem like he'd had a good choice in a long time.

~

Maureen was still awake when she heard the stone hit the window. With everything that went on that day, the *crack* on the glass took her by surprise. She had forgotten what night it was. Conor was snoring in the bed above hers, while Fiona and Michael were asleep in the bunks opposite. The house was quiet—her father and Uncle Frank hadn't come home yet. The kids wanted to wait up for them and she originally agreed, but gave up an hour before and sent the kids off to bed with the promise that their father would be there the next morning. She just hoped she hadn't lied to them.

She scanned the front yard. Nothing. If anyone looked out, they'd never know that Leo was hiding around the side of the house, but she did. Tuesday was their night—a night no one else knew about. It was one of the only times when she didn't have to be a mother to her siblings, when she could be sixteen and sneak out with a boy. They saw each other at school, and their friends and family knew they were together, but with all that Maureen had to deal with, the nights they met were the only times they got to spend alone.

She stood at the window for a few seconds, just until he peeked his head out. Any more stones hitting the window might wake the kids up. Once he saw the curtains open, he'd know she was awake and making her way downstairs. It took about a minute to slip her dress back on and find her shoes in the half-light, taking them in her hands before going to the door. All the places to step that wouldn't send creaking noises reverberating through the house were mapped out in her mind, and she crept down the stairs in near silence. Her only worry tonight was running into her father and uncle coming home, but the clock in the foyer told her it was only ten thirty. They probably wouldn't be back for hours yet.

The night air was still warm, and she felt beads of sweat on her palms as she glanced back at the house. Nothing was moving. Leo was waiting on the corner, 100 yards down. He greeted her with a kiss on the cheek and took her hand. A rush of exhilaration washed through her as they ran together back toward his house, three blocks away. She always enjoyed the feeling this part brought.

Leo's parents' house was dark as they arrived, and he led her around the side to the shed at the bottom of his well-manicured yard. They didn't speak until he pushed the door open, letting her in first. She knew where the matches were and reached up for them. She lit the candle and the interior of the shed was bathed in golden light. The drapes that Leo pulled over the window would act as extra protection against being caught, but still they kept their voices to a whisper as they began to speak.

"It's so good to see you," Leo said. The candlelight danced in his dark-brown eyes and turned his tanned skin the color of amber resin. They sat down together and took a few moments to kiss. It felt good to lose herself, to escape the thoughts bouncing around inside her mind, but she couldn't keep them at bay long and broke away from him.

"My father came back today," she said. "He just arrived out of the blue—no letter, no telegram, nothing."

"He's back? Why didn't he let you know he was coming home?"

"He said he wanted it to be a surprise, but my guess is he lost his job and got sick of living in a tent and shoveling dirt for a living."

The level of anger in her voice seemed to make Leo uncomfortable. "You don't sound too happy he's back."

"I want to be, but in all the time he was gone, I never dreamed he'd come back like this. He didn't have a suitcase, or any belongings. He arrived with a new suit and whatever he could carry in his pockets—like he was running away or something. It's hard to explain."

"Does he have a job here? Wasn't that the whole reason he left in the first place?"

"No. He doesn't have a job or the money for us to get a place of our own. It seems like the last two years has been for nothing. He says he's going to see his old manager and try to get something like his old job back, but I don't know what's out there with the economy still in the toilet like it is. He also has some crazy idea about going to work for his uncle in Germany."

"Germany?"

"I told him no. He's not leaving us again."

"Do you think he'll go?"

"I don't know that he has any idea of what to do next. We can't stay in Maeve's house forever. There's even less room now that he's there. Do you have any cigarettes?"

Leo reached for a pack he'd stashed on one of the shelves and gave her one. She lit it off the candle and they both sat down.

"I don't know how I feel," she continued. "Or if he's even going to stay. Maybe he'll be gone in a few weeks and we'll be right back to where we were yesterday, and every day for the past two years." Maureen took a drag. The smoke seemed to catch in her throat, and she had to fight not to cough it back up. Her father wouldn't have approved of her behavior. No one would have. She exhaled the smoke and held the cigarette to her lips again.

"Uncle Frank says he has some work for him and they disappeared after dinner together. Dollars to donuts they'll come back drunk in the middle of the night."

"Maybe he'll get a job and everything will be like it used to be again."

"When we were kids and my mother was alive? Yeah, I'd like to believe that, but somehow..."

"Somehow what?"

"I can't make myself. It's like there's two parts to my father's life—when my mother was alive and then after. He turned on a pivot. She got sick really quickly."

"That must have been awful."

"Father was already unemployed then. The bank went under six months before, but it was Mom's death that really changed him. He stopped trying to look for work when she was sick because he couldn't bear to leave her, but when she died, he gave up. He didn't try looking for a job...just left. It was as if he wanted to get away when we needed him most."

"How do the kids feel about him?"

"They worship him. I'm glad they do. I just hope he doesn't let them down again."

"Are you going to introduce me to him?"

Maureen stubbed out the cigarette in a makeshift ashtray

and smiled. "I'll give him some time." Leo looked a little hurt so she reached across the table and took his hand to comfort him. His fingers curled around hers. "Let him get used to being back first. I'll bring you over for dinner."

"The dreaded dinner with the father-in-law, eh?"

"Yeah. I'd say to bring him a bottle of scotch to soften him up, but that's not legal."

"He'll have to settle for some of my mom's marble rye bread."

"He'll love it, and he'll love you too, just like I do."

She leaned across the table and kissed him. They stayed in the shed another 30 minutes before Leo walked her home. The streets were quiet as they went, but she couldn't shake the feeling that she might meet her father and uncle on the way home. It was after midnight when they arrived. The house was dead: no lights on, no sound. He left her at the corner, as he always did, but this time she dared to kiss him on the lips to say good night. A bright smile flashed across his handsome face, and he turned to make his way home without another word.

Maureen walked the last few steps alone, making sure to take off her shoes as she ascended to the front door. It was unlocked, and she pushed it open. Maeve had laid out blankets on the couch where her father would sleep, but he wasn't there. Upstairs, she changed in seconds. She was lying down, her eyes heavy, when she heard noise downstairs. The sound of footsteps and then hushed voices in their wake. *They're home earlier than I thought.*

Frank said good night to her father and then came up the stairs. She was wide awake now, her father downstairs asleep on the couch. She wanted to go to him, for him to take her in his arms and sing to her as he had when she was a little girl, but she didn't. She rolled over and went to sleep instead.

3

Jim O'Grady was waiting on the porch and waved as Seamus strolled up. It was a fine evening, and his old boss was drinking a glass of lemonade. He stood up and shook his hand as Jim's wife, Gertie, emerged from the house to say hello and offer a drink. He accepted and took a seat beside Jim overlooking the street. Seamus was wearing the suit he came home in—it was the only thing he had. He knew he should buy some more clothes, but the thought of spending money right now was more than he could bear. It was a good suit, perfect for a job interview—if he could get one.

He still hadn't given Frank an answer about working for the bootlegger. His brother-in-law was starting to get impatient, and couldn't seem to understand Seamus's reluctance.

Jim offered him a cigarette, but Seamus had his own. A few seconds later, both men were puffing away. Jim was sixty and had a son Seamus's age working oil rigs in Texas. He showed Seamus a photograph of his grandchildren as his wife came back with the drinks. Seamus handed back the picture while Jim smiled. He'd aged these last couple of years. The last vestiges of his brown hair had given way to gray, and he had deep lines in his skin now that defined his face.

"How is your family?" Gertie picked up her husband's empty glass.

"The children are good. Maureen's done such a fantastic job with them. I couldn't be prouder."

"She's a good girl," Gertie said. "It's a crime when children have to grow up so fast like she did. When I think about her poor mother..."

Jim appeared to recognize that his wife was about to cry and stood up. "I'm sure Seamus appreciates your thoughts. Go on inside now." She nodded and retreated. Seamus took a sip of the cool lemonade. It was a warm evening, and he took off his jacket.

"Sorry about that," Jim said. "Gertie lets things get the better of her sometimes. Especially when it comes to Marie and your kids."

"Not at all. She's a sweet lady. I need to hear that every so often."

"How long are you back?"

"A week. It hasn't been quite the triumphant return I envisaged when I was digging dirt in the Midwest."

"What did you do when you were away?"

"Christ, what didn't I do?" He held his hands out. The blisters had healed, but the calluses never would. "There's a world out there I never thought I'd be a part of—not until the crash, anyway. I've done things I never thought I'd have to, made choices I never dreamed of."

"It's been a hard time for everyone."

"I wanted to ask if you knew of anyone hiring right now."

"For finance jobs? Like what we used to do?" Jim shook his head and finished his glass of lemonade. "I wish I did. You were good at that kind of work. I'd recommend you in a heartbeat, but the bank runs have destroyed the industry. Thousands of them have gone under since the crash. The runs are still going on. Nothing's changed."

"That's what I thought you'd say."

"I wish I had better news for you. You don't deserve any of this."

"You'll let me know if you hear of anything?"

"Of course."

"How's retirement?"

"Forced retirement? Not great. My pension was all but wiped out. We're scraping by on savings, and whatever Gertie makes from sewing. It isn't what I dreamed about either, those 35 years working for the bank."

"It all seemed so easy back in '29."

Jim laughed and stubbed out his cigarette. "We got caught in the greed trap. We're paying the price now. Have you had any interviews? Anything?"

"Nothing. The banking industry is hanging on by its finger-nails. I may as well run for president as get a job in finance—I think winning the election'd be easier. I can't even find a job digging ditches or working on the docks."

"Roosevelt's going to win the election. He's promising better times."

"I can't feed my kids on a politician's promises. Even if he does come through, when's that going to be? Next summer? Next fall? I need something today."

"What are your options?"

"If I can't get a job? I don't know. My uncle has a factory in Germany, and my sister's been in touch with him about a job there. That'd pay well, I'm sure. I could leave again, but Maureen, my oldest, is already angry at me. I thought she'd cool down after a few days but, it doesn't seem I can do anything right. She'll be seventeen next year. She's so smart, too. I know she wants to go to college, and she has the grades to get in, maybe with a free ride. If she goes away before I get back, I'll lose her forever."

"Would you consider moving and bringing the children with you?"

"I'd consider about anything at this stage...except leaving them. I won't do that—make the same mistake twice. The problem with moving to Berlin is we don't have the money. I'd have to go ahead of the kids and send for them once I earned their passage over."

"So you'd have to leave them behind."

"I don't think I can do that."

Seamus took a sip of his lemonade. The sky was turning an orange hue as the shadows lengthened. He wasn't going to tell Jim about the job loading and delivering booze, but it was the only option he had left to keep his family together. The vise was closing around him with no escape.

They sat there a while, talking about the old job. Jim still kept in touch with many of his ex-employees. Some had found work since, but many moved on to California, Texas, and even to Alaska.

Gertie came out after an hour passed and asked if Seamus wanted to stay for dinner, but he refused with a polite word and said goodbye to his old friend. He walked home through the descending darkness, a feeling of loneliness overwhelming him. He imagined Marie walking beside him, and the feeling of her skin against his. The image faded too quickly and suddenly he saw her in the hospital bed, lined and worn, old before her time.

The man was the head of the family—that's what he'd always been taught by his father, and society as a whole. Then why wasn't that the case in his family? He deferred to Marie's better judgment so many times during their marriage that it became the norm. He didn't see any problem with living their lives that way—

a partnership dedicated to the same cause. Why should he have claimed to have superior insight? Because society demanded it? The truth was that he, and the family, were bereft without her, rudderless on the most raging sea he ever could have imagined. He tried to silence his thoughts so he could hear her voice. He stopped on the street a block from his sister's house and closed his eyes, but the voice was from his memories. He couldn't hear her anymore. He needed her now, but she was gone.

The children were already at dinner when he walked in. Maureen glared up at him and he almost expected her to tap her wrist or to point at the clock on the wall. The thought that he was a disappointment to her tore him to shreds. He went to each of the children, kissing them on the head, but stopped short of his eldest. Frank wasn't home.

Maeve looked at him with jaded eyes. "Have you eaten?"

"No, I wanted to have dinner with my family."

Patricia shifted in her seat as he slipped a chair in between her and Fiona. His daughter smiled at him between mouthfuls. Maeve brought his food, and he asked each child in turn how their day had been. Who was their favorite teacher? What was their favorite subject in school?

When dinner was over, he went to his sister, who was clearing the plates. "Let me help you," he said.

She looked at him as if to refuse, but then relented with a smile. He picked up the children's plates and brought them to the sideboard.

"You go and sit down," he said.

She didn't seem to require a second invitation and took off the apron in seconds. He was halfway through washing the dishes when Maureen came into the kitchen.

"You need some help?" she said.

"No, you do enough, sweetheart. It's about time I started pulling my weight around here." She nodded and started to leave. "I'd love some company, though. Can you stay a few minutes?"

"Ok."

She stood against the kitchen table with her arms crossed. He put a glass on the drying rack and looked at her as he put his hands back into the water. She was so beautiful, it made him want to cry.

"I want you to know I'm trying," he said. "I was just at my old manager's house, in the faint hope that he could help me get something like my old job back."

"Can he?"

"Hundreds of banks have gone under in the last three years. Thousands. It doesn't seem possible right now."

"So, are you going to leave again?"

The water sloshed in the washbasin. Seamus pulled out his hands. "That's the last thing on my mind. I just want things to be back the way they were."

"Let me help."

"No, I'll do it."

"You wash, I'll dry."

He nodded and she moved beside him. She picked up a tea cloth and started wiping a pan from the drying rack. They worked in silence for a few seconds, just the sound of the water, the dishes, and their breath. Being beside her was enough to make him happy. He couldn't leave, no matter what. He'd die before he lost her.

He wanted to apologize to her for casting her in the role of a single parent. He wanted to get down on his knees and beg her forgiveness for stealing her childhood away from her. But his father's voice, his thick German accent, asserted the need for strength above all else: Never show weakness. Maureen was just like him—he'd resented his father too.

"I think Uncle Frank has a job for me, working at the docks."

"With him?"

"Yes. I wasn't sure I should take it. I've no experience doing that, and I wanted to build back my career."

"But it's a job. Will you have to work the same hours he does?"

Seamus thought of Frank and the time he spent gambling and drinking with his friends. "No, I don't think I'll have to be away as much as that."

"I hope it works out."

"I've decided to accept the job. It's the only way to keep us together, and as generous as Frank and Maeve have been with letting us stay here, we need to get somewhere of our own." He handed her a glass. "It isn't what I wanted to do, but nothing lately has been."

"Not since Mother died."

"No."

The washing up was almost done, and he reached to the bottom of the basin for the last knives and forks. He washed them as one and put them in the rack. He took a tea cloth and started drying with Maureen. Not knowing what else to say, he reverted to the default conversation of schooling. She was doing great—as she always did. The other kids were too. Conor had the propensity to be naughty, but the teachers dismissed that as a sign of his age.

"Do they talk about their mother often?" Seamus asked as they finished.

"Not so much anymore. Not since you first left."

The words sliced at him because he didn't have to leave. He could have toughed it out. He shook those thoughts from his mind. *No use in torturing myself. The past is past.*

They were finished, the kitchen clean. "Thanks for helping," Seamus said.

"No problem," she said as she went to the door. He was still standing at the sink when she turned back. "Don't mess this up, Father. We're relying on you."

He nodded, and she walked into the living room to check on the children before bedtime.

~

Two weeks passed. Seamus had ceded to the inevitable and took the job Frank offered him. Lying to Maureen and the kids was the hardest part, but this would only be until he got back on his feet—a temporary solution to their most pressing problems. The hours were antisocial, mainly in the afternoons and evenings, and he hadn't seen the kids much since he started the job. But the cash was coming, and so would time with the children. They'd have enough to move out of Maeve's house soon. He hoped the banking industry would return and he could get something like his old job back, so this was about putting in time until then. Running some illegal booze to people who would have bought it somewhere else anyway seemed like a small price to pay for the chance to get their lives back. He started out loading the trucks, then moved into taking inventories, tracking payments. His bookkeeping skills were valuable, but not so much as to keep him from getting his hands dirty.

Every few days he took his turn to do deliveries. He'd been to several towns in Jersey so far; Haddonfield, Tom's River, Trenton. Tonight's trip was farther south, to Wildwood. He was riding in a truck filled with cases of Canadian whiskey. A man he met the day before called Fred Baskin was driving. It would be Seamus's turn to take the wheel on the almost three-hour ride home once the delivery was made.

Fred was smoking a cigarette with the window down. He was a few years older than Seamus, perhaps forty-five. They hadn't spoken much in the hour they'd been on the road. It was ten o'clock at night, and the truck's headlamps shone funnels of bright white into the gritty darkness of the road in front of them. The forest of the Pine Barrens seemed to be closing in around them on both sides. They hadn't seen another car for 10 minutes. The only sound was of the tires on the asphalt below.

Seamus broke the silence. "You been doing this long, Fred?"

"About two years," came the reply.

Seamus waited a few seconds for Fred to continue, but when it seemed like he could wait all night for that to happen, he spoke up again. "You ever seen any trouble on the road?"

"Been stopped a few times by cops who didn't know who they were dealing with, but it all gets sorted out in the end. You ain't worried, are you?"

"No, course not. You got kids?"

"No. I never had time for any of that."

"You got a wife?"

"You always ask this many questions?"

"Just trying to make conversation."

Seamus stared out of the window, but the darkness made them mirrors and all he saw was his own reflection. Silence descended in the cab again. Seamus was thinking about Marie and how she loved walking in the summer rain when Fred spoke.

"See that pickup behind us?"

Seamus lifted his head to look in the rearview mirror. Two balls of burning white light pierced the darkness behind them. "I see it." He watched the truck for a few seconds. It was gaining. "It's not a cop."

"Probably nothing, but let's see," Fred said and pushed his foot down on the accelerator. Their truck surged forward. The lights of the pickup receded into the darkness for a few seconds before coming back closer than before.

"He's picking up speed," Seamus said. He tried to make out who was driving and how many there were, but all he could see was the glare of the headlights.

"I can't go much faster than this," Fred said. "I guess we'll see what they're after in a minute or so."

He threw his cigarette out the window. Seamus kept his eyes on the truck behind. It was still gaining and almost on them now. "Do we have anything in the cab for this?"

"For what?"

"For a sticky situation?"

"No. We're delivery boys, not soldiers."

The pickup was on them now and moving into the other lane, as if to overtake. Seamus brought a greasy palm to his forehead. Fred kept his eyes on the road as he applied the brake. They crested a hill on the road, and a new glare of lights came from in front of them. Beside them now on the right, the pickup's driver was holding a sawn-off shotgun out the window, pointing it at Seamus in the passenger seat. The lights ahead were of another pickup parked in their lane. Fred pumped the brakes.

"We've got trouble," Seamus said.

"Let me handle this," Fred said as the truck came to a halt.

Two men were standing by the pickup parked on the road, each with a gun in their hand. *How did they know the truck was coming? Someone must have tipped them off.* The pickup that had been following them stopped on their right. Neither Fred nor Seamus dared move.

"Get on out of there now," said one of the men as he motioned with his pistol. "Come on. Don't make us come up there and get you." He was about twenty-five and dressed in a plaid shirt and black pants. He seemed to be the oldest of the three men, and he was the one who spoke again as they got out. "Line up there on the side of the road."

Seamus kept his eyes down as he moved to stand beside Fred. Both men had their hands in the air. One of the hijackers, a boy of not more than nineteen, pointed the sawn-off shotgun in Fred's face.

"Do you boys know what you're doing here?" Fred said. "Do you have any idea who you're stealing from?"

"Do you have any idea who we are?" the kid with the sawn-off said. His pathetic mustache hung like a rat's tail over his top lip.

"Think about this," Fred said. "Our boss is not a man you want to mess with. Get back in your pickups and go home to your mommas."

"Who are you to talk about my momma?" one of the men said. The other two laughed. Seamus saw in their eyes that they'd been drinking. He knew what they were going to do. The forest was a few feet behind them: They'd cut him down before he got there. What about Fred, who was older, heavier? Perhaps he could talk them out of this.

"If you steal our truck, our boss will send men here. They will find you, and they will kill you. With pain. I'm asking you not to do this," Seamus said.

"If I wanted your opinion, I'd tell you it," the young man said. The others laughed again. "Let's get on with this," he said. "On your knees." Neither man moved. "I said, get on your knees right now."

The oldest of the three men walked to them, holding up a revolver, pointing it at Fred's chest. "Didn't you hear what the man said? Get on your knees."

"I'll be damned if I'm getting on my knees for a gutter rat like you. If you want to end your lives here tonight, be my guest, but leave me and my partner out of it," Fred said. "Let us be on our way."

"Well, first you had to bring our mommas into it, and then you called me a gutter rat." He put the barrel of the gun against Fred's chest.

"You'd best pull that trigger, boy, 'cause otherwise you won't see next week alive."

"Whatever you say," he said and pulled the trigger. Fred fell backward, clutching his chest, blood between his fingers.

The young man started to turn to Seamus, but he was too slow. Seamus saw what he was going to do before the young man knew it. He went for the gun, twisting it in his hand and smashing him in the face with his elbow.

The other two men seemed stunned. It took them a second or two to raise their weapons. Their hesitation gave Seamus the time he needed. He raised the other man's gun and fired first, hitting one of them in the abdomen, the other in the hand he was holding the sawn-off shotgun with. One fell to the asphalt. The other screamed in pain, shaking his bloody hand as if he hit it with a hammer.

Seamus took the opportunity to bolt into the forest. The little light on the road from the truck and the pickups seemed to disappear immediately as he entered the tree line. He struggled to watch his footing, trying to move as quickly as he could.

He stopped behind a tree 50 feet back from the road. The old instincts had saved him. He was back in France in his mind, but had an old revolver in his hand now instead of his Army-issue rifle. Those boys would come again, just like the Germans. They knew they were dead if he made it back. He could stay there and pick them off, or he could run.

He moved just as he heard the two boys who could still walk enter the tree line. He supposed they were locals and knew these woods, but who really knew woods like this? No reason to come in there, particularly at night. He was confident he could hide and pick them off one at a time, but he didn't want to kill anyone. He just wanted to go home.

The boys were about 50 feet behind him but moving through the trees noisily—he'd hear them coming a minute before they reached him. The forest was so dense that there was no clear line of sight. *One of them is shot in the hand, and their buddy is on the road, bleeding from his gut. It's just a matter of outlasting them.*

They weren't going to let the other young man die on the side of the road, and besides, someone would be along sooner or later. They were going to have to clear the truck and the pickups off the road, and they didn't have enough men to drive them all now—not with the guy he shot.

Seamus proceeded in silence, aware of every step he took. His eyes began to adjust to the dark and he quickened to a steady pace. The sounds of the boys behind him—blundering through the trees, snapping twigs and rustling leaves as they went—grew dimmer and dimmer. A few minutes later, they faded to nothing.

When he was sure that they weren't following anymore, Seamus crouched down to wait a little longer. He found a comfortable padding of leaves and took a seat. The cops would be along soon. He couldn't go back to the road. They'd find Fred's body and whatever those idiotic boys left behind. Fred was right. The boys had killed themselves tonight.

Seamus decided to wait there until first light and then make his way back to a town or a road, or somewhere he could get home from. And then what? Go back to running booze? When he arrived back in Newark sometime tomorrow and reported back to Ted at the warehouse, what consequences would he face for what happened tonight? What if they thought he was in on it?

Management would write that one shipment of booze off as a loss and be done with it, but they wouldn't forget the hijackers. Or him. They'd ask for a description so they could get to them before the police did. As it was, two were going to need medical attention, but the one he presumed was the leader— the one who shot Fred—might get away with it if Seamus didn't tell the gangsters who to go after. It was up to him. He was the only witness, but couldn't go to the police unless he wanted to do some time himself.

The choice was between telling his bootlegger masters and knowing that his word would mean the boys endured an agonizing death, or lying to his bosses and hoping the police dealt with it. One thing was for sure—this wasn't who he wanted to be.

∾

Maureen was awake first and went to the bathroom to wash up. The children were still asleep, but it was almost seven o'clock and she needed to wake them soon. The water on her face revitalized her. She dreamed she was a little girl again last night, alone with her parents, before Fiona and Conor came. So she must have been four or five. Michael wasn't in the dream, but the essence of the pictures she saw in her mind told her that he existed at that time. The dream itself was brief—just her and her parents walking in the park. Her father picked her up and put her on his shoulders, just as she remembered. They walked until they came to a river. Her mother dived in and was gone. They went after her, screaming her name, but she disappeared. There was nothing left of her, just the diminishing ripples where her body sliced into the water.

Maureen's heart was thumping as she woke, her entire body pulsing with frustration. Seeing the children sleeping brought her back. She regained her composure in a few minutes and was ready to get on with the myriad practicalities that constituted her day.

Michael was awake when she went back to the bedroom, and she heard Maeve getting the girls out of bed next door. Maureen thought about Leo as she shook Fiona and Conor awake. They'd been meeting in the night for a few months now, not because she wasn't allowed to see him, but because it was dangerous and fun. His parents were in bed before nine most nights, which gave them all the freedom they needed. His father ran a local grocery store and had to receive the daily bread delivery at work before five in the morning.

The last time she was there, two nights before, Leo mentioned taking their relationship further than kissing. It had been hard to hide her discomfort. She blushed and covered with the fact that they were both just sixteen and had nowhere to go to do such things. The risks associated with something she knew nothing about made her nervous.

The children marched into the bathroom, each waiting their turn to wash their faces and brush their hair. Then the girls went back to the bedroom to get changed while the boys waited downstairs. Maureen and Fiona got dressed for school in five minutes. Michael was at the door as Maureen opened it.

"Father's not here," he said.

Maureen pushed past him and descended the stairs. The blankets Maeve set out for him every night were still folded at the end of the sofa. The thought that he came and went while they were asleep crossed her mind, even though it'd never happened before.

"Maybe he was working late and had to leave early," she said to her brother. Conor and the cousins were standing with them too. Maeve was in the kitchen starting breakfast. Maureen went into her.

"Do you know where my father is?"

"No," she said and shook her head. "Frank's still in bed, so he's not with him. He was working late last night, wasn't he?"

"It's not like him to stay out all night."

"No, but I'm sure he's fine." Maeve's eyes didn't echo the sentiment of her words, having seen her husband disappear too many times. Sometimes for days on end.

"Never mind that. We need to get the children ready for school."

The ever-present call of duty forced Maureen's thoughts back to the present, and she went to the kitchen to help prepare breakfast and get the lunches packed for each of the children.

Ten minutes later, Maeve, Maureen, Michael, and the four children were sitting at the kitchen table eating porridge when the sound of the front door opening cut through their conversation. Maureen dropped her spoon and stood up. Her aunt put a hand on hers as if to tell her to leave it—the men did what they did, and it wasn't theirs to question why. But that wasn't good enough, and the concern she felt for her father's well-being superseded any gender roles she might have been expected to fulfill at that moment.

"Stay in your seats." Maureen left for the front door.

The look of shame, of regret, in her father's eyes struck her dumb. She almost went to him, but stopped a few feet short. Several tiny pairs of eyes were peering around the frame of the kitchen door now. His new work clothes were torn and ragged, and his face and hands were a mosaic of tiny cuts and scratches. His hat was gone. His eyes were ringed by dark black bags. It looked like he hadn't slept.

"What happened?"

"I had to make a delivery. The truck driver was off sick. I was south of Atlantic City when the truck broke down. It was the middle of the night and I had to walk through the woods to get to a phone."

"Why did you have to walk through the woods?"

Her question seemed to stir some anger in him. "It was the fastest way to get help."

He walked past her and upstairs to the bathroom. None of the children spoke as Maureen turned to go back to the kitchen. Something in his demeanor told her he wasn't telling her the truth.

Who is this man? Why is it always a lie?

She tried to think of a time when he lied to her before they lost everything. She couldn't. It was hard to reconcile him with the man he was before the crash, before they lost their mother and their house. She thought to go to him, but the look in her aunt's eyes told her not to.

Maureen went back to her seat at the kitchen table alongside the girls, trying to suppress the white-hot rage she felt toward her father. *How could he show himself like that in front of the other children? They still worship him, even if I don't. Their loyalty has stood up to so much, but it won't last forever.*

The clock on the wall signaled it would be time for school soon. Duty called once more. Maureen herded her siblings back toward their seats.

"Where was Father last night?" Fiona said.

"He had some trouble with a truck he was driving."

Maureen finished her porridge and brought the children upstairs to brush their teeth before school.

4

The sound of knocking on the front door jolted Seamus from his sleep. It took him a few seconds to realize where he was, but the surroundings brought him back. The knocking came again, and he called out to say he was coming. He kicked off the sheets and turned his body around to get off the couch. It was just after one o'clock. The few hours of sleep he got weren't nearly enough. Maeve didn't seem to be in the house—he was glad of that.

Ted from the warehouse was at the door, with two other men wearing gray suits.

"Did we wake you?" Ted said.

"No, I was just getting up."

"How about we wait out here while you get dressed?" Ted said. The other two men took a seat at the table on the porch.

"Ok," Seamus said and closed the door behind him. A terrible sense of foreboding washed through him like a polluted stream. He knew why they'd come. He'd soon have to make a choice about the boys who held them up last night—the same boys who murdered Fred. He changed into a shirt and a pair of slacks before going back out to the three men waiting on the porch.

"Hello," he said.

"Seamus, I didn't introduce you to my colleagues. This is Salvatore Torricelli." Salvatore had a large, round balding head and piercing black eyes. He stood up to shake Seamus's hand. "And this is Giovanni Mello." Giovanni was smaller, with a tight black beard and an ugly scar down the side of his face. "We wanted to see how you were doing. It must have been a traumatic night."

"I'm fine. A few bumps and bruises, but nothing serious."

"I wish we could say the same for poor Fred." The two men beside Ted nodded their heads. It didn't seem like they were there to talk. "So, what happened?"

Seamus recounted the story from when he saw the pickup truck tailing them to when Fred got shot.

"You shot two of them?"

"One in the lower right abdomen." Seamus stood up to show the men. "And the other in the hand."

"Good work," Salvatore said.

"I took my chance to run into the forest by the road and hide out there. I knew I wouldn't have to wait long because they needed to get their friends to a doctor. They couldn't spend all night searching the woods for me."

"Seems like you can handle yourself," Salvatore said.

"I did some time in France during the war."

"Did you get a good look at the men who pulled you over?" Ted said.

Seamus took a second to respond. All three men were staring at him. "No. They were wearing handkerchiefs over their faces. It was dark too. I tried not to look at them. I thought I'd have a better chance at surviving if I didn't."

"So you don't think you could pick them out?" Ted asked.

Seamus could see the face of the man who shot Fred as clear as day.

"No. I don't think I could."

"This is important," Ted said. "Our employer can't stand for the likes of this, not if we're to be a viable business."

"No, I'm sorry. I don't know."

"Not to worry," Salvatore said. "You shot two of those guys, right? They can't just go home riddled with bullets. Someone's gotta get the slugs out."

"Where's the gun now?" Giovanni said.

"I dumped it in the woods."

"Smart guy."

"I'm sorry about the shipment—"

"You've been with us how long? Two weeks, and this happens?" Ted said.

"Seems like one hell of a coincidence," Salvatore said.

"Are you implying I had something to do with it?"

"You'd better hope we don't find out you did," the Italian said. Each word was a threat.

"I only just got away with my life. Find those guys. They'll tell you I knew nothing about it."

"And if we don't find them? You're not too forthcoming with helpful details."

"It all happened so quickly, and as I said, they were wearing handkerchiefs."

"I'm sure we'll clear this up soon, but look at this from our perspective," Ted said. "Either you're bad luck, or you're in on it. Either way, we can't have you round anymore."

Seamus wasn't sure whether to feel relieved or devastated. "Should I expect a visit from the police?"

"No, that's all been taken care of. We had someone go out and clean up the scene when you called in this morning. You don't need to worry. We've already talked to the local cops. We're going to handle it," Salvatore said.

The three men got out of their seats. "We won't keep you any longer," Ted said. "You can come down to the warehouse later and clear out your stuff."

The three men stood up and left. The boys who held them up last night were going to be dead soon. The police were their only hope, and it seemed like they were willing to let mob justice take its course. There was no escaping that, no saving them, but would they rat him out? Would they make up something about him under duress to save themselves more pain? How could they? They didn't even know his name.

Ted and the other men drove off. Maeve walked out from around the side of the house where she'd been weeding and stood by the porch, gardening gloves on, staring at him with her mouth open. He couldn't have seen her. How much did she hear? She couldn't know what Frank was doing.

"What are you involved with?"

"I had to make a delivery last night. I didn't ask what it was."

"That man said something about getting held up. What were you delivering?"

"It turns out it was booze," he said. His mind was racing, trying to get ahead of her in this conversation. He was finished with that dirty business, but Frank had to make his own choice. Maeve knowing what he did would force his hand, and Seamus couldn't allow that.

"Is that why you were out all night?"

"Yeah. It wasn't like that. We had some trouble with the truck and I ended up getting stranded in the Pine Barrens somewhere."

Telling his sister a half-truth made the act of lying easier. He hadn't lied in years before the last few weeks...maybe since he was a kid. Circumstance had changed him, had turned him into things he never thought he'd become.

"What happened to the truck? If the police find it—"

"The truck is fine. It got towed. The police are none the

wiser." He stopped a few seconds to gauge her reaction. She seemed to be buying it. "I want to tell you that I'll never be doing anything like that again. I took a chance—a stupid chance. I regret what I did, and I'm finished with it now, anyway. I lost the job."

"Is Frank tied up in this?"

"No." The words pinched as they passed his lips, as if they were studded with barbs. "He has nothing to do with what happened. He doesn't know anything about it."

Maeve took off her gloves and threw them down on the dirt. "What happened to you? I feel like I don't even know you anymore."

She walked up the stairs and into the house. He thought to go after her, but realized that warning Frank before he came home was a more pressing concern. Living there would be close to impossible if Maeve forced Frank to quit. It was going to be hard enough with what his sister knew now anyway.

The vise tightened a few more degrees. He felt it, squeezing his insides out. He went inside, apologized to his sister, and assured her that he was done.

"So, what now?" she said. "You're unemployed again."

"What would you have me do, then? There's nothing out there."

"I don't know. What I do know is that I want my brother back. I don't like this version of him."

She went to the kitchen and washed her hands. He stood alone in the foyer a few seconds before he went to the door.

It was a fine day, and he walked across town with his jacket slung over his shoulder. People passed him on the street, but he didn't see any of them. A river of thought washed through his head.

Will the kids be better off without me? How much longer will this Depression last? Perhaps with a new president, things might return to some semblance of what they were, and I could get a job where I don't have to risk my life or integrity. How long will that take? Six months? A year? What about Germany?

Frank was in the warehouse, as he hoped. He took the news well and thanked Seamus for giving him advance warning.

"I know how to handle her," Frank said. "I'll feed her a line, but I'll have to throw some blame your way."

"I understand."

His sister being mad at him would have to be the price to pay for not undermining Frank. Things might be awkward for a while, but then, things already were.

"They won't have me anymore—not after last night."

Frank nodded, seeming to realize there was no way back. Seamus went to the office and found Ted. He quit on the spot. Ted shook his hand and thanked him, and Seamus walked out, unemployed again. He was 50 yards down the street when he heard Frank's voice calling. He stopped as Frank ran to him and thrust a briefcase into his hands.

"This is a little keepsake from me and the boys—just to say thanks."

Seamus opened the briefcase and saw two bottles of fine malt whiskey. It felt like the last thing he needed, but he thanked Frank and shook his hand again. He walked away, thinking about going somewhere to drink. He went to the riverfront and found a quiet spot overlooking the water. The briefcase opened with an audible *clack* and he reached in, took one of the bottles, and screwed off the top. He held the top of the bottle to his lips as Maureen's face came into his mind. He remembered being there—not quite at this spot, but close by—with her and the kids when Marie was still alive. He saw those memories play out in front of his eyes like a movie. Smiling, Marie turned to put a hand on his shoulder. Michael was teaching Conor to swim, holding his body out in the water. Maureen and Fiona were jumping off the riverbank, seeing who could make a bigger splash. It was perfect. Every moment of it.

He screwed the top back onto the bottle and stood up. He dusted off his pants and walked home, keeping the memory of that day by the river front and center in his mind as he went. The kids would be home from school in an hour or so, and he was determined to take them back to the river, to relive some of the golden times of the past. New energy surged through him as he bounded up toward the house. He hadn't changed—only his circumstances had.

He rounded the corner to the street Maeve and Frank lived on and saw the mail carrier out doing his rounds. He recognized Seamus and gave him some letters, which he leafed through as he walked up the steps. One was addressed to him. He put it down on a table in the foyer, along with the briefcase. Maeve was in the kitchen. He apologized for what she saw earlier and assured her that nothing like that would ever happen again. She took his words with good grace.

He went back to open the letter, the stamp on which was German. He slipped in a letter opener and ripped the top of the envelope off. He scanned the letter and called his sister into the foyer.

"Did you write to Uncle Helmut?"

"I told him about your situation."

"He wrote me back," Seamus said. "It seems he wants me to come to Berlin to work for him."

"What does the letter say?"

"That he needs a good man to hand the factory over to. My family is welcome. I'm to go to a lawyer in the city next week for the details of the job, and for money to cover my passage."

"So?" Maeve said.

Seamus smiled. "It would be a good job, and if he pays for the children to go too, I don't see why we shouldn't."

"He wants to hand the factory over to someone? What about Helga?"

"Maybe he doesn't think she's up to the job?"

"What age is he now?"

"Seventy-five, I think," Seamus answered. "He was fifty-three the last time we saw him."

More than 20 years had passed since either of them saw Helmut—not since they moved back to America, after their stint in Berlin, in 1910—but Seamus could still remember his uncle's broad smile and gregarious nature. They kept in touch for a while, but it was two years since Seamus wrote to him. The last he remembered of his uncle was when Helmut threw a party to celebrate his nephew's return to America after nine years of living in Berlin. Seamus was fifteen at the time, and Helmut insisted he was old enough. Maeve was only thirteen, so she was confined to the house with a babysitter that night.

Noisy children interrupted his thoughts, and Jennifer and Patricia burst through the door and ran to their mother. She was still holding the letter, but they didn't seem to notice. Seamus took it and put it back in the envelope.

"How was your day?" he asked. Conor ran to him and gave him a hug. Seamus picked him up and spun him around.

"Who wants to do something fun?" The children cheered. "You remember that time we went down to the river?"

"We went to the river lots of times," Maureen said.

"Let's go again today. Let's do something together while the weather's still warm. Homework can wait," he said to Maeve. "It's what Helmut would do. He was never one to miss out on some fun."

"I'll start getting the girls ready."

Thirty minutes later, they were all down by the river. Michael and Conor were skimming stones; Fiona and her cousins were climbing trees overlooking the water. Maureen sat down on the riverbank alone. Seamus joined her.

"I had to quit that job." She looked up as if she were about to snarl at him. "It didn't feel right to leave, but... I couldn't stay. You're going to have to trust me on that. There's something else. Another opportunity."

"In Germany?"

"Yes. It'll be a big change for us and we'll all have adjustments to make, but we'll be together. That's all I want—I don't care where."

Seamus put his arm over his daughter's shoulders. They stared out at the river without a word between them.

~

The lawyer's office was in the city. Seamus got dressed up in the one suit he owned and met his sister in the foyer. She wore a smart blue dress with a cream-colored hat. Seamus adjusted his tie in the mirror, and they set out for the train station. The gray sky above seemed fitting. Rain started as they reached the train station and they huddled under Seamus's black umbrella as they hustled inside.

Conversation turned to their uncle as they waited on the platform for the train into the city. Seamus remembered touring Helmut's metalworks factory with Maeve when he was around ten, and she was seven or eight. Helmut introduced them to some of the workers on the factory floor. Seamus's favorite part was operating the machinery—under the supervision of his uncle. Helmut let him keep one of the metal forks he made, and he kept it in his room for years. It was gone now—lost in the move back to America. Helmut was a wealthy man then. He and his wife and daughter lived in what had seemed like the biggest house Seamus had ever seen back when he was ten. It was hard to know how much he was affected by the Depression since he was always so upbeat in his letters.

The train arrived and they took a seat by the window.

Rivulets of rainwater flowed down the windows, obscuring their view. The talk of their uncle led to the inevitable mention of their father.

"Do you think about him much?" Maeve asked.

"I wish I could say I didn't, but I think about the choices I made as a young man all the time."

"He was wrong to cut you out of his life. Mother never would have allowed it."

"No, she wouldn't." Memories of his mother formed in his mind. Remembrances of her were gentler than those of his father. He remembered her holding him, singing the songs in the Irish language she spoke as a child. They were so different. Sometimes he wondered what she'd seen in his father. She came over from Ireland alone. Her family only had enough money to send her, the oldest daughter. The ship was bound for Boston, but high winds and rough seas forced the captain to tie up in New York City. His father worked at the docks, and found her crying and alone. She knew no one in New York. The person she was to meet was in Boston but she never made it there. Seamus was born two years later, in 1895.

"I think about her more, but the old man... He's still there, in the back of my mind," Maeve said.

"Barking orders, no doubt."

"Sometimes."

His mind went to the funeral in '26. It was the natural thing to think of, considering he hadn't seen his father for eight years prior to that. Not since he got home from the war. Not since his father told him that he'd disgraced his German heritage by fighting against the Kaiser. He never met Fiona or Conor, and only knew the other two children as babies.

"You'd have to search hard to find a more stubborn man," Seamus said, trying to smile. "His principles were more important to him than his own grandchildren. His Kaiser was more important to him than his son."

The train pulled into Penn Station. Seamus stood up first but let his sister go ahead of him. The carriage emptied out and they joined the crowd making its way up the stairs. The rain had stopped as they came out onto the street. The lawyer's office was close enough that they could walk. It was years since they were in the city together.

Seamus didn't verbalize his thoughts. They talked about the children as they went, but Seamus was thinking about Helmut's offer: *How much will the job pay? How long will it take to save enough to put money down on a house?*

His cousin Helga, Helmut's only child, never married, and was still in Berlin. Her mother was dead 10 years and Helga was all Helmut had left. She had been working at the factory since she left school. Neither he nor Maeve ever felt close to her. They didn't keep in touch.

They came to the lawyer's office and proceeded up the stairs. The secretary greeted them and took their coats. Seamus tried not to think about what he was going to do next as he sat there. He tried to clear his mind, watching the traffic below. He thought of Maureen and the other children. This was right for them. They'd be a family again.

The lawyer appeared—a stout man in his fifties with an impressive bushy mustache below a red drinker's nose. He greeted them with a handshake.

"Howard Baines. Good to meet you. Follow me. Take a seat."

They followed him to the two chairs set up opposite his desk and sat down. Baines engaged them in some small talk for a few minutes about where they were from and how they knew their uncle in Berlin so well. He seemed impressed when they told him that they lived there for nine years as children.

"We should get on—I don't want to keep you all day." Baines reached for an envelope on his desk. He held up a letter in German and began to read. Baines had been chosen for his fluency. He got through the first few lines of legalese before he brought his eyes up to them and then continued.

To my nephew, Seamus and my niece, Maeve:

I'm an old man now, and my memories have faded with the passing of time. I still cherish the years you spent here in Berlin. It was the closest Helga ever had to the brother and sister her mother and I couldn't give her.

I've appreciated your letters over the years, especially the photographs of your beautiful children. I still have them all hanging over my desk to remind myself of what's really important in life. That's a question an old man ponders more and more as he realizes that the end is nigh, and the only answer that I've been able to settle on is family.

I never had the joy of a large family. Your father, stubborn old goat that he was, was my only sibling, and I've few cousins to speak of. Helga never married, and though she's been a faithful and dutiful daughter, you both—and your children—are at the forefront of my mind now. All I've ever wanted was to pass down what I've built in this life to those I love, to assure them of a secure future.

It's for this reason that I extend the offer to you to travel to Berlin to take up a position working with me. I need a good man by my side, and I know you're that. Life has been cruel to you these last few years, but I hope you see this opportunity as a fresh start, and the chance at a new life for you and your children.

The lawyer cleared his throat. Maeve reached over and took her brother's hand, sensing something important was coming.

Maeve, I'll always remember you as the little girl I bounced on my knee. I've never forgotten the sound of

YOUR LAUGHTER. I HOPE YOUR OWN CHILDREN STILL HEAR IT
EVERY DAY.

I'M SENDING YOU THE SUM OF $2,000. YOU'VE DONE SO MUCH
FOR YOUR FAMILY. IT'S THE LEAST YOU DESERVE. I HOPE THAT YOU
CAN USE IT TO MAKE YOUR GIRLS' LIVES BETTER. I'M ONLY SORRY IT
ISN'T MORE.

Seamus turned to his sister as a lone tear ran down her cheek.

"Thank you," she said, as if her uncle were in the room.

"And Seamus..." Baines continued reading from the will.

ALL THESE YEARS, I'VE THOUGHT OF YOU AS THE SON I'VE
NEVER HAD. I DIDN'T AGREE WITH YOUR FATHER ABOUT WHAT YOU
DID DURING THE WAR. YOU WERE SENT TO SERVE YOUR COUNTRY
AND DID SO HONORABLY. I CAN'T IMAGINE HOW HARD THAT MUST
HAVE BEEN FOR YOU, BUT YOU HANDLED IT WITH GOOD GRACE, THE
BEST YOU COULD.

I KNOW YOUR LIFE'S BEEN HARD SINCE THE CRASH AND SINCE
YOUR WONDERFUL WIFE DIED ALL TOO SOON. I WISHED SO MANY
TIMES THAT I COULD REACH OUT AND HELP YOU, BUT YOU WERE SO
FAR AWAY.

I MENTIONED EARLIER HOW I RECOGNIZED THAT FAMILY IS THE
MOST IMPORTANT THING IN THIS WORLD, AND HOW I WANT TO PASS
ON MY LEGACY. IT HAS BEEN MY LIFELONG DREAM TO PASS ON MY
FACTORY—TO MAKE SURE THE RITTER FAMILY TRADITIONS ARE
UPHELD.

HELGA IS A GOOD WOMAN, BUT SHE'S NOT THE RIGHT PERSON
FOR THE JOB. THAT'S WHY I WANT YOU TO COME TO BERLIN: TO
LEARN THE BUSINESS WITH A VIEW TO ONE DAY TAKING THE REINS
FOR YOURSELF.

The words hit Seamus like a truck. He felt like he was in a
dream. Baines kept reading.

YOU'VE ALWAYS BEEN SMART, ALWAYS HAD A GOOD HEAD FOR NUMBERS. I'M SURE YOU WOULD BE RUNNING THAT BANK BY NOW IF IT WASN'T FOR THIS DAMNED DEPRESSION. I KNOW YOU CAN MAKE AN EVEN BIGGER SUCCESS OUT OF MY FACTORY. THE ONLY PROBLEM IS, OF COURSE, THAT YOU'RE ALL THE WAY OVER IN AMERICA.

I'M SENDING YOU THE SUM OF $2,000 TO BOOK PASSAGE FOR YOU AND THE FAMILY TO BERLIN. YOU CAN FIND YOURSELF A HOUSE TO RENT—SOMEWHERE FITTING LIKE CHARLOTTENBURG, THE NEIGHBORHOOD I LIVE IN. YOU ALWAYS SAID LIVING IN BERLIN WAS ONE OF THE HAPPIEST TIMES OF YOUR LIFE. NOW YOUR CHILDREN WILL HAVE THE OPPORTUNITY TO SAY THE SAME.

I KNOW YOU'RE THE RIGHT MAN FOR THE PROJECT. I'LL BREAK OUT A BOTTLE OF MY FINEST SCHNAPPS IN ANTICIPATION OF YOUR ARRIVAL.

YOUR UNCLE,

HELMUT

Baines put the letter on the desk.

Seamus blinked his eyes. He felt cold, and turned to his sister. She smiled at him, not mirroring the sense of shock he felt. Baines confirmed the money for their passage to Germany would be available in a week or so.

"I'll leave you to talk," Baines said and let the office.

"So, what do you think? Moving back to Berlin?"

"I think I'm in shock," Seamus said. "I knew it was coming, but it seems real now. Germany has been hit hard since the crash. The little kids would follow me anywhere, but what about Michael and Maureen? What about their lives here?"

"We were there for nine years, and Helmut was right—it was a wonderful time in our lives. It'll be the same for them."

"But I was fifteen when we came home. Maureen is sixteen. Michael is fourteen. If we go there now, they may never leave."

"And what would be so wrong with that? Germany is a

wonderful place, full of arts and culture and learning. They already speak the language."

"It's as if you've been preparing them all this time."

"Perhaps I was. What about you? How do you feel about going?"

"I've nothing in America. There's little to keep me here except the children—"

"Those children are stronger than I ever thought possible. With everything that they've been through, moving into a big house in a fashionable neighborhood in Berlin is going to be the easiest thing in the world."

"They're strong... Like their mother."

"But they need a father. You're what they need most now. And if this is the chance you have to take to be that for them, you need to go."

Seamus stood up and looked out the window. The sun was coming out from behind the clouds, sending down sabers of golden light. He thought of his time digging ditches in Ohio, and of Fred's bloodied corpse on the side of that dark road in New Jersey. *Will moving to Berlin be as hard as what I've already been through? Will it be any worse than sleeping on the couch in my sister's house with my four kids packed into one room upstairs?*

"I'll talk to the kids about it tonight."

"That's a good idea, but ultimately the decision is going to be yours."

"I know," he said. "That's what makes it so difficult."

This moment was pivotal. He'd remember his life as before and after this moment in years to come. Was this what he'd been waiting for? He went back to the desk and slumped down in the chair. A strange brew of fear, trepidation, excitement, and relief was swirling around inside him. Moving the family to Berlin, having the children settle into new schools, and finding new friends, would be a massive undertaking, but they'd be

together. That one thing would make all the other pains that
went with it worthwhile.

He wracked his brain for any news stories about Germany
in the last few months. The volatile political situation there had
led to an uptick in violence on the streets, but the upcoming
elections, which were set to happen around the same time as
that in the US, would bring order back...or so an editorial he
remembered reading claimed. Germany was a civilized country,
a place he knew that he could feel at home in. They all spoke
the language. He thought back to friends he'd known there,
places he visited, his old teachers, and days at the lake. They'd
have money, and anywhere was good when you had that.

Baines came back, and they stood up and thanked him for
his time. He reminded Seamus that he'd send the money for
their passage to Germany in the next few days. They shook his
hand and left the office.

The sun was still shining as they stepped out onto the
street. Seamus felt like he'd never be in New York City again.
He looked at everyone and everything as they walked, drinking
in the street scene with his eyes. This part of his life was
coming to an end. He just hoped the children would be as
excited about it as he was.

"What will you do if the children don't want to go?" Maeve
asked him.

"It's my decision to make."

"What if Maureen decides not to? She's a young lady now,
with a life of her own to lead."

"She can't just stay here without her family. I know she'll be
the hardest sell, but what would she do?"

"She might want to prepare for college. You know how
ambitious she is."

"I know," he replied, "but there'll be plenty of opportunities
for a razor-sharp young lady like her in Germany. I hear it's

quite a progressive place these days. I'm sure she'll recognize that."

"Who are you trying to convince? Me or yourself? You'd better hone those persuasive skills on the way home. You're going to have to sell your dream to the children."

Seamus knew his daughter's ties there would be hard to break, but her loyalty to family would supersede them. He was confident she'd agree to come. Leaving her behind and breaking up the family would render all these actions as pointless. This was their chance to be together, to have the regular, steady life he craved for them. It didn't matter where—just that they were a family.

~

The children had eaten dinner and were playing in the front yard when Maureen saw her father and aunt returning from the city. She was sitting on the porch reading a book as they approached. Michael was playing football with Conor and threw his father the ball. Seamus caught it with one hand and threw a spiral back. Michael dived onto the lawn to catch it. He came up smiling, with grass stains on his bare knees.

Maureen was looking after the children alone: Frank was wherever Frank was most of the time. She had gone well beyond the point of asking or even wondering where her uncle disappeared to. She put down the book and stood up as her father and aunt approached. The sun was setting behind them, blotching the skyline with red, orange, and pink, like some celestial work of art. Her father locked eyes with her, seeming to ignore the others as soon as he saw her. She sat back down and picked up her book again. He took off his hat and took a seat opposite her. A feeling of dread descended upon her.

"What's the book?" he asked.

"*Brave New World*." She held it up.

He nodded to himself with a smile, as if it fit the moment. "Is it good?"

"It's exceptional, but something tells me you're not looking to discuss literature right now."

"I can never hide anything from you."

"I could argue that."

He ignored her comment and leaned in. "I wanted to tell you first, before I sit down with the others. Uncle Helmut offered me a job working for him in the factory—"

"You're not going to Berlin," she snapped.

He closed his eyes for a second and sat back in the chair. She wanted to lean forward, grab him by the lapels, and shake the information out of him. Her aunt came up behind him and said hello. Seamus shot her a look that told her to keep moving, so she went inside without another word.

"I won't go if you don't agree to come with me." Maureen felt her heart seize up in her chest. Her father kept talking. "Helmut set aside money for our passage and to get set up. He wants me to take over the running of the place someday. I haven't seen the accounts, but I could make a good living—"

"But we live here, in America. We've never even been to Germany. I don't know the first thing about the place."

"You speak the language."

A flash of anger ignited within her. "I never thought you would hold that against me."

"Nobody's holding anything against you."

His gentle tone was likely meant to dull the anger she was feeling, but instead she read it as patronizing, riling her up more.

"And you want to uproot the entire family." Her voice was loud enough that the other kids were looking now. Her father rubbed his eyes. Had he expected this to be easy? Leo flashed into her mind. *I can't leave him! It would be forever.*

"I know this is a huge thing to ask of you, and your aunt

suggested that you might want to stay here to finish out school. She said you can stay with her if you want to do that, but I don't think I can bear to leave you behind."

"So, you want to get rid of me when for almost two years, I've been the only parent they knew?"

"No, no. That's not it at all. I just wanted to give you the option—"

"Like you gave us when you left? I don't remember you asking our opinion two years ago when you dumped us here."

"I'm trying to make up for the past now. Can't you see that?"

"By tearing us away from the only home we know?"

"We can't stay here. It isn't fair to Frank and Maeve. This is their house."

"What about school and our friends? Michael's on the football team. They don't even have that in Germany."

"There'll be other friends, and other sports, and a fresh start for all of us. I'm not saying it will be easy. This isn't what I would have chosen, but I don't see that we have any other choice."

Michael glanced up at the mention of his name. "What are you talking about?"

Her father seemed to change gears and beckoned him up, along with the other two children. Jennifer and Patricia started toward him too, but he told them to stay where they were.

"Let's go inside," he said. He brought them into the house and sat them down at the kitchen table, speaking in German this time. Maureen was still seething, but let him explain the situation to her siblings, speaking to the little kids in much the same way he had to her. Conor was first to talk when his father finished.

"Will we get our own house?"

"You'll get your own rooms," his father said.

The children smiled, their eyes wide. They seemed sold by

that one notion. Maureen couldn't believe they let him off the hook so easily.

"Will we have to stay there forever?" Fiona asked.

"No. We can come back here in the future. I don't know when that would be, but we can leave whenever we want."

He looked around at the three younger children. He seemed to be taking nourishment from their enthusiasm. "What d'you think?"

"We get our own house?" Fiona said. "It sounds great!"

Michael spoke next. "I'll miss my friends, but not sharing a room with my sisters."

"We won't miss sharing a room with you," Fiona said. "You snore."

He looked shocked by the accusation, so Maureen felt she had to weigh in. "You do."

"It's a fresh start. I know it's in a new place, but we'll have things we don't have here. I don't know what I'll do if we don't take it. The money I brought home is almost gone. I can't find a job."

"But you had a job, with Uncle Frank," Maureen said.

Seamus shook his head. "That wasn't the right job. You're just going to have to trust me."

"When would we have to leave? Can we stay until the end of the school year?" Maureen said.

"We don't have that much time. Helmut wants me to get over there as soon as possible. It's going to have to be next week."

"Next week?!" Maureen couldn't believe the words coming out of his mouth. The other children seemed utterly unfazed, however.

"Can we bring our toys?" Conor said.

"We can get new toys when we arrive. I hear they have all kinds of wonderful toys in Berlin."

"So we're leaving next week? We're leaving the country?" Maureen said.

"It's not forever—especially for you. You can come back if you want to go to college here."

"And leave them? They're the only reason I'm even considering going! They need me here and they'll need me there. I'd never desert them. We're not making any decisions tonight, but we'll think about it, won't we?"

The other kids nodded. She saw the effect her words had on her father: He sat back in his chair and the excitement in his face melted like a snowball in the summer sun. She felt a pang of guilt, but the truth was, she was happy to hurt him at that moment. It felt like justice.

He stood up from the table and hugged each one of them in turn.

"I'll never leave you again," he said and walked out of the kitchen.

≈

Maureen was awake when the stone hit the window. She got dressed and ready before opening the drapes. Leo saw her wave to him and left to wait for her up the street. The kids would sleep through a hurricane, so she didn't have to tiptoe out of the room. It was her father on the couch she worried about. He was an even heavier sleeper than the children, but while the chances of him catching her were low, the consequences would be significant.

She stopped to listen at the bottom of the stairs. The soft sound of his snoring told her the way was clear, and she tiptoed to the front door. It closed with a tap and she carefully kept to the side of the wooden steps from the porch to the walkway. She was panting as she rounded the corner to where Leo was waiting for her. He greeted her with a tight embrace. He had no idea what she was about to tell him. That could wait until they were alone in his father's shed—when they were comfortable, and the setting was more private.

They walked together, holding hands. The avalanche of sadness was about to break. It would be easy to say they'd stay in touch, that they'd write, and maybe he might even promise to wait for her, but she knew all of that was window dressing. Whatever they had between them would end tonight, and she was already looking back on it. *It's a strange feeling to remember a moment you're participating in.* It was as if she constructed it from her own memories, and she and Leo had parted ways years before. She could feel his hand clasped around hers, but she was already thousands of miles away.

They stopped outside his house to see if any lights were on, but as always, every window was dark. It was almost midnight, and the streets were silent as death. There was no one and barely any sign of life anywhere, apart from a few lights flickering through lace curtains or the faint sound of a radio playing through an open window. It was as if they were all alone in the world, beholden to no one but themselves.

Leo led her around the side of the house, but she knew it so well, she could have walked with her eyes shut. Leo took her and kissed her as they stepped inside the shed. She returned the sentiment, enjoying the feel of his lips against hers, unsure of anything more than that. A few seconds passed before she broke away and sat down. He took the chair opposite her, reaching across to take her hand. She decided not to tell him yet. *Best wait. Enjoy this while you can.*

They spoke of other kids from school and the stupid things that went on. They spoke of their teachers—the fun ones and the mean ones. They spoke about things she never got to think about in her life as a pseudo-mother to her siblings. She sat and listened to him tell her about his cousin's new job in the city. The pressure to tell him began to build inside her.

"Do you have any cigarettes?" she asked.

"Yeah, sure," he said and went to the top shelf where he kept them behind a flowerpot. He handed her one and lit it for her. He sat back and sparked up his own before continuing on the story. She looked at her watch—it would be time to leave soon.

"I have to tell you something," she said, interrupting his story. "It's important."

Once again she felt like she was watching the scene more than participating in it. She didn't want to be there, didn't want to do this to Leo. She resented her father more than ever in that moment for putting her in this position.

"My father is going to take the job his uncle offered him in Berlin."

"He's leaving you again? He can't—"

"No. We're going with him."

Leo's brown eyes dropped. He grabbed her hand across the table with both of his. "No! You can't do that."

"He said he wouldn't go without us."

"Do you have any say in this?"

"He said he wasn't going to force us, but we need a space of our own. And since he lost his job with Uncle Frank…"

"I can't believe this. When does he want you to leave?"

"Soon. A week or so. My father's going to book the passage out of New York tomorrow."

"Well, what about us? Surely that's one of the most important things in your life?"

The tears were flowing down her cheeks now, thick and heavy.

"I can't let my siblings go without me. As important as you are in my life, they're my priority. I have to be there for them."

"But to a foreign country?"

"We're German—half-German, at least. We all speak the

language. I'm scared, but they're excited. We'll be together and have our own house. They can't see past that."

"When did you find out?"

"Only a few hours ago."

"And the decision's already made? You're leaving?"

"I wish it didn't have to be this way. I don't want to leave you."

She stood up and he embraced her. He held her as she wept in his arms.

The thought that her father would be around every night occurred to her. They would be a family again, sitting down having dinner in their own house. It didn't seem like too much to ask for. It was something Leo had every day of his life.

"You don't have to leave," he said. "Let them go. You can stay here and continue school. We can go to college together—"

"Aunt Maeve did say I could stay with her..." she said, immediately regretting telling him.

"Well, then, you should stay."

"I won't let the children go without me. They need me...and I need them. My father too."

"What about me? Don't you want to be with me?"

"Of course I do."

"We can get married. I love you, Maureen."

"We're too young."

"We could get married with permission from our parents."

"And where would we live? We're both still in school. I can't let my father take Michael and the children to Germany without me. I don't trust him to look after them."

She didn't necessarily believe any harm would come to her siblings without her to look after them, but knew how difficult it would be with just her father. She wanted them to be a family, just like they were before her mother died. But the thought of leaving Leo tore her apart.

They sat talking for a few more minutes, covering the same

ground over and over, before she realized she had to leave. Staying was only making things more painful. "I have to go. It's so hard seeing you like this." She wiped a tear from his eye. "You're a wonderful boy—"

"I'm a man, and I want to marry you."

What about what she wanted? Her ambitions didn't include getting married while still in school, or becoming a mother before the age of twenty.

"I'll look after you," he continued.

"I want to go to school and get a job."

"You don't need to do that. I can get a job and one day take over my father's store. You don't have to waste your time getting an education you'll never need."

She brushed aside the sting of his words. This wasn't the time to fight. "I want more than that."

"I know how smart you are, and one day our children will be too." He wrapped his arms around her and pulled her close. "Come inside the house with me. The bed in the spare room is empty. My parents will never hear."

The truth was she didn't want to, and certainly wasn't going to out of some sense of obligation.

"No. It's time for me to leave." She unwrapped his arms and went to the door of the shed they'd been meeting in for eight months. They embraced again. He kissed her. A few seconds passed before she drew back to look into his eyes again.

"This isn't the end for us," he said. "I'll write you every day."

The pain built to a crescendo inside her. It felt like she was coming apart at the seams. "I can't believe I have to leave you."

They stood there a few more minutes promising each other over and over that they'd ride this out and write every chance they got. No one was going to keep them apart—not her father or anyone else. Their parting seemed to tear a hole in her. She was sobbing uncontrollably as she walked out

An air of finality hung over her walk home. She felt

changed. The tears dried after a minute or two and left her evaluating the things he said. Would he have said those things about marriage and children and her not going to college if she wasn't going to Germany? Did it even matter now? Leo was old-fashioned, like his father. That didn't mean he wasn't worthy of love. She was more determined than ever to make her own way in life and not have to bow to the expectations of men like Leo —or her father.

The house was dark as she arrived home. It was almost two o'clock in the morning. They'd taken to meeting much later since her father had come home. She did everything she usually did—keeping to the side of the stairs to avoid them creaking and waiting to listen before going inside. She opened the door once she was sure no one was stirring and made for the stairs, not daring to look over at the sleeping figure of her father. Her foot was on the first step when she heard his voice and her blood turned to ice.

"Maureen." She closed her eyes and took her foot off the step. "Come over here."

Her father was sitting up on the couch. The floorboards creaked under her feet as she walked over to him. She took a seat in the armchair perpendicular to the couch. It was hard to make out his face in the half-light, but the tone of his voice did little to disguise his anger.

"Where were you?" he said. "Don't lie to me."

"I was with someone."

"Who, Leo Bernsen?"

"Yes, and I had to say goodbye to him tonight because of you and your insane scheme to uproot the family."

"Don't try to turn this around on me."

"So what if I was out with a boy? Don't you dare try to give me a hard time about it."

"What if something happened to you? What if we needed you here?"

"Needed me for what, exactly? It's the middle of the night and all the kids are asleep. I wish you'd never come home. You know that? I just had to say goodbye to someone I love tonight because of you."

"You wish I never came home?"

She wondered if she was going too far now, but the anger inside her wouldn't let her stop.

"I worried about you every day you were away. I heard some of the stories from other kids in school about what goes on with those men riding the rails. The other kids teased me about it—called you a bum."

"That's not true, and you won't have to worry anymore. I'm with you and we're going to be together, no matter where that might be." His voice was weaker now. The anger seemed to be gone, replaced by loss, longing, and pain.

"Have you any idea how hard it was for us, not knowing where you were half the time or what you were doing?"

"I wrote as much as I could."

"Yeah, but you never really told us what was going on, did you? You always made it seem like you were at a holiday camp."

"So, in trying not to worry you, I only worried you more?" He reached over to where he left his pants and into the pocket for a pack of cigarettes. He lit one up and pulled an ashtray up on the coffee table.

"Can I go to bed now?" she said.

"I'm sorry about your boyfriend, but you'll meet so many more wonderful people in your life."

"Don't give me that line. I'm just about the same age you were when you met Mother. What if your father had taken you away and played down the feelings you had for her—dismissed them like they were nothing?"

"I'm not trying to do that. I didn't choose for things to be this way."

"So you keep on saying."

"Did you mean what you said before?"

"About what?"

"About wishing I never came home?"

"I don't know right now. I really don't."

He stubbed out the cigarette. Smoke hung in the air between them like cobwebs in the darkness. "Go to bed. I don't want to see you anymore tonight."

She stood up without another word and he lay back down on the couch. Maureen stopped at the bottom of the stairs. She looked back, wanting to say something else, but she didn't and walked up the steps to her bedroom.

5

The last week in America was a whirlwind of tearful goodbyes that seemed to pass in seconds. Seamus was grateful that the fights with Maureen had abated. Her anger was simmering below the surface now, but he knew it was just lying dormant, not gone.

She invited Leo to the house the night before, perhaps to introduce him, or perhaps just to stick the knife in farther. Either way, Seamus was left with a residual guilt that was hard to suppress. It would have been far easier if Leo was rude or unfriendly, but he seemed like a fine young man. He shook Seamus's hand as he left with a confident stare, declaring that he'd be seeing him again in the future. It was hard to know what to say back to the young man, except to wish him luck. Maureen seemed to appreciate him meeting Leo. She hadn't shouted at him once since.

The boat to Germany was leaving in a few hours. Seamus's suitcase was already packed, with so few personal items that it was only half-full. Everything he owned in the world was ready to go in ten minutes. Maureen and Fiona had more trouble.

Maeve and the girls helped them sort through their clothes, laying out those they wanted to bring and those they'd leave for the girls.

Maureen led her siblings downstairs to where her father was standing in the kitchen. He had begun talking to them in German all the time. His command of the language was rusty, but improving. He was learning from them.

"Is everyone ready?" he said. Fiona was about to speak when he cut her off. "Well, you're going to have to be soon, because we sail in a few hours." He raised his voice at the end to elicit a cheer that Conor and Fiona delivered. "There's something we need to do before we go." He looked each one of them up and down, evaluating what they were wearing. They each looked respectable.

"Come with me," he said. He led them out the door and onto the street.

"Where are we going?" Maureen said.

"To see your mother."

The clouds above their heads covered the sun, rendering everything below a light-gray hue. They walked together, 20 minutes across town, to the graveyard where they laid their mother to rest just over two years before. Michael went first, pushing the gate open for the others. They trudged up toward the grave in silence. Being there seemed like the only time they were ever all quiet together. Fiona was already crying as they got to the grave. Maureen read out the words on the gravestone as she held her sister. It was something she'd taken to doing each time they came there.

"Here lies Marie Anne Ritter, loving wife, mother to Maureen, Michael, Fiona, and Conor. Taken too soon. 1897–1929."

No one spoke for a few seconds. The only sound was Fiona crying. Conor seemed in a daze. Seamus knew he had to be the one to break the silence.

"Marie, my love, we've come today to say goodbye. We've had the most amazing opportunity arise. We're going to Germany later on today. I know that you'll be with us, but we won't be able to come here anymore, not for a while. I want to tell you how proud I am of all of our wonderful children, and especially Maureen, who took on your job when I left. I don't know where we'd be without her today." He lifted his eyes from the gravestone to Maureen's. "The children want to say a few words now."

Each of them took a turn to speak to their mother.

"Hello," Michael said. "I miss you. I'm sorry I can't come and see you here anymore. Not for a while at least. We're going to Germany for a while to live with Uncle Helmut. Father got a job over there. I'm excited. I can't wait until we're all together in our own house. Oh, and one more thing—Maureen thinks she's you. Tell her she's not."

"Ok," Seamus said. Fiona went next. She stepped forward, barely able to get the words out. A few mumbled words about loving and missing her mother crossed her lips before she stood back. Conor was next.

"We miss you. I wish you were still here. I want you to come with us. We all do."

Seamus scooped him up in his arms and hugged his young son. "I'm proud of you, son."

Maureen went last. A tear ran down her face as she began. She rubbed it away as soon as it came, seemingly annoyed at herself for showing it in front of the children.

"Goodbye, Mother. I've done my best to keep us together. I just hope I'm not going to have to work quite so hard anymore."

"You won't," her father said.

"We're off to live in Berlin for a while. I was terrified when I first heard, but I'm not scared anymore. I know you'll be with us and we'll all be together." Fiona took her hand. "It might be a while before we're back here, but I'll still think about you every day. We all will. It doesn't matter where we are—I know you'll always be with us."

They stood there another few minutes, only saying a few whispered words until Seamus announced it was time to go. They were out on the street again when Maureen asked, "What was she like when you first met?"

Memories flooded his mind. "We were only kids. I was seventeen, she was fifteen. She was fresh off the boat, just like my mother was, from a little village called Spiddal, in the west of Ireland. I think I knew the moment I saw her that I wanted her to be my wife. She was working as a maid in one of my friend's houses. Her accent was so thick you almost had to wave it away from your face as she spoke."

He smiled. "I never met anyone more wonderful. She was strong too—she won the argument over what names to call you kids four times out of four. You were named after great-aunts and -uncles back in Ireland none of us ever met."

"Do you ever hear from her family?"

"Not since she died. Her parents are long gone. Her younger sisters used to write, asking about you, with news of your cousins, but the fact that we never met any of them made it harder to stay in touch."

"And then everything went out the window when you left," Maureen said.

"A lot of things did, yes."

Maeve and the girls were in the kitchen when they got back. They prepared a special lunch. Frank came home in time to eat, and they all sat down together one last time. Frank had a bottle of red wine and poured each of the adults a glass, including Maureen. Seamus wasn't sure how he felt about her drinking. Frank noticed his discomfort and roared, laughing as he topped up her glass. They toasted family.

Time moved so quickly he barely felt it pass and the children left to gather their bags. They came back downstairs with wet eyes. Maeve and her two girls said goodbye with hugs and cards they made. More tears. Seamus almost felt a few himself. He embraced the girls in turn, thanked his sister one more time, and left.

Frank gave them a ride to the wharf in his new car. They boarded their ship, bound for Hamburg. The children took places at the railing as the boat eased from its moorage. They waved down to the people on the dock they didn't know, screaming goodbyes. Seamus was standing next to Maureen. She looked up at him.

"How do you feel?" he asked. "Just a little excitement?"

She looked at him for a long second, as if wondering whether to let him have this moment. "I'm glad we're all together," she said. He knew better than to try to hug her, and settled for the smaller victory.

They stayed there until the city dissipated into nothing, and all there was to see around them was the vast emptiness of the ocean.

~

Three slow days passed. The children grew tired of staring out at the endless blue horizon and of the few toys they'd been able to bring. They found some friends among the children of other families on board and played hide and seek in the countless nooks and crannies of the ship. Michael found another boy his age who had a football. He and his new friend spent hours passing it to each other, fighting the constant looming threat of the ball falling into the ocean. Maureen took to her books, both for pleasure and to study. She had her mind set on becoming a doctor. Seamus feared for her in a male-dominated profession. That didn't seem to deter her, however, and she studied on.

Seamus spent much of his time alone in the lounge, reading books on management, and even one he found on the metalworks industry. He knew numbers and finance, but hadn't set foot inside a factory since visiting the one he was to work in all those years ago. This would be a different experience, and he wanted to be ready. The factory was a going concern, with a staff of about three hundred full-time workers. It was profitable, but he guessed a little antiquated. His first job would be to modernize it, minimizing waste. It was challenging to plan in any detail without being there, but he was trying.

Helga was a mystery to him. He sent her a telegram a few days before they left, telling her that he looked forward to working with her. She didn't respond...or at least, he didn't receive any reply by the time they left. He wondered how much interest she had in taking over the business. He tried to remember her. She was ten when he last met her and a quiet, well-mannered girl. He couldn't remember ever playing with her. Maeve knew her better but had little to say past that she was studious, along with knitting and sewing and other pursuits best performed alone. Helga was the polar opposite of her gregarious father.

When the boat was in international waters, Seamus went to the bar and ordered a beer. The laws of the United States no longer applied. Escaping the ridiculousness of Prohibition was something he'd been looking forward to. The bartender handed him a frothy beer in a tall glass. Seamus studied it a few seconds before taking a sip.

"Thing of beauty isn't it?" said a man sitting alone beside him.

"Sure is. And we don't have to worry about the cops busting in. It seems like we've got it made out here in the middle of the ocean." He took another sip and turned to the man. He was in his late twenties, with sharp blue eyes and slicked-back hair. "What has you going to Hamburg?"

"I'm a journalist. I just got a job working for the *Times*, and my first posting too. I studied German history in college and speak the language, so they put me on the boat over. Should be plenty to write about, anyway." He extended a hand. "Clayton Thomas."

Seamus shook his hand. "I'm set up over here," he said, motioning toward the table where he left his books. "You feel like talking a while?"

"I'd love to. Nothing else to do, is there?"

"Not a whole lot."

They made their way over to the table. Seamus cleared his books off to make room for their drinks. Clayton was drinking some kind of orange cocktail with fruit floating around in it.

"So, where are you going to be based?" Seamus asked.

"Berlin. Right smack in the middle of the lion's den."

"Same. With my four kids."

"You're moving to Berlin with your four children—"

Seamus cut him off before he could ask about their mother. "Just me and the children, aged sixteen, fourteen, eleven, and seven. Their mother's no longer with us, I'm sorry to say."

"My commiserations."

"Thanks."

Clayton sat and listened as Seamus talked about the letter from Helmut and the decision to move to Germany. He told him about leaving the kids for two years and his struggles to find a job when he got back. He stopped short of describing his brief time as a bootlegger and shooting those idiotic boys on the side of the road in New Jersey. He thought of them many times since, but knew that they'd dug their own graves that night. Some things were impossible to come back from.

"And the children are happy to move?" Clayton asked.

"Yes. Much more so than I thought they'd be. Where are you from?"

"Manhattan. Born and raised on the Upper East Side. My father owns a chain of drugstores in the city. My brothers work for him, but I went to journalism school instead. I guess you could say I was the black sheep of the family." He finished his drink and lit up a cigarette. "I don't have any attachments, so when the Berlin posting came up, I jumped at it. You know where you're going to live when you get over there?"

"Not yet. We'll stay in a hotel until we get something. My uncle suggested Charlottenburg, but we'll see. We lived in Wedding when I was a kid."

"Why did you move to Germany back then?"

"My father had some business interests there. He never talked about them much. He worked with my uncle for a while, but it went sour. My father wasn't the type to share unnecessary details with his children."

"You know much about what's going on in Germany these days?"

"I've been reading what I can since I found out I was going to be living there. Seems like a bit of a mess right now—politically and economically."

"Yeah, there's a bit of a tug-of-war going on with the conservatives, the center, the Communists, and the hard right all wrestling for power. The hope is that the election in November will sort everything out, but I don't see it. The last one didn't do that. The system's not set up to elect clear winners."

"What about this Hitler guy? I've read his name a lot He's the leader of the NSDAP?"

"Yes, the *Nationalsozialistische Deutsche Arbeiterpartei*, also known as the Nazi Party."

"I've heard the term thrown around a few times."

"Hitler's an interesting one. He casts himself as a man of the people, an ordinary guy fighting against the political elites."

"Is he?"

"He was a corporal in the war, whereby President von Hindenburg was the head of the entire German Army, so there may be a little truth to his role as an ordinary man. That doesn't make him any less radical or potentially dangerous."

"How widespread is the fighting on the streets?"

"It's there. Mainly the Nazis' bullyboys, the SA, or the Stormtroopers going after their Communist rivals, but civilians get caught up in it sometimes."

Seamus drank some of his beer, thinking about what he was getting his children into. Could it be any worse than what he left behind? Shooting men on the side of the road?

"It's not anarchy over there by any means," Clayton said. He obviously saw the look on his companion's face. "It's a country of laws, just like our own. I'm hoping the Nazis get wiped out in the next election. Hitler isn't one for compromise. He's more of a death or glory type, and he's put all his eggs in the basket of the next election. The Nazis are the biggest party in parliament right now."

"The *Reichstag*."

"Yes, exactly. But if things don't go well for them in the election, it could be the end of Hitler and his mob. I'm hoping that's what'll happen, anyway. The economy is improving. The only way was up from where they were two years ago."

"I know the feeling."

"I don't think we'll be hearing too much about our friend Hitler after the upcoming elections, and good riddance when he goes. He's a narcissist. The Nazis' entire policy is based on blaming others for the loss of Germany's greatness, whether it be the establishment, the Communists, or the Jews. I read his book, or at least as much of that tripe that I could stomach."

"I've heard of it—what's it about?"

"The betrayal of the German forces at the end of the war, and the path to return Germany to greatness...as he sees it."

"What betrayal? They were beaten in the field of battle."

"It's one of many fantasies he's concocted to shift the blame for losing the war. And he's obsessed with the Jews—how they're an inferior race to the racially pure German supermen."

"Supermen?"

"Yes. A made-up race called *Aryans*. He continually says the Jews are parasites, trying to destroy German culture and all that's good in the world from within. It really is so ridiculous. It stretches credibility that anyone could believe it, but millions do."

Seamus finished his beer. "Do you work for the German Department of Tourism by any chance?"

Clayton laughed. "The world is full of men like Hitler. I'm sure the German people will come to their senses and give him a swift boot up the rear-end."

"I hope you're right."

"I don't want to worry you. I've been to Berlin twice in the last three years. I've always found it a charming and lively place. They have some problems there, but look at me—I'm going back. I'm sure you and your family will make a wonderful life there no matter what the political situation is."

Michael arrived at the table, red-faced and panting. His new friend Charlie was beside him. Seamus introduced Clayton to his son. Michael shook hands, but was more concerned with getting money for a Coke. Seamus pressed a dime into his palm after forcing him to promise to share with his friend. The two boys ran off.

"Do you play poker?" Clayton asked.

"A little. You know of a game?"

"There's always a game somewhere. Maybe later. You want another?" Clayton motioned to the glasses on the table.

"Please."

Clayton stood up to get another round of drinks while Seamus thought about what he said. Germany was under the rule of the Kaiser when he lived there. He'd heard his mother complain about the war culture there at the time, but being a young man, dismissed it as boring or irrelevant. It seemed less so now. Clayton arrived back with the drinks. He changed the subject, talking about where he went to college and his journey from being a fledgling reporter to being a foreign correspondent. Seamus enjoyed the conversation and settled down. He was sure Clayton was right. Hitler and his wide-eyed bigots would soon be gone, and life could resume as normal.

The entire world seemed to be in flux right now. Germany was no exception, but it was still a nation of great thinkers and inventors, the home of Beethoven, Goethe, and Heine. A few crazy bullies weren't going to erase all that by appealing to the base instincts of the downtrodden. He sat back in his chair to enjoy the conversation.

~

The ship docked in the Port of Hamburg a week later. The journey down the Elbe lent a sense of anticlimax to the end of the trip, as they could see land on either side but not the port itself. Once the city came into view, a party atmosphere on the ship commenced. Crowds gathered on deck let out a cheer as the boat docked, and minutes later, people were walking along the gangway onto solid ground.

Seamus was almost as enthusiastic as the children. It had seemed like an interminable journey across the ocean. Everyone had a smile on their face—even Maureen. Perhaps the excitement of the new life they were to embark on was taking effect on her at last, and the pining for Leo would stop now.

Seamus put his arm over Michael's shoulder. This was the new beginning they needed. The time on the ship began a chance for him to be a father again. He made all the decisions, whether that was where they went to dinner or who they played with. It felt like he was warming up for the real world and the new responsibilities he was taking on as a single parent.

It was hard to say if Maureen was happy to be relieved of

her role as parent. She didn't relinquish it easily, and the children still went to her. He supposed they always would, but she had her own life to live. It was time for him to take hold of his responsibilities and make up for the mistakes of the past. A few hiccups were to be expected, but he hoped the trust that had been eroded was being restored bit by bit, and their confidence in him was growing.

Clayton appeared from behind them, his suitcases in hand. A gust blew up, and he dropped one to hold onto his hat. He greeted each of the children by name. They turned to say hello before focusing back on the crowd waiting on the dock below.

"You got anyone to meet you?" Clayton asked Seamus.

"No. We were planning on getting the train to Berlin tonight."

"Same. I know where the station is. You can come along with me if you'd like. I figure I owe you that much for fleecing you in cards the other night."

Seamus smiled. "That'd be about the least you owe me after that." Clayton was quite the poker player. He and the other men at the table were relieved that they were only playing for a pittance.

The ship's horn let out a massive blast, which excited the children even more. Fiona and Conor were jumping up and down now. Seamus waited until the crowds dissipated before letting the children get in line to disembark. Once he gave the word, Fiona and Conor bolted like greyhounds out of a trap, and he had to call them back to remind them to bring their suitcases along. Clayton did his best to help them with their luggage but was struggling with his own.

Maureen led the family along the gangway and onto German soil. She turned to them as soon as she set foot on the dock with an enthusiastic smile. Clayton led them through the crowd, the sound of English fading out. Harsh German consonants were everywhere, but somehow Seamus didn't feel like a stranger. It felt like a homecoming of sorts.

There wasn't enough room in the taxi for all of them, so Clayton gave them the address of a restaurant he knew and went ahead to get a table. It felt momentous to speak German to a native, and Seamus let Michael do it. The taxi driver nodded, but didn't share Michael's enthusiasm and loaded their bags in the back of the car without saying a word.

Hamburg didn't look much different from any other city. The street sellers and businessmen in suits could have been in downtown Manhattan as much as here, but the excitement in the car didn't wane. Seamus wondered if the kids noticed the political notices plastered on every wall they passed. The vehicle stopped at a red light beside a billboard. It was covered in Nazi election posters declaring that communism had to be stopped and Adolf Hitler was the man to save Germany from it.

The taxi pulled up outside the restaurant. Seamus paid the driver with some of the German currency he managed to procure on board the ship. It was just enough to get them to Berlin and settle there in the hotel. The rest of their savings, still in dollars, was in the money belt he'd worn in the work camp.

Clayton waved to them as they made their way into the busy restaurant. Fiona was first to join him, and he greeted her with a handshake. The children took their seats. Michael insisted on ordering for everyone else at the table. Clayton laughed as the young man dealt with the waiter in perfect German. They ordered schnitzel, sauerbraten, and bratwurst, not because they wanted it, but more because they thought they should get into the local culture. Clayton and Seamus both ordered beers. Every adult in the room seemed to be drinking it. Seamus waited until the meal was over to ask his friend about the election posters. They spoke in English.

"I saw them everywhere on the way here. All the parties were represented, but the Nazis more than any other."

"They're the biggest party in the *Reichstag* right now and are looking to take the next step and secure a majority, but I don't see it."

The thought of the Nazis securing a majority made Seamus more than a little uneasy, but he knew better than to voice his concerns in front of the children.

~

The journey to Berlin was three hours. Maureen's resentment toward her father, which she thought had peaked in Newark when he forced her to leave Leo behind, was boiling over again. Her father and Clayton were in the dining car having their third or fourth drink of their time in Germany so far. It seemed he found a kindred spirit. The children peered out at pretty towns set amid rolling emerald hills, seemingly content that he left them in her care again. Their standards for him were so low that they didn't seem to care that he said he'd be gone 30 minutes. It was almost 45 now.

Is this to be my life here? Am I to be left stuck with my brothers and sister while our father drinks beer? He makes such a big deal of wanting his family with him, yet he seems to take any opportunity to dump them on me.

She'd seen flashes of the man he was before her mother died. Things got better and better...and then he did something like go to the drinks car and she was back feeling this way again, dreaming about Leo. His words about marrying her—and her not needing to work or better herself in any way—gave her pause these last few days. She hadn't admitted it to anyone, but was beginning to think the time was right to break up with him. She didn't want to end up like her parents: married at eighteen, a child a year later. But that was what he wanted.

If she went back to him, she was sure he would be as good as his word. He'd doubtless ask her to wait for him to take over his father's store, and then she'd become a wife and mother, married to the local green grocer. Or she could stay there and see what Berlin had to offer. College, and her dream of becoming a doctor beckoned. Her family was here, and maybe in time she could love again. But it was too early to think about other boys. Leo was in firm possession of her heart for now at least.

Fiona pointed out the window at another pretty village. It was as if they were in a dream. Everything seemed different there, yet somehow as if she'd seen it before. Michael spoke of home a lot since they left, and apart from Maeve and the cousins, the little children had hardly mentioned it all. They were caught in the exhilaration of the moment. It was infectious.

Loud raucous laughter cut through the air. Three young men wearing brown uniforms were making their way up the aisle. They were all young and fit, but one boy—blond and toned, with high cheekbones and bright blue eyes—was so handsome, she couldn't help staring at him.

"What's that funny cross on their arms?" Fiona whispered in English.

"The armband?" Maureen answered. "I think it's the symbol of the group they belong to,"

"What group? Like the Boy Scouts?"

"I think so."

The three boys were only a little older than her, perhaps nineteen or twenty years old. Two of them had brown hair. They barreled through the narrow space between the row of seats. Maureen let herself look up at the handsome boy again.

"I wonder what that symbol means," Fiona said.

The handsome boy stopped. "You're American?" he said in English.

"German," Maureen said in their language.

He didn't seem to buy what she said. "No, I heard the little girl." The blond one said in German, "You're Americans." The other two stopped to see what their friend would do. The atmosphere changed. The look in the boys' eyes told her they were trouble. Maureen peered down toward the dining car—no sign of her father. *Where is he?!* A flash of panic surged through her as the young man took a step toward where they were sitting.

"I think I'd like to talk to the pretty American," he said. His friends smiled. "Move out of there, kid," he said to Fiona.

Maureen curled her arm around her sister. "Don't move," she said in German. She brought her eyes to the handsome boy, who seemed to be the ringleader. "Our father will be back any second."

"And what's he going to do?" the young man sneered. "We're just trying to be friendly—and welcome you to the greatest country in the world."

"Soon to be the greatest again," one of the other boys said.

"Yes. Once Herr Hitler is in power," the blond said. "Once we've rid ourselves of the Jews and the Bolshevists. Why don't you come over here and sit down on my lap? I'll tell you all about it."

The other men laughed, but the blond didn't move. Maureen could see he had no intention of leaving. The smile faded from her face, and he held out his hand. The carriage was half-full, but none of the other passengers seemed to acknowledge what was happening in front of them.

"Please leave us alone. I'm here with my family."

"Well, then, leave them, pretty girl. Maybe you and I could take a trip to the bathroom together, and get acquainted." The other two roared, laughing.

Michael stood up. "That's enough. Move on," he said. His voice was quaking.

"Oh, so the little American thinks he can come over to our country and push us around, does he?" the blond youth said. He stepped up to him. Michael looked like he was about to cry but didn't back off. Maureen stood up, and the blond boy grabbed at her. Michael deflected his arm, but the German slapped him across the face.

The noise of the slap reverberated through the carriage like a whip, and everyone was looking now. Michael fell back on the seat and the Stormtrooper was on him, pummeling him with his fists as her brother tried to defend himself. Without thinking, Maureen jumped up and onto the Stormtrooper's back. The other two moved in.

Conor was crying, calling out for their father. Fiona tried to get up, but one of the louts pushed her down. Maureen swiped at the handsome boy's face. One of the other louts grabbed her and she fell backward, almost on top of her sister.

That seemed to be the final straw for one middle-aged lady sitting down the aisle who got up, saying she was going to the ticket inspector for help. What the fat old ticket inspector could do was unclear. Maureen staggered to her feet again as one of the other boys stepped in to grab her. The blond was on Michael again, who was protecting himself with his arms across his face.

A loud roar erupted through the carriage as their father ran in. The last remaining thug went to fend him off, but received a punch in the face for his efforts. Clayton was behind him and rushed the boy on Michael. Seamus went for the one who had his hands on Maureen next, breaking his nose with a closed fist. Clayton had the blond by the arms, and Seamus unleashed a punch into his midriff as the ticket inspector arrived.

The portly old man shouted at them to calm down. Seamus whipped around. The boys backed off, sweat pouring off their brows and panting like dogs.

"What on earth is going on here?" the ticket inspector said, as if he were talking to a bunch of naughty children. Maureen felt hatred bubbling up inside her, choking her.

Who do these boys think they are? Who told them they had the right to do this?

Her father was drinking with his new friend when they were attacked—absent when they needed him most. *Some things never change.*

"That idiot attacked us," Maureen said.

"No need to call us names," the blond boy said. "We're SA. Stormtroopers—Hitler's finest."

Maureen wanted to rip the smile off his face with rusty razors. They weren't ashamed in any way. One of them held a handkerchief to his bloody nose, but the other two were still smirking.

"I heard the ruckus in here and came back from the dining car with my friend. These boys were attacking my children." The ticket inspector stared at him with dull brown eyes. Seamus held out his arms. "Can we have them removed from the train, at least?"

"What happened?" the ticket inspector asked the blond Stormtrooper.

"We were just passing and that girl asked us to come over." He pointed at Maureen. "I was curious, but when I went over, she hit me. Her brother here stood up and got in my face. I had to defend myself."

"That's a lie!" Michael said. "They came over and started harassing us—"

"Save it," the ticket inspector said. "The police at the next stop have already been alerted. You can tell them your stories and they'll figure out what went on. In the meantime, you three come with me."

He led the three SA men away. They left, but not before hurling insults at Seamus and Clayton under their breath.

Seamus went to the children. "Are you ok? Did they hurt you?" Conor hugged him, but Fiona stayed still in her seat.

"They attacked us," Michael said. "They were pestering Maureen and I stood up to ask them to stop and one of them hit me. But I wasn't going to let them push me around. We didn't start it."

Maureen was glad Michael was doing the talking, as speaking to her father was beyond her at that moment. He should have been there for them, not sampling the local beer. She could see the rage still rippling through him as he sat opposite her. He opened his mouth to speak to her.

"Don't," Maureen said to him, smelling the beer on his breath. Fiona nuzzled into her as Maureen pulled her close. Several people got up to tell Seamus what had happened, and a few offered to speak to the police on their behalf. He thanked them and they sat back down.

Why didn't they help when the boys were attacking them? Were the people that afraid of the Brownshirts? Did they have that much of a hold on the ordinary citizen on the street?

The train came to a halt at a place called Breddin, which the conductor told them was about an hour from Berlin. Maureen hadn't looked at her father in the 10 minutes since he tried to speak to her. She hadn't responded to his apologies, and he stopped trying. The anger she tried to conquer on the boat trip over was reemerging.

The ticket inspector spoke to them. "Can you come with me, please?"

Seamus nodded. It took a minute to get the luggage together. They inched off the train, past the other travelers who suddenly seemed less interested in being involved. But it didn't matter. Maureen was sure the police would see sense, and those hooligans would spend the night behind bars. A few passengers apologized for the behavior of the young Stormtroopers. Their words added a spattering of water to the flame inside her.

The ticket inspector led them onto the platform at Breddin, assuring them that there would be a train within minutes of whenever their business with the police ended. The police were waiting, the SA men already with them. None spoke as they walked over. Clayton went with them. One policeman was in his twenties, the other much older, about fifty or so. The older man took a notebook out of his pocket. His bushy mustache danced above his lip as he talked.

"So, I've had a few words with the boys. They told me their side of the story. What did you see?"

"I missed the start," her father said. "I'll let my daughter explain."

Maureen stepped forward, eager to tell her side. The young policeman smiled at her. The older one, who was about a foot taller than her, bent over and looked at her as if she were Conor's age.

"We were minding our business. That one heard my sister speaking English." She pointed to the blond Stormtrooper. "He came over to speak to me, making inappropriate suggestions."

"That's not what happened at all. I welcomed her to the Fatherland. She's probably a Communist."

"That's enough," the policeman said.

"My brother stood up for me and that thug hit him."

"That's not what he or his friends said." The policeman closed his notepad. "I think it's best if we left this, and you get on the next train to Berlin. I'll make sure these boys don't get on. You'll never see them again."

"What?" Seamus said. "You're not going to arrest these idiots? They attacked my family. My son is only fourteen. That hoodlum hit him."

The Stormtroopers knew better than to answer this time.

"You broke his nose," the policeman said. "A grown man like you hitting a man half his age?"

"I was defending my children."

"And these young boys are trying to defend our country. They might be a little over zealous at times, but their intentions are good. They're going to apologize and we're all going to get on with our day. Aren't you, boys?"

The Stormtroopers nodded, the mirth from earlier now absent.

"You can't be serious," Maureen said. She felt like she was going to explode.

"Apologize, boys," the policeman said.

The SA men murmured an apology through barely opened lips.

"That's not good enough at all. I want these men charged," Seamus said.

"Maybe you're the one who needs to be brought to jail," the policeman said. "You broke his nose. There's another train to Berlin in five minutes. If you and your family aren't on it, I'll be bringing you to the station."

The policemen turned and led the Stormtroopers away. None looked back.

"Where are they going? They're leaving together? Get them back here now!" Maureen said to her father.

He looked at her with a pained expression on his face, but no, that wasn't good enough.

"What would you have me do? It's best we get on the next train like he said—"

"No, it's not. Get them back here," she said. It was hard to control herself. They were in public, and the kids were looking at her. "They can't just get away with doing that. This is your fault."

"I'm sorry, Maureen," her father said. "There's nothing we can do."

"They're in cahoots with the police," she said. "We've only been here a few hours. Why did you bring us here?"

Her father looked like he was searching for the right words, but there were none.

Fiona knew better. "Let's get on the next train. I want to get to the hotel." She clutched her sister's hand and led her away, joining Michael and Conor. All four of them stood together. Her father came to them as they were standing on the platform.

"I'm so sorry," he said. "I should have been there for you."

"Not drinking with your friend in the dining car," Maureen said.

"It's ok, Father," Michael said. "You got that one guy a good one."

"Yes, a great one," Conor said and gave his father a hug.

Maureen couldn't believe what she was hearing. Were they going to forgive him that easily? It was all his fault. Another train pulled up a few seconds later. She didn't speak to her father for the rest of the journey.

~

The train steamed into Berlin's Lehrter Bahnhof as the sun was setting over the River Spree. Seamus cursed the SA boys as the train came to a halt. They had sucked the joy out of the final leg of the journey to Berlin. Arriving in the city for the first time with the family after an arduous journey should have been a moment to savor for the rest of their lives, but the children greeted it with hardened, tired faces.

Seamus wasn't going to give up on them. He picked Conor up and pressed him against the window, but there wasn't much more to see than the station itself. Still, he pointed to the sign that read BERLIN and managed to elicit some enthusiasm. He apologized to Maureen again, but she still wouldn't even look at him. This was the beginning of a new life, but it felt more like they were arriving home from vacation.

The station displayed an air of grandeur he hadn't experienced in settings such as this one before. The ceilings stretched high above their heads as if they were in a cathedral. Banks of windows let in the golden light of the setting sun.

Clayton dropped his suitcase and wished them goodbye. He had a dinner date with one of his new colleagues, and Seamus knew he had to get the children to the hotel and to bed. The young journalist gave Seamus his contact details.

"I have some people I want you to meet—a bunch of expats. Next week sometime."

Seamus put the folded note into his breast pocket. "I'll be in touch."

The young man turned to Maureen and the others. "Welcome to Berlin. I can assure you that not everyone here is nearly as nasty as those ruffians on the train. You're going to love the city, and you'll have your new house."

"We're going to get our own rooms!" Conor said.

"I can't wait to see them," he said with a smile. "And Maureen, go easy on your father. He's doing his best."

Maureen glared at him. With that, he disappeared into the crowd.

"Let's go," Seamus said and took Conor by the hand. The children followed him through the crowd. Their mood lightened as they made it out onto the street and got into a taxi. Conor and Fiona were rapt during the ride to the hotel. They stared out the window as if they were at the pictures. The taxi driver took them to a simple hotel in Wedding, the area in the center of Berlin where Seamus lived with his parents as a child. The surroundings weren't as instantly familiar as he thought they might be. It felt different than he remembered.

They booked two rooms, one for him and the boys and the other for Maureen and Fiona. They were used to sharing, and the fact that it wouldn't be for much longer made it all the more fun. At least, he hoped so.

Seamus took Maureen aside as he was leaving to go to his

room. Fiona was in bed, and she was in her nightdress. He fumbled for the words as she stood in front of him.

"I am so sorry for what happened earlier—" he began.

"You were drinking with your friend." She almost spat the words.

"I'd never let anything happen to you and the children." It never used to be like this. This was all new.

"You weren't there for us. We were only in the country a few hours—the country you dragged us to."

The thought to argue with her sparked in his mind, but he resisted the urge. "I will never let anything like that happen again," he said, but she didn't look like she believed him. "Good night. We have a big day ahead of us tomorrow."

"Good night," she said and turned to walk back to the bed she was sharing with her sister.

Seamus felt his heart constricting in his chest. There was nothing more he wanted in this world than to be there for her and the children, but he'd failed them again.

6

October 8, 1932

Seamus drew back the curtains to reveal the street below. Commuters walked by reading newspapers and smoking cigarettes. He stayed at the window a few minutes, watching the city rouse from its slumber, looking for clues about how this new life would be. Michael and Conor were still asleep, though he had slept little himself. The SA boys from the train had infected his mind like a virus. There was no escaping the truth—what had happened was his fault. He had to do better. *Just when I was starting to get somewhere with Maureen.*

He closed his eyes, fantasizing about saving Maureen from a rabid group of Brownshirts, facing them down on the street and chasing them away. It had felt good to punch that lout. Would he need to protect them again here? Were the Brownshirts a danger to ordinary people, or was his family just unlucky on the train? Did their prejudices stretch to any foreigner, or was their hatred confined only to Jews and Communists?

He was sure that it was only bad luck. It could have happened anywhere. The SA would break up and scurry back to their holes once Hitler and the Nazis disappeared after the election, and then all he'd have to worry about was every boy who came calling to the house for his daughters.

Michael's voice interrupted his thoughts. "Morning, Father."

"Good morning."

He wanted to ask him how he felt, and if he forgave him for what happened on the train, but he didn't. Conor opened his eyes.

"Who wants to go on an adventure?" Seamus said. The boys looked at him with surprise in their eyes. "I'm going to arrange to meet Uncle Helmut at the factory later. Who wants to come with me?"

They both responded with gusto.

Seamus went to the girls' room and knocked. Maureen told him through the door they'd meet him in the lobby, and 20 minutes later they were in a café drinking hot chocolate and eating freshly baked bread rolls smeared with butter and raspberry jam. Maureen spoke little and glared at him over her cup. The children finished their food, and he sat back to drink his coffee.

The stories in the newspaper were dominated by the upcoming election. Hitler was campaigning in Munich, his stronghold, and promising to return Germany to greatness. Seamus folded the paper and put it down on the table.

"Let's go and see Uncle Helmut's factory," he said.

The three younger children cheered and smiled. Maureen wasn't as enthused, but seemed to agree to the plan. "Can we see some of the city beforehand?" she asked.

"Of course. That's what I was planning to do with you after

breakfast. There's so much to see. I just need to make a phone call first."

Seamus paid the bill. He was excited to see his uncle and the factory where they'd be working together. He took the letter his uncle sent him with the address and checked it over one more time before leading the kids out onto the street. Being in the city felt surreal. Just a few weeks before he was in Ohio, digging trenches and sleeping in a tent. Now he was in Berlin. It was about 45 minutes down to the Brandenburg Gate, but the children didn't protest. They wanted to walk, to soak up the sights of their new city.

"Let's get going. I think a walking tour is the best way to travel on our first day."

Conor grasped his hand and they left.

They stopped on the bridge over the Spree to stare down and throw stones into the water. He watched his eldest daughter as much as he could without her noticing. She seemed impressed by the lively and beautiful city they'd moved to. The idiots on the train were almost forgotten, the only reminders the ubiquitous election posters, most of which seemed to espouse the greatness of Hitler and his Nazi Party. A few minutes later they were walking through the Brandenburg Gate, marveling at its magnificence.

"It's hard to believe we're going to live here."

"I know," Maureen said. "I feel like a tourist."

"You'll settle in soon enough. Once you start school and find friends, it'll seem like you've been here your whole lives."

"It's a beautiful city," she answered.

They entered the Tiergarten, the city park just beyond the Brandenburg Gate. The children ran ahead, leaving Maureen with her father. They didn't speak for a few seconds as they watched the children. An awkward silence descended. He knew he had to say something.

"Maureen, I just wanted—"

"I shouldn't let the kids run too far ahead," she said. She left him standing alone and went to Conor, who was trying to climb a tree. Seamus found a bench to sit on and watched the children playing for a few minutes, thinking about all that was to come.

~

The factory was only a few minutes away by taxi, and they went there after lunch. The children looked at each other as the car drove down streets with boarded-up houses and unkempt trees lurching onto the road, like wraiths guarding the way. They pulled up to a large black gate. Seamus asked the driver to sound his horn. A few seconds later, Helmut appeared, a beaming smile on his face. His neat beard was in sharp contrast to his curly gray hair, which ran wild around his head. His expensive suit was the only indication that he was a rich man.

"Seamus!" he shouted. "And the kids! Get out here and give your great-uncle a hug."

Seamus paid the driver and barely had time to get out of the car before his uncle grabbed hold of him.

"You look great," Seamus said. "I can't believe it's been 22 years."

"I haven't aged a day, have I?" Helmut said.

"Let's not go crazy," Seamus answered.

The kids filed onto the pavement. None were impervious to Helmut's energy, and all were smiling in seconds. He hugged each one before turning to Seamus again.

"They're still smiling...even with everything they've been through. I'm so glad you're here."

"We're glad to be here," Seamus said.

"It's exciting," Michael said.

"I can't wait to see the factory and all the machines!" Conor said.

Helmut smiled. "It's Saturday, so all the workers are home with their families, but they'll be back on Monday. I'm sure your father will bring you back to meet them."

"Of course," Seamus said.

"I'm so looking forward to getting to know you all," Helmut said.

His uncle hadn't changed a bit. They walked with him across the empty lot toward the factory.

"What do you make here?" Conor asked.

"Lots of different things. We cut metal sheets, and weld steel. We polish it and make knives and forks and pots and pans. We make the iron railings you see outside houses, and even gates, like the one you just passed though. Lots of things to do with metal."

They arrived at a wooden door and he reached into his pocket for the keys. The children looked at each other in anticipation as he pushed the door open. It wasn't quite the wonderland they were expecting, and they seemed a little disappointed by the industrial presses and idle metalworking machines. It took them a few minutes to walk around, peering at every workstation. Seamus imagined the presses working. It was so ridiculous—he hadn't been inside a factory since he toured this same one as a kid. He was relying on his imagination to form a picture of what the working day would be, but his future was coming into sharper focus.

"Who wants to see your father's new office?" Helmut said.

The office was on the second level, and Helmut led them up metal stairs that clanked under their footfalls. He pushed open a black door to reveal Seamus's new office. Michael ran to the chair behind the desk, delighted that he was the first to sit in it. Seamus went to the window and peered down at the factory floor. He turned around to speak to his uncle.

"I can only imagine what it's like with all the machines working."

"How are you feeling about taking a job here?"

"Excited. Terrified. The usual."

"You'll do great," the old man said and placed a hand on his shoulder. "I'll teach you what you need to know. No one's expecting miracles on the first day."

"Thank you for this opportunity."

"Thank you for coming here, and bringing these wonderful children with you."

Helmut whirled around to the kids, before his nephew had a chance to answer. They were already getting bored of the trip to their father's new workplace. "Who wants to come back to my house?" He held out his hand, counting on his fingers. "I have cakes, and chocolate. I have soda pop, and bon bons."

"Me! Me!" Conor and Fiona shouted in unison as if they'd practiced it. Maureen and Michael agreed also.

Helmut was very much as Seamus remembered him—a showman. "But first," he said. "I have a surprise."

"What is it?" Michael asked.

"It wouldn't be a surprise if I just told you, would it? Follow me."

Helmut walked out of the office with the Ritter family in tow. "What's going on?" Maureen asked her father.

"I have no idea," he replied.

Helmut was almost skipping as he went. It was hard not to smile. He led them outside, around the side of the factory, where a black Ford Model A was parked.

"What do you think?" Helmut said.

"Is that your car?" Michael said. "I like it."

"No, Michael, it's not my car anymore. It's your father's car now."

"What?" Maureen screamed.

"Helmut, I couldn't possibly—" Seamus spluttered.

"No, you can and you will. This is my gift to you and your wonderful family. The car is to welcome you to our country."

Michael, Fiona, and Conor ran to the car, pulling at the door handles. Maureen seemed to be in shock. "Can we go for a ride?" Michael asked.

"It's your father's car, ask him. But why doesn't he take us to my house for lunch first?"

Seamus hugged his uncle. "Thank you," he said in his ear.

"Let's get going. Helga's waiting for us. She's eager to see you too," Helmut said.

They all got in. Seamus sat behind the wheel, incredulous of how lucky he felt in that moment.

They arrived at Helmut's red-brick house 20 minutes later. Seamus pulled into the driveway and stopped outside the front door. There was another car parked in front of the garage. The children spilled out onto the gravel. Helmut led them to the door.

"It's far too big, but what else was I to spend my money on? I never thought we'd only have one child. I always imagined a whole gaggle of them running through here. I've been alone in the house for years now, so it'll be nice to hear other voices echoing through these old halls."

"We'll be around all the time. We live in Berlin now. You and Helga are our family."

Helmut cupped his nephew's head. "That's everything I wanted."

The food was already laid out on the table in the dining room, and the children made for it so quickly that Helmut bellowed with laughter.

"The last time I was in a house like this I was trying to rob the place," Seamus said so no one else could hear.

"What?" his uncle said. "Come and have a beer with me."

Seamus told the kids he'd be sitting in the back yard, and they should follow them out as soon as they were finished eating. Conor nodded his head, as his mouth was too stuffed full of cake for him to speak.

Seamus took a seat on the patio with his uncle. The sun was doing its best to burst through a layer of clouds.

"I want to thank you again. I can't tell you how much we needed this. My whole family."

Helmut patted him on the hand. "My pleasure." He paused a few seconds before he continued. "Before we go any further, I should tell you, I'm sick…I don't know how long I have."

"What?"

"It's serious. I'm sorry to spring it on you like this, but I wanted to tell you in person."

Seamus was struck with grief. "What is it?"

"Some blood ailment. What does it even matter? The doctors can't make head nor tail of it. When Maeve wrote to me, I realized how much I wanted you to be here for my last time on Earth, no matter how long that might be."

"Of course. Do you want me to tell the children?"

"No. Not yet anyway. I don't want them to feel sorry for me. I want to live free of that." He took a pack of cigarettes out of his jacket pocket. "Can't do me any harm now, can they?" he said and let out a thunderous laugh.

Seamus heard voices inside the house and stood up as he saw his cousin Helga greeting the kids with warm embraces. She was thin as a greyhound, dressed in dark colors. Her hair was slicked back, and she moved across the hardwood floor like a ghost. The news Helmut told him weighed on him, but he tried to ignore his feelings.

"Cousin Helga," Seamus said and went inside. She flashed a crooked smile as he held out a hand. Her touch was cold, but her gray eyes were warm.

"Welcome," she said. "I'm sorry I'm late. I met the children. The girls are so pretty, and Michael and Conor are fine young men. I'm looking forward to getting to know you all better."

"Thank you," Seamus said.

Helga left the children there and she and Seamus walked

outside to the patio where her father was sitting. He stood up and greeted her with an embrace.

"You're smoking again, Father?" she said.

"Oh, God, it's the only thing that makes me feel good anymore."

Helmut insisted on fetching a seat for his daughter despite her and Seamus's protests.

"How are you feeling?" she asked Helmut.

"I'm doing great. I have my nephew and his children here all the way from America. And I have you. How could I be better?"

"He's been like a child himself, awaiting your arrival these last few days," she said with a smile.

"Your father just told me about his illness," Seamus said.

"Yes, it's been a difficult time," Helga said. "I've tried to get him to slow down, but he won't. Maybe now that you're here…"

They spoke about Seamus's trip across the ocean for a while before the inevitable subject of the factory came up.

"There are certain unsavory elements among the workers," Helga said.

"Unsavory?"

"Here we go," Helmut said.

"Yes, I've gotten to know them over the years, as I'm sure you will also. My father is too kind. He doesn't keep up with the times. His mind is stuck back in the days of the Kaiser."

Helmut shook his head and lit up another cigarette. "What do you mean?" Seamus asked.

"He isn't aware of the hidden dangers in our society."

Seamus thought of the Stormtroopers who accosted his family on the train to Berlin. It seemed the dangers his cousin spoke of weren't so hidden anymore.

"Radical political thoughts have infiltrated almost every element of our city. With riots and violence on the streets, the country is in serious need of a new start. We have to wipe away the mistakes of the recent past if Germany is to retake its place among the great powers of the world."

Seamus didn't like the direction her speech was taking. "What has this got to do with the factory?"

"Some of our workers have become unduly influenced by radical ideology."

"The ideas of Hitler and the Nazis?"

She looked shocked at the notion he was suggesting. "Oh, no, of course not! Hitler and his party are trying to save Germany from the abyss we're all hurtling into. It's the Bolshevists, the Communists, that I'm referring to." She lit up a cigarette.

"Now, Seamus, didn't you know the Nazis are trying to save us all?" Helmut said in a sarcastic tone.

It took Seamus a few seconds to regain his composure. She was one of them—like the thugs on the train, like the baying crowds in photographs of Hitler's political rallies. Helga was a Nazi sympathizer, but her father didn't seem to share her views.

"How do you know who the factory workers support?" Seamus said.

"They've been seen at rallies, and attending Communist meetings. Andrei Salnikov, who works in the metal polishing section, is an outspoken Communist. He moved to Berlin after Stalin came to power in Russia. I'm convinced he's a Russian agent, sending back—"

"Sending back what exactly? Knives and forks?" Helmut said.

Helga pursed her lips, looking like she was about to relent before starting in again.

"Berlin might be the reddest city in the world after Moscow. The Bolshevists are everywhere, and they threaten the fabric of our lives. If they take over, everything we hold dear in our lives will disappear, including the factory that my father holds so dearly."

"I can't fire people because of their political inclinations," Helmut said.

"Why not? Do whatever it takes to protect your legacy. The factory is your life's work. If they get their way, they'll take it from you." She stubbed the cigarette out in the ashtray on the table and looked toward the horizon.

"The factory is like a model of Germany as a whole. If we don't eradicate those who would destroy us from within, like a worm eating the core of an apple, then we'll all perish together."

"How can I even consider—"

"I'm not asking you to do anything today. I just want you to be aware of the ideologies inside the place that could sink the ship. I want you to keep an eye out."

"What about the Nazis in there? Surely there are other National Socialists on the floor," Seamus said.

"We don't have to worry about the hardworking patriots among us."

It was hard to believe she was saying this, but she had a right to her opinions. She could exercise her right to vote in the upcoming elections, as those who leaned Communist or otherwise also could. He wondered what she would have done if she inherited the factory. *Would she have gotten rid of all the so-called Bolshevists on day one?*

He was beginning to understand why Helmut brought him over to show him the reins. Perhaps misogyny wasn't the reason Helmut chose him.

"I'll be sure to watch for any tensions that arise on the factory floor, but as long as it doesn't affect the quality of their work, I won't be firing anyone because of their political beliefs," her father said.

"It will start to affect their work. I can guarantee you that."

"What about your beliefs? Will they influence your attitudes to certain workers here who don't agree with your political leanings?" Seamus asked.

"My beliefs?" she said. "I believe in Germany, and that the German people should sit prime among the greatest in the world. I believe in a future where we all have what we need to live happy and productive lives."

Seamus wondered about the *happy and productive* future she dreamed of, and who would pay the price for it? "I'm glad you want what's best for this great country."

Her eyes seemed to be boring through him like diamond-tipped drill bits. They spoke for another few minutes before she went inside to use the bathroom.

"You see why I brought you over now?" Helmut said. "She's been like this for years."

"There's no talking to her about it?"

"I've tried. She's convinced that idiot Adolf Hitler is going to save us all. I can't have someone like that inherit my factory alone. She's my daughter, and I'll never deny her, but I have a duty to my workers, no matter what their political ideologies are."

Helga came back with the kids and a football under her arm for the boys to play with. Maureen sat with the adults. Helmut pulled up a chair for her and asked her question after question, enthralled by every word she said.

The night was drawing to a close when Helmut put his hand on Seamus's forearm.

"Can I show you something?" the older man said.

Seamus nodded and followed him back into the house. Helga had left a few minutes before. The children were still playing in the backyard. Helmut led him up the stairs to his bedroom and flicked on the light.

"There's something I wanted to show you."

He went to the wall and pushed back a painting of the royal palace to reveal a safe. It took a few seconds to get it open.

Seamus stood in silence as he reached in and pulled out a large necklace. The massive diamond pendant sparkled in the light. It swayed as he held it by the silver chain.

"This is precious to me—far more valuable than money, though it might be worth more than the house."

"It's beautiful."

"It was my mother's. She never had a daughter. I wanted to give it to Helga the day she got married, but I don't think that's going to happen now. It was my mother's last wish that this be given to a Ritter woman, and that it remains in our family. I want you to give it to Maureen one day."

"You can give it to her yourself."

"We both know that's not going to happen."

He handed the necklace to Seamus. It was heavy. He'd never had something so valuable, so beautiful in his hand before.

"This will be your responsibility when I'm gone." Seamus tried to interrupt him but his uncle cut him off. "Just promise me you'll give it to Maureen. It's all my mother wanted."

Seamus took a few seconds to marvel at the necklace one more time before handing it back. "Of course, Helmut. You have my word."

His uncle smiled, took one last look at the necklace and deposited it back in the safe.

～

Maureen agreed to babysit if Seamus taught her to drive. He accepted her offer and gave her some money for her trouble too. She smiled as he pressed the notes into her hand.

"Nice doing business with you. Conor and Fiona will be asleep by nine. Will you be home before me and Michael go to bed, around eleven or so?"

"I doubt it. I'll see you in the morning." He wanted to hug

her but figured it was still too soon, so he thanked her again and went to the other children instead. Leaving them in the hotel room didn't feel good, but Clayton arranged to introduce him to some of his friends that night, and they had a marvelous afternoon in Helmut's house. He kissed Fiona and Conor good-bye. Maureen was standing against the wall with her arms folded over her chest. He wondered whether it was worth it to stay to talk to her about why tonight was important to him, but realized that he was already going to be late.

"I appreciate this," he said.

"We'll see you tomorrow morning" she said and shut the door. He made his way down the stairs to the lobby. A taxi took him to the Eden Hotel, where Clayton was waiting for him in the lobby. Seamus took off his hat as he saw the young journalist was with four others—a woman and three men. They all stood to greet him. A brief picture of Maureen standing by the hotel room door fluttered into his mind, but he dismissed it as quickly as it came—there'd be time to deal with that situation later.

"I'd like to introduce you to some friends of mine," Clayton said in English. "This is Linda Murphy." A lady about his age with dark-red hair and brown eyes stepped forward to shake his hand. She was exquisitely dressed in a gray dress that hugged her slim figure. "Linda is foreign correspondent for the *Chicago Daily News*. She's been in the city 13 years now, and knows the place better than just about anyone."

"Nice to meet you," Linda said.

"This here's Arnold Muller." A tall man with a long beard and icy blue eyes greeted him with a handshake. He was wearing an elegant blue pinstriped suit with a matching tie.

"I'm with the *New York Post*," he said.

"This is Tom Lewis, from the *Baltimore Sun*. He's fresh off the boat too—only been here a few weeks." Tom was in his late twenties, like Clayton. He was as tall as Linda, but with powerful shoulders bulging from his gray blazer.

"And our resident German, I'd like to introduce you to Hans Litten. Hans is a lawyer. He's stared down the Nazis in court more than once." Litten was in his late twenties. He had thick brown hair; a clean-shaven, boyish face; and wore round glasses.

They took their seats once more and returned to their drinks. Seamus flagged down a waiter and ordered a beer before joining them.

"I was here only a few weeks when Rosa Luxemburg was executed right here in the lobby of this hotel," Linda said. "It was one of the first stories I covered. That and the January uprising that she was a part of. The country was a mess back then."

"Even more than now?" Clayton asked.

"It's solid as a rock now compared to back then."

"Who was she?" Seamus asked.

"A Communist leader trying to bring her ideals to bear on the country."

"And the Reds are still trying," Tom said.

"It was a tug-of-war between them and the Social Democrats. Democracy won, but only after calling in the troops to put down the Reds. They beat Rosa with rifles before dragging her out to the Tiergarten to finish the job. The whole country's been in upheaval since the war. There might have been a little ray of hope, but then the markets crashed in '29."

"Yes, people lost their faith in the new democratic system when their life savings went down the tubes," Arnold said. "It's been clinging by a thread ever since."

"And that's where Hitler and his mob come in?" Seamus asked.

"Yes. They took advantage of the chaos and discontent after

the Depression began. Germany was one of the hardest hit countries in the world. Unemployment skyrocketed, and people began to listen to Herr Hitler's rhetoric about returning Germany to its former greatness with new enthusiasm," Linda said.

Seamus got his drink from the waiter and took a sip. "We had a run in with some SA thugs on the train over from Hamburg."

"Charming lot, aren't they?" Tom said.

"I'm not sure charm would be their strongest asset," Seamus said.

Linda lit up a cigarette before continuing. "The Nazis are shrewd. They use the Stormtroopers to beat up and intimidate their opponents—"

"The Communists?" Seamus asked.

"Mainly, but others too. They have a deep-rooted hatred of Jews. As I said, they use the SA to bully their enemies, but always in a way they can deny. There's no trail that directly leads back to Hitler or any of the other leadership. They may seem like blathering idiots, espousing their bigoted rhetoric, but they're clever swine. Of course, Hans held their feet to the fire in court last year. He had Hitler on the stand... For how long? Two hours?"

"Three," Hans said.

"What was the case about?" Seamus asked.

"Three Communist workers were murdered by a Nazi mob at a dance. I summoned Herr Hitler to court to prove that the leadership in the party was aware of the murderous intent of the SA who attacked the dancehall," Hans said.

"How did he wriggle out of it?" Seamus asked.

The others put down their drinks, leaning forward in anticipation. They must have heard the story 100 times, but seemed eager to relive it again.

"Hitler claimed that the SA was an organization of intellectual enlightenment." Hans shook his head, a bitter smile on his face.

"As if the Brownshirts are going around changing people's minds with their concise and practiced powers of persuasion," Arnold said.

"It was all there in the official pamphlets the Nazis distribute—all the language to rile up the troops. Hitler's arguments that the Nazis are a legal and ethical party were as ridiculous as those brown uniforms his minions wear," Hans said.

"He had the Austrian corporal red-faced and wild with rage. It was one of the most wonderful things I've ever seen," Linda said. She slapped Hans on the shoulder.

"So what happened in the end?" Seamus asked.

"The judge saved him. One of my main goals was to prove collusion between the police and the SA Stormtroopers. The investigation into the deaths of the Communists workers was a joke. The judge stepped in and saved Hitler just when I had him where I wanted him. It proved my point about the collusion on the spot. The Nazis suffered some losses for a few months afterward, but Hitler is like no one else. He's been down and out more times than anyone can count, yet he always comes back somehow."

"And now he's head of the biggest party in Germany," Seamus said.

"And vying to become chancellor after the next election in a few weeks," Hans said.

"I admire your courage in facing him down," Seamus said.

"I have to do what's right to defend my country from people like him and his cronies," the lawyer said. "My personal safety isn't what's paramount."

Seamus sat back in his seat and raised the beer glass to his lips. It was awe inspiring to be in the company of someone so courageous. No one spoke for a few seconds. It was hard to follow such a noble and brave sentiment. Seamus just hoped what Clayton told him on the boat on the way over to Germany was true—that the Nazis would be wiped out in the election and crawl back under the rocks they came from.

The conversation at the table remained focused on politics for most of the rest of the night. Seamus kept up with the others drink for drink, but his choice was beer. They were sipping gin and were ready for bed by the time midnight came. Only he and Clayton, who'd also been pacing himself, were ready to go onward from the hotel to sample some of the city's famous nightlife. Seamus bid good night to his new friends and promised to meet them again the next time the group met for drinks. They were eager to find out how he got on with the factory and how his children would adjust to their new lives in Germany.

Linda gave him a hug to say goodbye, all earlier inhibitions eradicated by the gin. She left to return to her husband, a diplomat and a teetotaler. As she put it, she "had to drink for both of them." She didn't have children, and the others weren't married. Seamus tried to convince them to come along, but it was beyond them, and he had to comfort himself with their promises to join him next time.

"I don't know the city as well as they do, but I have somewhere in mind we can go," Clayton said after the others left.

"Lead on," Seamus answered. "I want to sample some of the delights of the place before work takes over."

He followed his friend out into the cool night air, where he hailed another taxi. Clayton gave instructions to the driver, who nodded and put his foot down. The two men got out at Potsdamer Platz. Seamus had to strain his neck to peer up at the massive building with giant neon lettering in front of him.

"The *Haus Vaterland*?" he said. "The Fatherland House?"

"You're going to love it," Clayton said and made for the door. "It's the entire world under one roof. Five stories of fun. There's a massive cinema, the biggest café in the world, a Bavarian beerhall, a Spanish wine cellar, a Turkish café, and even a Wild West bar with cowboys in full Western getup twirling lassoes, if you're missing home. And that's not even the half of it."

"I think I'd like to see the Wild West bar. That sounds too ridiculous to even imagine."

"Let's start there and see where the night takes us."

The crowds swelled as they made their way inside to a spacious lobby area with stairs leading off in several different directions. Hundreds of people milled around, and the two men joined a line to walk up the stairs to the fifth floor. They passed at least a dozen different restaurants and bars on the way up, each packed with eager partygoers. Some seemed drunk, others as if they hadn't touched a drop. He and Clayton were somewhere in between.

The American Wild West bar was everything he imagined it might be, and more. They pushed back saloon doors and made their way to the wooden slab that constituted the bar. It seemed fitting to order whiskey from the cowboy-hatted bartender. The music was loud jazz, played by a band dressed head to toe in stereotypical cowboy gear.

"Shouldn't they be playing country music?" Seamus asked his friend. He almost had to shout to make himself heard.

"Should any of this be the way it is? I stopped trying to make sense of this place two minutes after I walked in."

Several beautiful showgirls in oversized frilly dresses made their way up onto the stage and started to dance. The crowd gathered in front of them, cheering them on. It was like nothing Seamus had ever seen before.

Clayton smiled at him and they clinked their glasses together. "I told you it was a good time."

"It's certainly that."

The room was crowded, and Seamus heard the sounds of French, Italian, English, and several other languages being spoken. The two men stopped to have a conversation with a newlywed couple from London who were just as amazed by the surroundings as they were.

Seamus excused himself and pushed his way through the crowd toward the stage where the showgirls were performing. It was hard to place the dance. It seemed to be a distant cousin of the cancan with a Wild West twist. Whatever it was, the crowd was lapping it up like camels at a desert oasis. Seamus finished his whiskey, reveling in the burning sensation traveling all the way down to his stomach. The women on stage, dressed in their frilly pink dresses, were moving so quickly it was difficult to focus on any of their faces. It was plain to see they were beautiful, but somehow, they all looked the same. Their painted faces and beaming smiles made it hard to differentiate one from another.

He slalomed his way back to where Clayton had been standing, but his young friend was nowhere to be seen. Seamus looked around the crowd, searching for the journalist, or the young English couple they'd been talking to. He settled back against the bar to wait, happy to peer out at the crowded dance floor in front of the band and the dancers performing on stage.

The sound of someone arguing grabbed his attention, and he whirled around. A young man in a blue suit with a thick black beard grabbed at a pretty woman in her mid-twenties in a gray chiffon dress. She pushed him away before another woman stepped in, her back to Seamus. The second woman grabbed at the man. He pushed her, and she stumbled backward. Seamus didn't want to get involved, but enough was enough. He strode toward the fight, pushing past the second woman without even looking at her. Before he knew what he was doing, he'd pinned the man against the wall. The man reared up against him, and before Seamus had a chance to speak, threw a punch at him. Seamus deflected his fist with his forearm.

"Calm down," Seamus said.

"This has nothing to do with you," the young man hissed. He was several inches smaller than Seamus and seemed to know when he'd met his match. He backed off.

"What's going on here?" Seamus said. "Are you all right?"

"I'll be fine once he leaves me alone," the woman in the gray dress said.

"Get going," Seamus said.

The man in the blue suit pointed his finger at the woman in the gray dress. "This isn't over, Greta."

"Just leave me alone, Jens. I don't want to see you ever again," she said.

Jens pushed past Seamus and faded into the crowd.

"Thanks," Greta said.

"That's quite all right. I'm glad to help. Who is he?"

"An ex-boyfriend who can't take no for an answer."

Seamus turned to the other woman. He realized he hadn't looked at her yet.

"Are you hurt?" he said, but the words stuck in his throat and came out as a whisper. Her face was exquisite. She was wearing a black sequined dress that hugged her slim figure. She had deep-brown eyes and lightly tanned skin that stretched over high cheekbones. Her short brown hair was pushed back from her face.

"No," she answered. "Thanks for helping us out."

She stood silent for a long second, waiting for him to speak. Her friend moved forward just as he managed to get the words out.

"It's my first time in here. I only got into the country yesterday."

"I was wondering about that accent," the woman said.

"I'm American, but my father was German."

"What's your name?" she said.

"Seamus," he said. "It's not too hard to say. Spelling it's a different matter."

"I'm not sure I understand," the lady with the brown eyes said.

"My mother was Irish. It's a long story."

"Well, thank you for your help, Seamus," the woman said. Greta pulled on her arm, but her eyes never left his.

"We should go," Greta said.

The woman nodded. "It was nice meeting you, Seamus."

"It was a pleasure meeting you. But you know my name and I don't know yours."

"It's Lisa," she said. "Maybe I'll see you around sometime."

Seamus was caught between not wanting to be pushy and not letting her go. He scanned her finger for a wedding or engagement ring—it was bare. He stopped wearing his a few months after Marie had died. Strange to think of her in a moment like this.

"How about later on tonight? There's so much to this place. It seems like you'd need to come here every night for a month to see it all."

Lisa looked at Greta with a smile on her face. "Come to the ballroom in about an hour. You'll see me there."

Fire flashed inside him, like he was Maureen's age again. "How will I see you? That place is huge."

"Trust me. You'll see me," she said with another smile.

"Ok, I'll be there in an hour."

"Ok," she said as Greta led her away.

Seamus watched the sparkle of her dress fade into the crowd until it disappeared like stars behind a cloud. He took a deep breath and went to the bar to order a beer. It had been 20 years since he spoke to a woman like this. He was a little out of practice. His mind harkened back to when he met Marie. It seemed like a lifetime ago. A part of him didn't feel right talking to other women like that. It didn't feel proper to want anyone else. His wedding ring was gone, but the indentation in his finger was still there when he touched it. Marie was gone too, but the indentation in his soul would remain forever.

Clayton arrived back alone. "Sorry, pal, I went to the bathroom and got stuck talking to some people. Everything all right? You look like you've seen a ghost."

"There was a bit of a scuffle. I had to step in to defend a couple of ladies."

"Pretty ladies?"

"You could call them that. One in particular."

"But you said there were two, didn't you? Where are they now?"

Seamus wasn't used to this. It was so long since he even had a conversation like this with another man. It seemed a whole world was opening up to him.

"She told me she'd see me in the ballroom later. So, we have plans."

"Did she say where? Have you seen the size of that place?"

"No. She just said we wouldn't miss her."

"This should be interesting," Clayton said and turned to order a beer at the bar.

They stood there for another 45 minutes, watching the show and the maelstrom of people around them. Seamus tried to be as casual as he could, but knew he wasn't fooling anyone —particularly an intelligent guy like Clayton. The younger man laughed as Seamus suggested they go upstairs.

"Lead on, my friend," Clayton said. "You have a date with destiny."

The ballroom was the biggest he'd ever seen. The dance floor was full of darkened bodies pulsing to the jazz music the full band onstage at the back of the room was playing. The lighting behind the stage glowed blue and red. An open microphone stood in front of the drummer, a lonely spotlight shining down. The dance floor was surrounded by dozens of tables, where people sat drinking, laughing, and bopping to the beat of the music. The bar at the side of the room was 100 feet of white marble with mirrors colored gold on the walls behind. He'd never seen anything quite like this place.

"You see what I mean when I said you might have some trouble finding her in here?"

Seamus scanned the dancefloor and saw 100 faces darkened by the dim light. There must have been 1,000 others, at the bar or sitting at tables. Finding Lisa would be like picking out one grain of sand on the beach, or a leaf in the forest.

"She said I'd see her."

"I've heard that line a few times before."

Seamus dismissed his friend's comment and went to the bar. He ordered beers for them both. They turned around, their elbows on the white marble as they surveyed the room. Seamus thought about the children and felt a pang of guilt for leaving them. How long would it be before Maureen was coming to places like this? He didn't feel old in that room, but there were many people far younger than his 37 years, and older too. Everyone seemed to be there—except Lisa.

"You ever come close to getting married?" Seamus asked.

"Yeah. Katie Cook almost snared me back in college."

"What happened with her?"

"I'd love to tell you that I moved on, or she asked too many questions, but that wouldn't be entirely true." He picked up his glass of beer and stared into the gold liquid before downing a gulp. "She left me for one of my best friends. They're married now with two little girls. They even invited me to the wedding."

"Did you go?"

"I was never one to miss a party," he said with a smile.

The music stopped and the crowd on the dance floor went still. The lights on the stage faded out, and all was dark save for the one spotlight shining on the empty microphone stand. The crowd cheered. Seamus put his beer down and moved closer to the stage. Clayton followed him as they pushed their way through the crowd. An air of anticipation was building in the room, and several people screamed out approval. The spotlight went out, and the room fell into near darkness. Several women screamed in faux fear.

The spotlight flicked back on to reveal a figure standing in a black hood. Seamus and Clayton were almost at the front of the dance floor, just a few feet from the stage now. The lights behind the stage flashed on, and the figure threw back the hood to reveal her face. A blonde woman with dark makeup grabbed the microphone as the band started. The crowd erupted as the singer launched into a song in English. Several dancers came onstage, cavorting behind the singer in black hula skirts and studded brassieres. Seamus laughed as he recognized Lisa among them.

"She did tell me I'd see her."

"You're not likely to miss her up there."

Seamus wasn't naïve enough to think she'd wave to him, or even look at him while she was working. They only exchanged a few dozen words, but seeing her up on stage brought a smile to his face as if he knew her. The song ended and Seamus and Clayton applauded with the rest of the crowd. The drummer started the next song with a solo that got the whole crowd dancing, Seamus and Clayton included. It seemed normal there to dance alone, or with friends.

The two men remained at the front of the stage for much of the next hour. Lisa stayed behind the singer with the other dancers, performing her choreographed moves. The whole scene was enrapturing: the lights, the stage, the band. It was almost impossible to look away. Clayton was talking to a girl when Seamus turned around to him. Two minutes later, he and the girl were at the bar and Seamus was alone, but it didn't matter. The singer launched into another song, the people on the dancefloor crooning along.

Clayton came back a few minutes later, alone. Seamus asked him what happened to the girl he was dancing with, but his words were lost in the music. Clayton just smiled and clapped him on the back. The song ended, and the singer thanked the crowd. The act was over. Lisa and the other dancers waved and ran off the stage. The band kept playing. It was almost two in the morning, but the night was still young.

The two men sat at an empty table. Seamus didn't want to admit it in front of his young friend, but he was tired and sweaty from dancing. His bed in the hotel was luring him in like a siren's call, but one thing—one person—made him stay. Clayton didn't have any intention of leaving just yet and lit up a cigarette. He went to the bar for more beer, but Seamus said he'd had enough. A sensible thought about how he'd feel the next day crept into his mind, and besides, he'd need a clear head to talk to Lisa if he ever managed to find her again.

They sat at the table for a few minutes talking about the spectacle they witnessed, and still were witnessing with each passing moment. Seamus felt lucky to have met Clayton. Through the young journalist, he seemed to have found a social group to plug into. He just hoped the children were as fortunate. The thought to get up to try to find Lisa occurred to him, but he realized she was likely backstage getting changed. What would she want with a man like him, anyway? It was ridiculous to think she might have been interested. What age was she? She couldn't be more than in her late twenties. A beautiful, confident woman like her must have dozens of suitors lined up outside her dressing room. He was embarrassed. Trying to talk to a dancer in a nightclub? He hadn't even been to a nightclub in about 10 years. He felt like a fish, flapping its fins on the dock, gasping for the safety of the water.

Clayton suggested they go out to the windows, where a dozen patrons stood peering down at the street. The scene was quiet below—a stark contrast to the frenzy of activity in the club, even at almost three in the morning. The two men looked out the windows for a few seconds and then sat down, Seamus with his back to the dance floor. They lit up cigarettes. They started talking about Hans Litten, the lawyer they met at the Eden Hotel earlier that night.

"I admire his courage in going up against Hitler," Clayton said. "It's awe inspiring, really, to dedicate yourself wholly to such a noble cause, but I'm not sure how wise it is to make an enemy of someone as powerful as Adolf Hitler."

"If you take a shot at the king, you shouldn't miss. It seems Hitler's as powerful as ever."

"Hans is betting that he and the Nazis get wiped out in the election. That's what he was trying to achieve—to reveal them for what they are, and let the people decide from there."

"That's the thing about people—you can't always trust them to do what's right, even for themselves."

"Hans is a Jew, so this is personal to him."

"It's hard to comprehend that level of courage," Seamus said. He noticed Clayton's face change. A look of surprise came over him before a wide smile wiped it out. He was looking over Seamus's shoulder and nodded at his friend to turn around.

"There you are," came a female voice just as Seamus turned around. Lisa was standing over him, a pearly white smile on her face.

Seamus stood up, trying—and failing—to keep his cool. He dropped his cigarette onto the floor. She let out a giggle as he reached down for it, almost burning his fingers on the lit end.

Clayton stood up. "I'm going to the bar for a while. I see someone over there I want to talk to. It's about time we caught up again."

"Nice to see you," Lisa said as Clayton walked away.

Seamus was still standing in front of her, captivated. "Would you like to join me?"

"I'd love to," she said. She took the seat opposite him, the one Clayton had been in.

"How about a drink?" he said.

"No, thanks. I try not to when I'm working. You can get into a bit of a spiral, you know?"

"I can imagine, being in this atmosphere all the time. I wouldn't know myself. This is the first time I've been to a nightclub since Julius Caesar was a boy."

She laughed for a few seconds. "What brings you here tonight?"

"My friend I met on the boat over from America. We arrived yesterday."

"Yesterday?" She smiled as she reached into her bag for a cigarette. He lit it for her, shaking out the match before throwing it in the ashtray. "Why did you come? Are you a tourist, or something else?"

"It's very much something else. I came over to work with my uncle managing his factory. I lived in Berlin for a few years as a kid and got to know him then."

"What does the factory produce?"

"All things metal, from knives and forks to pots and pans to...other things I can't think of right now. To tell you the truth, I have no idea what I'll be doing."

Lisa laughed again. He still couldn't figure out why she was there talking to him. *I'm thirty-seven, and I have four children. Does she think I'm handsome?* Marie frequently told him he was, but that was years ago.

"I don't want to bore you with the workings of a factory I know nothing about," he said.

"You're not boring me at all. Well, the workings of the factory do sound boring—I'll admit that—but even most solid, lucrative careers aren't exciting all the time. I used to dream of dancing on stage as a little girl, and now I do it five nights a week right here in the Haus Vaterland. Sometimes I wonder what I'd say to myself as a little girl if I could go back, you know?" Seamus nodded.

"Dreams aren't always what makes you happiest." She stubbed out her cigarette. "Sometimes I long for something boring where men aren't leering over me and I don't have to have a permanent smile tattooed to my face. Boring sounds ok to me." She looked off into the distance before bringing her eyes back to his. He was just about to speak when she beat him to it.

"What's America like? I've seen so many movies and read so many books. It feels like I know the place even though I've never been there."

"It's a mixed bag these days. The phrase 'The Land of Opportunity' has taken on a bitterly ironic tone."

"So the streets aren't paved with gold, then?"

"Not exactly."

"There goes my plan to get rich by marrying you."

"Do you speak the language?" he said in English.

"Not as well as you speak German," she replied in the same tongue.

He switched back to German. "It's different than it was a few years ago. It's barely recognizable from what I once knew."

"Is that why you took the opportunity to come here?"

Seamus wondered how honest he should be in this situation. "I've had some difficult years since my wife died and I lost my job."

"I'm so sorry."

"Thank you. The bank I worked in closed a couple of years ago and I had to leave town to look for any work I could find to support my children."

"What did you do in the bank?"

"Loans, pensions, mortgages, financial advice. All the fun things."

"Sounds fascinating."

"We can't all lead the glamorous life you do."

"Glamorous is one word for it, I suppose. How many children do you have?"

"Two boys and two girls. Maureen, my oldest, is sixteen. Michael is fourteen, Fiona's eleven and Conor is almost eight. Do you have brothers and sisters?"

"I'm an only child. Well, my brothers were killed in the war. I was about Maureen's age at the time."

"The whole thing was such a waste." Lisa paused, apparently wondering in what direction she wanted the conversation to go. "What did you do when you left your children? Who looked after them?"

"I left them with my sister in Newark. It's a city in New Jersey. Have you heard of it?"

"I've heard of New Jersey. New York is near there."

"Yeah, Newark is pretty close. To answer your question, I did whatever I could to support my kids. I sent home most of my wages at the end of the month."

"You must have missed them."

"Like a limb torn from my body."

She smiled. "That's a pretty gruesome reference, but I get it."

She took another cigarette and put it in her mouth. Once again, he lit it for her. Seamus turned around to see if he could find Clayton, but the young man was nowhere to be seen.

"My mother was sick a few years ago. My father was dead already and I told you about my brothers. I was all she had left. So I had to find the money to pay for her surgery," she said.

"What was wrong with her?"

"Cancer. They had to cut it out. We didn't have much, but I did what I had to do to find the money to save my mother's life."

"And did you?"

"Find the money? That's what brought me to this fine establishment."

Seamus wondered how much a dancer got paid, but didn't ask. "Was she ok?"

"She's asleep in the apartment we share right now, more than three years later. So it seems you and I may have more in common than we might have thought."

"It seems so. Who was that guy harassing your friend earlier? Do you see many like him in here?"

"Yes, it's the price we pay for prancing around in our underwear on stage. The men in here think they own us. That little boy, Jens, wants to push us around. Greta never should have gotten involved with him."

"You must get men trying to court you all the time."

"Like you, you mean?" Seamus held his hands up, not knowing quite how to answer. "Let's just say you're not the first man to try to talk to me after seeing me on stage—not the first man tonight, even."

"Why are you sitting here with me, then? What makes me different?"

"I don't know. Maybe it's your funny accent, or that childish look on your face."

"I'm honored. I'd raise a toast to that, but neither of us has a drink in front of us."

"I think it's still worth toasting," she said, holding up her fist. He held his fist up and bumped it against hers. They both smiled.

"Are you from here?" he asked.

"Yes. Born and raised in the city. My father used to run a hotel in Kreuzeberg. I grew up with tourists in and out of there all the time. People from France and Italy, from Poland and Austria."

"You speak any of those other languages?"

"Bien sur, mon ami," she said with a smile.

"You Europeans put us Americans to shame."

"You speak German."

"Only because my father insisted my sister and I speak it at home. I raised my children the same way. My sister too. They all speak fluent German."

"That should make the transition here a lot easier. How long are you planning on staying? Forever?"

"Forever is a long time. Maybe 10 years. How does 1942 sound?"

"It sounds so far in the future that I can't even imagine what we'll be doing then...living on the moon or something. Or under the sea?"

"It seems to me I'll still be living here, in Berlin."

"What about your children?"

"That'll be up to them, but give me a chance. I only arrived in the country yesterday."

Her entire face lit up as she laughed. She almost dropped the cigarette in her hand.

"I'm sure you'll find a wonderful life living here. This city's not perfect. It has more than its share of problems, but there's a place to find happiness."

"What happened to your father's hotel? Is your mother running it now?"

"No. It turned out my father wasn't quite the businessman he made himself out to be and we lost it back in '23. He died a year after."

"I'm sorry, I don't mean to pry."

"No, it's quite all right." She looked at her watch—the action he'd been dreading. "I think it's time I got home."

He wanted to keep her there, to somehow make this moment last, but it was after three in the morning now. His children were waiting for him in the hotel. "I should get going too."

They stood up together. She was six inches shorter than him. They walked in silence for a few steps before he spoke.

"I so enjoyed speaking to you tonight."

"I enjoyed it too, Seamus." Silence fell between them again. "I need to go backstage to get my things."

"Can I wait for you, and walk you out?"

"Ok," she said with a smile.

She took him back toward the stage. The band had long since stopped playing, and the dance floor was empty now. There were still some patrons sitting at tables sipping drinks, but most had gone home. Lisa disappeared through a door at the side of the stage. He spied Clayton talking to a group of people at the now almost-empty bar. He waved over to him and got the response he wanted—the young man seemed to understand that this was goodbye for tonight. He turned back to the group he was talking to, unperturbed.

Seamus decided he would make a point to call over at his apartment in the next couple of days. He tried to imagine what Lisa was thinking. What did she believe his intentions were? He had no idea what was expected of him, but he was a gentleman, and his conduct would be in line with how he was raised. He'd treat Lisa with respect. The door opened and she walked out wearing a blue coat and a navy beret.

"You're still here?" she said.

"I didn't have anywhere else I needed to be."

"Who does at almost three thirty in the morning?"

He walked beside her. "You must sleep all day."

"In my coffin," she said with a smile. "This lifestyle takes some getting used to. It's the nights when I get home at five in the morning that I long for that boring lifestyle we were talking about."

"You'd miss the bright lights, the razzmatazz."

"It's one thing coming here to enjoy yourself. Working here is entirely another."

"How will you get home?"

"I'll get a taxi home with some of the other girls. I know where they'll be."

They made their way down the stairs. The vast lobby was almost empty now, but not entirely. Several dozen revelers were still drinking and laughing, and the sound of jazz still boomed from the Wild West bar upstairs. Seamus knew what he wanted to ask her, but finding the words was another matter. She was so easy to talk to. Why couldn't he ask her?

They arrived at the front door and Lisa waved to a group of dancers she knew.

"Can I wait with you until the taxi arrives?" he said.

"Of course. Where are you going to live? Have you any idea?"

"My uncle lived in Charlottenburg. I think I'd like to live there. I have fond memories of his home from when I was a boy."

"That seems like a fitting place for a future captain of industry."

"Or at least one that has no idea what he's doing."

"You're an intelligent man. I'm sure it's like anything else—you just jump in the deep end and start swimming. You'll be fine."

She patted him on the shoulder, which felt wonderful. The taxi pulled up and the other girls motioned to her to get in. "That's my cue," she said. "It was so lovely talking to you. I wish you the best with your move to our fair city and your burgeoning business. I'm sure you'll take the metalworks world by storm."

"Lisa," he said as she went to walk away. "Can I see you again?"

She closed her eyes and shook her head. "Seamus, you're a nice man. You don't want to see me again, believe me. I'm more trouble than I'm worth."

"Why don't you let me decide that? I'd like to continue to get to know you."

She looked at him with wide brown eyes for a few seconds

as the girls in the taxi continued to call out. "I shouldn't do this, but ok. One time. I'll meet you one time."

"That's all I ask."

"You know the Romanisches Café on Kurfürstendamm?"

"I will after we meet there."

She laughed and held a hand up to the girls in the taxi. "I'll see you there for lunch on Wednesday at one o'clock. If you're late—"

"I won't be."

It was hard not to smile, and it seemed to be infectious. "Ok, I'll see you on Wednesday."

"Yes, you will."

She ran to the door of the taxi. She looked back at him before disappearing inside. The door shut and the car drove away. Seamus stood alone, dazed, for a few minutes. People passed him, but he didn't see their faces.

He moved back against the wall, slouching against it with a cigarette in his mouth. *What a woman! What a city!* He wondered what she meant by telling him she wasn't worth the trouble. Was that something young women said? He had no reference point and didn't want to go to Clayton like a little boy asking his older brother about girls.

The crowd outside the nightclub thinned to a few hardcore revelers. Clayton was nowhere to be seen, but could look after himself. Seamus flagged down a taxi and gave the name of the hotel to the driver. It was impossible not to think of Lisa, and of every curve on her face, during the drive home.

∿

The taxi driver said the block Lisa lived on was dangerous, and he had trouble in Kreuzberg at night before. After some cajoling from the other ladies in the cab, he agreed to drop Lisa at her door. She wasn't afraid. She knew the people there, and they knew her. The people the taxi driver was too scared to drive past were her neighbors.

She got out with a bright smile on her face, wishing her friends good night. There was no one out on her block except for Fritz Holder, a one-legged veteran of the Great War who seemed always to be awake when she came home from the club. He was sitting on the sidewalk with his dog, Harry.

"Don't you sleep, Fritz?" Lisa said as he looked up at her.

"It's hard to get any peace when you live on the street, Lisa. This is the only time I get to myself, when me and Harry here get some private time." He petted the mangy brown terrier. "Isn't that right, boy?" The dog wagged his tail in agreement.

"I'm glad you're getting some quality time, but I need to get home to bed," she said and bade him good night.

"Tell your mother I said hello," he said.

She carried on without replying. Her mother despised living there—didn't see anything good about an area she wouldn't have walked through alone five years before. Now it was the only place they could afford. The heady days of living in the hotel seemed like 1,000 years ago. Her old room seemed an immeasurable luxury that she hadn't appreciated at the time. What would her father think if he could see this place? Perhaps he wouldn't have gambled his fortune away, and they'd still have something. He got away with it: Death deprived him of the pain they were forced to endure in the wake of his poor decisions.

Then her mother got sick. She blamed her cancer on this place, even though the doctors said that it was impossible. She didn't believe them. It didn't fit the story she was trying to peddle to the world. Her mother was embarrassed by what happened to them and stopped calling her friends and family.

Lisa never understood that. Her mother cut herself off from the world she knew because of her shame. Their old friends,

and even the few distant family members they had left, soon
forgot about them...and her mother's wish came true.

Lisa came to the entrance to the apartment block and
pushed through the rickety old door. It was always unlocked.
Who would want to break in here, anyway? She shut it behind
her, making sure to lock it before she made her way up the
stairs. The paint was peeling off the gray walls. She wondered
when the stairway had last been painted—perhaps when Julius
Caesar was a boy. She chuckled to herself. It was five flights up
to her apartment, but she took the stairs with ease, even after a
night of dancing at the club, and wasn't out of breath when she
reached the door to their apartment.

She thought about the man she met as she opened the front
door. Why did she say she'd see him again? He was handsome
and charming, but there was something else about him she
couldn't quite place. Agreeing to meet him was an entirely
selfish act. Her instincts to warn him off weren't strong enough.
They'd been broken down by his smile, by the warmth in his
eyes. He had four children and just moved to Berlin the day
before—he had enough to worry about without her and the
mess of her existence dragging him down like an anchor. Still,
he seemed like a good man. Perhaps she could meet him the
one time she promised. She was sure he'd see sense after that.

She lit the oil lamp. There wasn't much fuel left, so she'd
have to make sure to extinguish it quickly. Her bag fell to the
floor with a gentle thud. It must have been past four o'clock in
the morning. Seamus kept her out too late, but perhaps it was
worth it to meet someone not trying to pretend to be something
they weren't. People like him still existed in this world. She
could draw comfort from that.

Her bed was calling her, but she checked the other room
first, as she did every night she came home late. She pushed it
open slowly so as not to make the slightest noise. Her mother

was asleep. A chink in the curtains let in the silver light of the moon, and it lay like a saber across her mother's face.

Lisa took two more steps and peered over her mother's body to where Hannah, her three-year-old, was curled up beside her grandmother. Lisa watched her daughter sleeping. The sound of her gentle breath was the sweetest music she ever knew, and she stood there for a minute or more, reveling in it.

7

October 10, 1932

Monday morning came and Maureen got Fiona out of bed for what was to be their first day in school. She had suggested giving them a little more time to settle in, but her father insisted. They were lined up and ready to go before seven o'clock, and after breakfast in the hotel room, they met their father and the boys in the lobby. He greeted them with hugs and asked if they were excited. Maureen could barely get the words out to answer him. His face echoed the disappointment inside him.

He took them outside to where he'd parked their new car. The prospect of riding through the city to school brought the excitement out in the children that their father craved, and Conor and Fiona even cheered as they got into the car. Maureen sat in front, with her father driving. There were as many cars on the roads in Berlin as there had been in Newark.

She tried to put aside her feelings. What was the point in speculating? It wasn't going to be easy to start in a new school, in a different language, albeit one they spoke fluently. She knew she was going to have to be there for her younger siblings. She'd save her energy for them and try not to waste it worrying about herself, or when Leo's letters might start arriving.

"Don't you want to be on time for your first day?" Fiona asked.

"I want to tend to your needs first. I'll go in after."

The sun was shining and the city was alive with Monday morning commuters. They drove past trams that spewed nicely dressed men and women onto the pavement before they hurried along to work. Several people on horseback rode past. People bought coffee and snacks from street sellers, and children with dirty, ripped clothes asked for spare change. Policemen directed traffic, stopping cars to let the trams and horses through. Their father bought them bikes the day before to afford them some freedom. They were hitched on the back of the car. *This is a great city, and now I have the means to explore it —if I ever get time.* For now, the bikes would be their way of getting home.

They arrived at the school in time for their meeting with the teacher they were to coordinate with. Her father had sent a telegram before they arrived with the children's details. The teacher was a gray-haired woman called Frau Bende, who greeted them with a warm smile and referred to them as *the American visitors.* She escorted them inside to her office, along with their father, and they sat down in front of her desk.

"Conor and Fiona can start school today, as they're still of age to enter the Volksschule. Maureen and Michael will have to take a test first unless they want to join the Volksschule also."

"What would that entail? How is the Volksschule different from the school they'd have to test into?" her father said.

"It's less of an academic focus. They could stay, progressing with children their own age until eventually graduating to learn a trade or take a position as a laborer."

"No way—not Maureen and Michael. They'll take the test to get into secondary school. They're clever children, just like their mother."

Maureen was glad her father spoke up for them. She and Michael excelled at school back home, and she was sure things wouldn't be any different here.

"Well, you're in luck. They can take the test to gain access to secondary school tomorrow, and if they pass, can join their new classmates next week," said Frau Bende.

"Excellent," Seamus said. "I know they'll make me proud."

He stood up to shake her hand. Maureen wanted to tell him to lay off, that he didn't have to try so hard, but knew how he'd take it and kept her mouth shut.

"The younger children can come to class now. They'll be separated by gender, of course."

"That'll be a different experience, but I'm sure they'll thrive," her father said.

He seemed to be doing everything he could to make his energy the primary driver of their transition to German society. It was as if he thought he could control what would happen just by his shaping his own attitude to magnify every positive detail in the situation, no matter how small. It was embarrassing.

They left the office. Frau Bende took Conor and Fiona with her, leading them down the hallway toward their new classrooms. Maureen wanted to go with them, to see where they were sitting and what their teachers were like, but she knew she had to let them go. Her father led her and Michael out of the school building.

"So, it looks like you two will have a little more freedom before school begins next week."

"Some time to explore the city on our new bikes, perhaps?" Michael said.

"That sounds like a great idea," Maureen said.

They went out to the parking lot, where her father detached

the bikes from the back of the car. "Just don't go too far," he said and reached into his pocket for some lunch money. "Try not to get lost. I'll see you at the hotel later on."

"Good luck on your first day at the new job," Maureen said.

The words seemed to stop her father's train of thought, and he paused. "Thank you, my sweet." Michael echoed what his sister had said. "That's all I needed," Seamus said and got back into his car. "Enjoy yourselves today."

They waited until he disappeared around the corner before getting on their bikes. The first stop was to be the Tiergarten and then, perhaps, the zoo.

~

Seamus told himself that the children would be fine as he drove toward the factory. Repeating that phrase over and over in his mind seemed to calm him. He tried not to think about what awaited him in his new job. After all, didn't he just have to seem like he knew what he was doing at first? Perhaps in this situation, it wasn't how good he was, but more how good he was perceived to be? His expertise would grow with experience, but until then he'd have to present a competent, and confident, front.

It was 15 minutes from the school to the factory. He had a brief thought of Lisa as he pulled up but dismissed it with a smile. There'd be time for her later. It was almost eight thirty, and the lot outside the factory was full of bikes chained to posts, and even a few cars. The workers had been on the factory floor since seven thirty.

It was time. He took a deep breath and pushed through the door. The sound of metal on metal filled the air, booming and clunking. Sparks lit up darkened spaces, and the shouting between the workers was just about discernible over the cacophony. It seemed like a different world. He stood there, just watching for a few seconds, unsure of what to do. *Look confident and decisive*, he said to himself. Helmut's face appeared over the balcony and he made his way down the stairs.

"Welcome to your first day. How are the children?"

"Settling in. Fiona and Conor started today. The other two will enroll next week."

"Excellent," his uncle said. "Let me introduce you around."

Helmut walked to the closest man, who was welding some sheet metal together with an open flame. The worker pulled up his mask to reveal a weather-beaten face and crooked teeth. Seamus introduced himself and held out his hand. The man pulled off his gloves and shook his hand. They walked the floor a few minutes, meeting various staff members, until they came to a man dressed in a suit looking at a clipboard.

"This is an important man around here," Helmut said.

"Herr Ritter," the small, balding man said to him. "My name is Gert Bernheim. I'm the factory manager. Shall we speak in your office?"

"Of course. Lead on," Seamus said, glad to have somewhere to go and someone to talk to.

Bernheim was almost a head shorter than him. He looked about fifty and had round black spectacles that rested on a thick nose. His face was clean-shaven, and his thin lips moved at a rapid rate when he spoke.

"I'll let you men get acquainted. I have some matters to attend to," Helmut said and went to his office.

Bernheim led Seamus up the stairs to the office. He opened the door and showed him to his new desk.

"I was in on Saturday," Seamus said. "It's quite a different story when all the workers are on the floor and the machines are going."

"It's a hive of activity. We like it that way," Bernheim said with a smile.

"How long have you been working here?" Seamus said. He motioned to Bernheim to take a seat. They both sat.

"I've been here 12 years. Your uncle is a good man. An excellent boss."

"I'm going to work every day to make him proud."

Seamus wondered if this man, or anyone else on the floor, knew Helmut was ill. He took a few minutes to talk about his background, leaving out the lost years riding the rails looking for work. It was easier to make it seem like the bank closed a few weeks before Helmut left the factory to him. No need for his new colleagues to know every detail of his past. He told Bernheim about his children and how his wife died. The older man sat and listened to every word, not interrupting him to ask needless questions.

When it came time, Seamus asked him about his life. He had two children, boys aged sixteen and seventeen. He was originally from Cologne, but moved to Berlin after the war. Bernheim had been too old to fight and hoped his boys never would have to either. Seamus echoed his sentiment, wondering how all these people would react if they knew he'd fought against the land of their birth. He hoped that unlike his father, they'd understand that he had little choice in the matter. He'd keep it to himself—no use stirring up needless animosity.

They went over the books, reviewing methods and suppliers. Bernheim seemed happy to tell him every detail he asked about. The factory was profitable, but a little antiquated. Seamus would have to tackle the needed modernization on another day. Helmut appeared through the door.

"Monday morning staff meeting," his uncle said. "I'd like you to address the workers after me."

"I'd love to," Seamus said.

Helmut had Bernheim gather the workers and switch the machines off for a few minutes so his voice could be heard. He stood on the balcony, looking down on them. They stood in silence, their visors in their hands and their hats off.

"Good morning. I'm going to keep it short today. I told you last week that my nephew was coming all the way from America to work with us, and I'm going to leave the talking to him. I'd like to introduce Seamus Ritter."

The crowd of workers gave him a round of applause. He felt like he should say something brilliant or profound.

"Yes, I'm American, but I spent much of my youth in Berlin. It feels good to be back," he began. Dozens of blank faces stared back at him. Talking to them like this wasn't going to do any good. He needed to get to know them, just as Helmut had, but he was committed to this now and had to finish.

He cleared his throat before continuing. "I want to thank my uncle for this opportunity and tell each one of you that I'm looking forward to working with you. I can assure you that you are valued as workers here, no matter what your political persuasions may be." Helmut nodded to him and he continued.

"The situation on the street is different than in our factory, and we will continue to stick together. I'll be working in the background to start off and your day-to-day manager will continue to be Herr Bernheim. We will let you know if anything comes about to alter any of our roles."

Seamus gestured toward his manager, who smiled back. "You all know him, but I don't want you to think you can't approach me. My door will always be open to you, and in time, I intend to get to know each and every one of you. It's been a sincere pleasure speaking to you today."

He dismissed them back to their posts, scanning their faces for some kind of affirmation, but there was none to be found. The workers flipped their visors back over their faces, or put on their goggles, and returned to their workspaces. It was impossible to make out what they murmured to each other as they shuffled back to the machines.

It was up to him to prove himself to them over time—one speech wasn't going to win them over. Seamus returned to his office alone. He sat at the desk, lit up a cigarette, and began to pore over the previous quarter's sales reports.

Fifteen minutes passed before he heard a knock on his office door. He left it open, so Helga poked her head through and greeted him. He told her to come in and take a seat. Her office was at the end of the gangway on the second floor, beside Bernheim's. She shut the door behind her as she entered and took a seat in front of him. She was a slight woman, and her narrow hips didn't touch the arms of the chair.

"I heard your speech," she said.

"I didn't see you in the crowd."

"I can't say I agree with what you said, but I suppose it's good to allay their fears. It's only natural to think things are going to take a sharp turn for the worse when new management takes over."

"I meant what I said. I've been in their position—being frightened for my job. In my case, my fears came true."

"I'm sorry to hear that." She reached for the cigarettes on his desk. "May I?" He nodded his head. A few seconds later, she was puffing away. He waited for her to begin speaking again, as the look on her face suggested she came into his office for a reason.

"What kind of a boss is your father?"

"The workers love him. I think you can see that already. Some of the staff have been working here for 20 years or more."

Good, then they can tell me what to do, he thought, knowing better than to voice his thoughts out loud. "He's a great man."

"He's too soft for his own good sometimes."

"I'm eager to learn from him, and you also. I'm looking forward to working with you."

Helga smiled. "There is something I wanted to speak to you about," she said.

"What is that?" He sat back in his chair.

"I know you're a little dubious about my political leanings, but that's only because you don't understand what Hitler has to offer this country. So, I have a proposition for you—come to a rally with me. Witness the good, ordinary people destroyed by the scourge of democracy, yearning for the chance to prosper once more."

"Come to a National Socialist rally? I don't think—"

"I'm not trying to convert you, although many who hear Herr Hitler speak in person see reason straight away. I'm just trying to make you realize the perspective of so many in this country. Hitler doesn't come to Berlin much. This city has become a cesspool of Bolshevists and liberal values over the past 14 years, but there is a rally this Friday in Potsdam. You know where that is?"

"About 45 minutes outside the city, as far as I remember."

"Please come with me, just to make your mind up for yourself. Don't let the poison the newspapers feed you in America blind you to the greatness awakening in Germany right now."

He'd barely ever heard anyone so forthright in their beliefs before. What happened to the shy little girl he remembered?

"I'll consider it—just to see what goes on at these events. I'm curious more than anything else."

"Thank you, cousin. Experiencing it will give you an insight that merely reading never could."

Helga got up and left the room. Seamus went to the window to stare down at the men working the machines below.

~

It was a fine sunny day for October, and Maureen and Michael wrapped the jackets their father made them wear around their waists as they cycled through the city. Maureen was still wary of the traffic and didn't trust her brother, so they made for the

Tiergarten, the park in the middle of the city, just beyond the Brandenburg Gate. They passed through the gate, continuing down as the trees on either side of the road seemed to envelop them. Soon, all they saw were green trees to their left and right and the long road stretching through the center of the park ahead of them.

They pedaled in silence, Maureen in front, until they reached the Victory Column, a gilded monument celebrating Germany winning a war long before they were born. A crowd of people was gathered on the steps leading up to it. The two children slowed to a halt and got off their bikes, making sure to lock them up against the railings. Maureen slipped the key into her purse, and they walked to the column itself, arching their necks to follow it all the way up to the sky. A golden angelic figure stood on top, holding what appeared to be a staff. A brief curiosity passed into her mind about who the sculpture was meant to be, and she made a mental note to look it up the next time she was in the library.

The crowd on the steps was perhaps 200 people who stood listening to a man in the same brown uniform the boys who attacked them on the train were wearing. Indeed, many of the crowd standing listening were wearing the same thing. Morbid curiosity drove her forward when she knew she should have turned and cycled away. She and Michael looked at each other.

"Don't get too close. I just want to hear what he's saying," she said.

He seemed to get the message. They moved toward the crowd, stopping just past where the last person was standing. The speaker was flanked by several intimidating-looking Stormtroopers who held flagpoles out in front of them. The flags seemed unique. They were red with a circle of white, and in the white was some kind of symbol in black. The scene was like nothing she ever witnessed before, and she felt a long way from home. Electioneering in America felt different than this.

Michael went to step forward into the crowd, but she grabbed his arm. There was no place for him among them. He seemed to understand and didn't move to shrug her off. She made out the banner hung across the column.

"Jobs, bread, and safety," she said under her breath. Michael didn't answer. They listened to the speaker.

"Make no mistake, the Red hordes are coming. They are gathering to invade, and will wrest everything we hold dear from us. They are godless, illiterate savages that will not stop until they've brought the great civilizations of Western Europe —particularly our own—to heel. Their plan for us is nothing less than domination and enslavement. Why? Because that is the very nature of the Communists. They have no tolerance for any other culture but their own. They have nothing but jealousy and contempt for the great societies of Europe. The secret of their Communist system is simple—some get a lot and the rest of the nation gets nothing. Jews get the money, more than they could ever spend in 100 lifetimes, while the working man struggles to survive. Stalin is the most dangerous man in Europe, but will our government stand up to him?"

The crowd shouted out "No!" The speaker, a man with a brown mustache who looked younger than her father, waited for their calls to fade before continuing.

"There is only one man, one party, willing to stand up against the threat from the East. That man is our dear Führer, Adolf Hitler, and his party of National Socialists." The speaker paused again as the crowd applauded. "He is the man to lead us through this crisis. This is existential: life or death. If the Reds come, they will destroy everything and everyone without mercy. A vote for Adolf Hitler and the National Socialists is a vote for our way of life. It is a vote for your children's future. Not just their economic future, but their very lives."

The crowd began to applaud again. A boy about Michael's age appeared in front of them wearing the now-familiar brown uniform with an armband. He handed Maureen a pamphlet. She didn't have time to look at it before the young Stormtrooper was talking to her.

"Are your parents concerned about the Bolshevist threat to our country?" His gray eyes seemed to pierce through hers.

"We just arrived here. We moved from America."

A smile came across his face, and suddenly the Brownshirt was a boy again. "You know Al Capone?"

Michael laughed, but Maureen didn't find the boy so amusing. "I've never been to Chicago," she said. The picture on the pamphlet was of a skeletal Soviet soldier on top of a flaming planet Earth.

"Would you be interested in joining our movement to save Germany?" the young SA man said. "We have roles for all ages. I've been a member since I was eleven."

"I really don't know enough about it yet," Maureen said.

"You're in the right place. The upcoming election will be the most important of our lifetime. It's our chance to put our current immoral society behind us and unite behind the Führer."

"I think it's time we moved on," Maureen said. The young Brownshirt seemed disappointed. They were walking back to their bikes when Michael began to speak again.

"Do you think that's true about the Russians? Do you think Hitler is the only person who can stand up to them?"

"God, I hope not," Maureen replied.

They returned to their bikes and continued exploring the park, but the speaker's words reverberated through Maureen's mind as they went. The thought of hordes invading from the East made her wonder if their father had made the right decision bringing the family to Berlin. Perhaps having nothing in America was better than having a home and a business here.

8

Wednesday, October 12, 1932

Seamus popped his head into his uncle's office. Helmut was on the phone and motioned for his nephew to sit down. He finished up the call.

"What's that little smile on your face?" Helmut said.

"I'm going to lunch. I'm meeting a young lady."

"You don't waste any time, do you?" the older man said and slapped the desk. "Where are you taking this lucky girl?"

"She suggested the Romanisches Café,"

"On Kurfürstendamm. I know it. Is she an artist?"

"A dancer."

"Best of luck. Don't hurry back. Take your time."

Seamus stood up and pointed to his watch. "Lunch is an hour. I'll be back then."

"No," Helmut said and put his feet up. "You came in two hours early this morning. That gives you three hours. Don't argue with me. And even if it doesn't go well, walk around and take in the sights."

Seamus smiled and scratched his head. "I'm not drinking, and I'll be back to finish out the day."

"If you insist. Let me know how it goes," he said. "It's been so long since I met up with a young lady in a café. I'll live vicariously through you."

Seamus laughed. "I'll see you later." He walked out of his uncle's office and to his car outside.

10 minutes early, he took a moment to adjust his tie and smooth down the sleeves of his blazer before he made his way toward the Romanisches Café. Kurfürstendamm was a hive of activity, and he had to zigzag through cars and bikes as he crossed the boulevard. His palms were wet, and he took a handkerchief out of his pocket to dry them off before proceeding toward the impressive gray building that housed the café. He took a seat outside, facing the street and the impressive view of the busy avenue.

He tried to think about something other than Lisa to calm his nerves. Michael and Maureen both took their entrance exams for secondary school the day before. Michael was uncertain about how he did and went to bed upset that he might have failed. Maureen showed her usual confidence, bordering on arrogance, in declaring the test easy. He was sure both kids would pass. It was always a rockier road with Michael when it came to school. At least it had been before he left two years ago. The children didn't seem to have changed as much as he thought they might in that time. They were still versions of him and Marie, with parts of his parents mixed in, making trying to understand them even more challenging.

A waiter came and Seamus ordered a coffee. Everyone around him seemed to be drinking beer. That would help his nerves, but he didn't want the workers to smell it on his breath after lunch. The last time he did anything like this, he was Maureen's age. He had no experience at romance as an adult. A magnificent Gothic church stood across the street, and he stood and craned his neck up to look at the spire as it ascended toward the heavens. Berlin was so different from America, where almost everything was new. The present seemed intertwined with history here, to the point where it was almost impossible to see where one ended and the other began. The archaic was unavoidable.

He sat back down in his seat and tried to ignore the fact that Lisa was already two minutes late. The waiter came back with his drink and asked if he'd like to see a menu. Seamus told him that he was waiting for a friend, and the young waiter bowed and walked away. Dozens of people sat around him, chatting and laughing. Only he sat alone. His thoughts drifted back to the conversation he had with his cousin two days before. It was clear she wanted to purge the factory workforce of anyone she didn't consider worthy of working there.

Seamus agreed with her about one thing—the factory did seem like Germany in microcosm, with differing political beliefs vying against one another. But unlike the Nazis, he wasn't interested in trying to crush opposing views. As long as the workers behaved and the factory remained profitable, Helmut wouldn't get rid of anyone, no matter what Helga advocated.

Time wore on. He'd almost finished his coffee. Lisa's words about being too much trouble and her warning to him about being late came into his mind. Perhaps she'd only been stringing him along, or made the decision that she was indeed too troublesome for him. He knew where she worked, but what was the point in going to the club if she didn't want to see him? He looked out onto the street as a large tram pulled up. He watched the people getting off, scanning their faces, but it moved off and he was still alone. It was almost one thirty now, and he was starting to feel like an old fool. He stared out at the traffic, his mind devoid of thought, when a voice interrupted him.

"Anything good out there?" Lisa said.

She was standing beside the table dressed in a floral dress. She took off her coat and beret and held them in her arms as she waited for him to answer. Several men at tables nearby were staring at her.

"I was beginning to think you weren't going to show," he said.

"It took me a while to make up my mind as to whether I would or not."

"I'm going to pretend you're joking and just offer you a seat." He stood up and walked around to pull out her chair. She sat down opposite him.

"I'm sorry I kept you waiting," she said.

He wanted to hear that she had a solid excuse and that it wasn't just a case of her making up her mind, but she didn't offer one. The waiter appeared again, breaking the slight air of awkwardness that had descended. Lisa ordered a beer. Seamus smiled as he asked for another cup of coffee.

"I don't usually drink at lunchtime," he said.

"A good choice considering your new job."

"Did you always want to be a dancer?"

"Yes, and an actress. I've done some acting too."

"Onstage?"

"Mainly movies. You can see me credited as dancer number twelve or nymph number six if you look hard enough at the credits of a couple of recent releases."

"What does it take to play a nymph?"

"A lot of flailing around. It's almost like having a fit, but on camera, and you have to do it over and over for hours. Those directors make you work for the pittance they pay."

"Sounds exhausting."

"It's the glamorous life of the Movie Extra Nymph. We're the unsung heroes of the nymph world. You're enjoying our wonderful city?"

"Very much."

"How was your first day? Did you whip the workers into shape yet?"

"No, but I've achieved my goal so far."

"To not let on that you've no idea what you're doing?"

"Exactly. It's a skill I'm perfecting."

"Sounds a lot like what I do."

"The time will come when I have to make a decision that will affect these people's lives, though. I just hope I'll be ready to lead them when they need me."

"I'm sure you will be, Seamus."

"I don't even know them yet."

"But you will, and they'll realize how lucky they are to have you as a boss when they need you."

"You don't know me either," he said and took a sip of his coffee.

"I don't even know your last name."

"It's Ritter."

"Nice to meet you, Seamus Ritter. I'm Lisa Geisinger."

Seamus stood and shook her hand. "Miss Geisinger, a pleasure. I do have one question—why did you agree to meet me? You must have so many men ask you out."

"I have a dozen men ask me out every night. I don't think I'm special—all the girls do. We're the personification of their fantasies: The dancer in the nightclub swinging their hips and smiling at everyone. That's what we're paid to do. But you have a warmth about you. I knew I could trust you. There are so many crazy men out there."

She reached into her bag for a pack of cigarettes. She took his lighter from the table and lit one up. "And I think I've met most of them. You're a family man—but not a married one. That's an important detail."

"You met me today because I'm boring," he said with a smile. "I get it."

"Sometimes boring is the best of things. Now, tell me about your children. How are they settling into life in the big city?"

"Good, I hope. The two little ones, Conor and Fiona, are in school now. Michael and Maureen start next week. Do you like children?"

The question seemed to make her uneasy, and she shifted in her seat. "I do, yes. I love children. Sometimes I think I should have been a teacher."

"You still can be."

"Oh, yeah, the parents would be overjoyed to find out their child's teacher used to dance in a studded bra with bananas wrapped around her waist."

"They wouldn't have to find out."

"Someone always does, and they always seem to tell everyone else."

"You think people would respect you less because of your past?"

"Wouldn't you?"

"Not in any way whatsoever."

"You always know the right thing to say, don't you, Seamus?" she said. "Let's make a proper toast this time." She picked up her glass, and he did the same. They clinked them together. "Here's to second chances—you coming to Berlin and me not having to play a nymph ever again."

"Here's to that," he said.

They each took a sip and put the drinks back down on the table with smiles on their faces. He told her about losing his job, losing his house, leaving the children with Maeve, and going searching for work. He didn't tell her any details about Marie, just that she died.

"I can't imagine how hard that must have been for you, to leave your children like that."

"It was, but Maureen was right. I can see that now. I left too soon. I could have done more to find a job, but my mind was elsewhere. Leaving was a selfish act. I needed to get away after my wife died. I couldn't handle the thought of looking for work and somewhere to live, and managing the kids too. Hitting the road was the easy option. I should have stayed."

"But you missed them terribly when you were gone and sent most of your wages home."

"Of course, but I wasn't there when they needed me most, and that's something I'll regret for the rest of my life."

"What made you come home? Did you finally get to the stage where you couldn't take being away from them anymore?"

"Yes, but that's not all of the reason."

It was hard to believe he was so honest, so forthcoming, with her. He couldn't remember anyone so willing to listen, so easy to talk to. Not since Marie. He didn't want to compare Lisa to her, certainly not at this embryonic stage of their courting, but she was his only point of reference. Marie was the only woman he ever loved, the only woman he ever even kissed. After she died, he didn't think that he'd be interested in another woman for the rest of his life, and he hadn't been until now. Lisa seemed different, and yet, he hardly knew her at all.

"What was the reason?" she asked.

"There was some trouble at the worksite."

"What kind of trouble?"

He shook his head and smiled before taking another sip of beer. A tram pulled up behind them and disgorged people onto the sidewalk. They both focused on it a few seconds before it pulled away. Should he tell her? She was looking at him again now, a cigarette in hand. Her brown eyes were expectant, but kind.

"I made a stupid decision." He stopped, wondering if he should go any further. *Will I scare her off? If I'm not honest with her now, what kind of a future could we have?*

"I met someone who convinced me to join him in a scheme to solve all of my money problems. It was a burglary, but the old man we were robbing caught us in the act. I barely got out of there with my life. The other man I went in with—the one who planned it all—wasn't so lucky."

She stubbed out her cigarette. "And I thought you were boring."

Laughing seemed the only way to respond. "I've shocked you."

"Why did you agree to do it?"

"Desperation. It seemed like a quick and easy way to get back to the children with enough money to make a difference in their lives. I was stupid. I know that now."

"For wanting to get back to your children?"

"No, that was the only good thing to come out of the whole episode. I was stupid to agree to something so dangerous with a group of men I didn't know."

"We all have regrets," she said. Her voice broke a little and faded out. "I don't hold what you did against you. Desperation can drive us so far from ourselves that we hardly recognize the person it turned us into."

The cigarette was shaking in her hand as she held it to her mouth. Was she about to make an excuse and leave? It was almost three o'clock. The lunchtime crowd had come and gone, and many of the tables around them were empty now. He knew he should get back to the factory soon, but leaving this woman was impossible. If he left her now, would he ever see her again? He wanted to make this moment last a lifetime. A few seconds of silence settled between them. It was obvious she wanted to speak, so he gave her the time to come up with the words.

"We've had our share of problems these last few years. My father was a decent enough man, but things changed after my brothers died in the war. He started drinking more and more, and staying out all night playing cards. I didn't think much of it at first, but then he started sleeping through the day and neglecting the hotel. My mother had to run the place herself. It was too much for her alone, so I started helping out. We saw my father less and less. That was in the days when inflation hit so badly that you'd have to bring a bag of money to the store to buy a loaf of bread." Her cigarette was almost burned out. She stubbed it out in the ashtray.

"My father had pawned all the valuables we had and then gambled away the hotel itself in a bid to regain what he lost. I remember the last time I saw him. He was in one of the empty rooms, propped up on the bed with a bottle of schnapps. I tried to talk to him, but he was so drunk I could hardly make out a word he said. If I knew that was the last time I'd ever see him alive, I would have tried harder. I could have put him to bed or gotten him some coffee, but I just left him there."

Lisa sighed and continued. "I hated him for what he did to my mother and me. I couldn't see past what the deaths of my brothers had done to him. The war made him a drunken degenerate who gambled away the last chance his wife and daughter had."

The life had drained from her face, and she was looking out at the passing traffic as she spoke. No tears...just the pain of regret in her eyes. She finished her beer and sat back. He gave her a few seconds to gather herself before he spoke.

"What happened to him?"

She looked at him across the table. "Why am I telling all this to a man I just met? I haven't told anyone this before."

"You don't have to tell me anything."

"No, I want to. The police discovered his body in the river a few days later, shot in the back of the head." A single tear broke from her left eye and ran down her cheek. "The police never found out who did it, but we knew it was the gangsters he fell in with. They took his money, then they took his life. And it's just been my mother and me ever since. Eight years now."

Seamus reached across the table and took her hands. They were cold to the touch, and he wrapped them in his, trying to warm them. He expected her to say she had to leave, but she didn't. A tiny smile spread across her face.

"What a first meeting, eh? I told you I was more trouble than I was worth."

"Shall we go somewhere else? Is there some hidden gem you'd like to show me? I'm a tourist after all."

"I'm sorry to tell you, but you live here now. You can't be a tourist in a city you live in."

"Says who? Can't I be a tourist for a day?"

The waiter came back to the table and Seamus paid the bill. They stood up. "Shouldn't you be getting back to the factory?" she asked.

"My uncle told me not to come back for three hours. He insisted—wouldn't let me argue."

"Sounds like my kind of boss!"

She put her coat and beret on. On the street she turned to him, inches away. He felt like he was swimming in her brown eyes.

"Have you seen the Berlin Palace? It isn't too far from here."

"Not since I was a boy, but I want to see it again today."

"Well, then, let's make it happen."

A tram pulled up and they jumped aboard. With no seats available, they stood beside each other, holding onto the railings as the tram trundled through the streets. It was too crowded to have the kind of conversation that he wanted to have, so they rode along without talking, just taking in the sights of the city. Seamus wondered about her politics and how to find out where she stood. He never would have suspected Helga to have been a Nazi supporter. What if Lisa believed the same things? It would be hard to see past that. A few minutes later, she tapped him on the arm and led him off the tram.

He gasped as he beheld the enormity of the Berlin Palace. It seemed to take up the entirety of his view, enveloping everything else around it. It was set just off the Spree, an almost equally impressive monument to Emperor Wilhelm I standing just in front of it. They stopped short of the palace, straining their necks to look up at it.

"How many bedrooms do you think they have in there?" he asked.

"About a thousand," she said with a smile.

They walked around the perimeter. He wanted to reach out and hold her hand, but was aware that it might be uncouth. He didn't want to risk anything at this early stage, so he kept his hands to himself.

"This is the first part of the city I've seen that isn't covered in election posters," he said. "Where do you stand on the issues? I just found out my cousin is an ardent Hitler supporter. She was warning me about the Communist threat within the factory itself on my first day there."

"I'm no fan of Hitler and his ridiculous policies. I read some of that book he published, just to see what he stood for. I couldn't get through it. It was nothing more than a diatribe against the Jews. What they ever did to him to make him feel that way is a mystery to me. I do find him handsome, though. He's a devastatingly attractive man."

Seamus went from relief to incredulity in a matter of seconds. "Wait, what?"

"Oh yes, that little mustache of his has haunted my dreams for years now. I just want to get my hands on it and—"

"Oh, right. I'm sure."

She couldn't hold in the laughter anymore. "You should see your face." She laughed so hard she was crying. "Oh, yes, he's such a dreamboat. A regular Douglas Fairbanks!"

"You had me there for a few seconds," he said. "I was wondering if you had a problem with your eyesight."

They walked on, talking about politics in hushed voices that passersby couldn't hear. She was disgusted with the entire system of government and the weak rule that plagued Germany since the war, but disagreed with Helga that the only way to start over was to burn the entire house down.

"I don't understand people who would vote for a party that will eliminate their opportunity to vote them out. What if everything they promised didn't come to be? No politician ever keeps all their promises, even the best of them. I'm amazed at these people who want to eradicate democracy, but there are a lot of them out there."

Seamus didn't ask any more questions about politics. He didn't need to. He supposed the beginning of a possible courtship was about vetting one another, and she passed every test. Did she feel the same way about him? Time would tell— nothing else. The next hurdle would be her meeting the children, but he stopped himself, realizing he was getting ahead of where he needed to be.

It was almost four o'clock, and as much as it pained him, he needed to get back to the factory and then home to his family. He didn't want to be the one to say it, but was wary of being too clingy, too needy. They found a bench across from the palace and sat down.

"So, your cousin is a Nazi," she said.

"It seems so. That sounds like a self-help pamphlet, doesn't it? *So, Your Cousin is a Nazi.*"

"Yes." She smiled. "It could be about how to talk to them without wanting to pull your hair out. I don't know what would be in the pamphlet, as just listening to them speak makes me want to scream, but there are better writers out there than me."

"And it seems a lot of cousins who are Nazis too."

"Unfortunately."

"I had drinks with some journalist friends the other night before I met you. They seemed to think the Nazis were on the way out. They said that the people were sick of them and the improving economy would sink their chances in the next election."

"I don't know. Hitler seems like the ultimate political survivor. You heard about his niece committing suicide last year?"

"The last couple of years are a black hole for me. I didn't follow much international news at all."

"He was living with her. Rumors abounded about the nature of their relationship. Supposedly he was domineering and protective over her, and she was a prisoner in the apartment they shared. They argued over a man she wanted to see in Vienna, and he left in a rage. The newspapers reported she shot herself with his pistol afterward."

"How did he react?"

"It nearly broke him. Her death sent him into a spiral of depression. Everyone thought he was finished, but he rose from the ashes of the scandal stronger than ever. So, forgive me if I'm not convinced by reports of his imminent demise. Nothing seems to stop that man."

"My journalist friends are more optimistic than you are, perhaps."

"I'd love to be blind to the truth, but I can't ignore it. The Nazis are a powerful force in our society and they're not going away anytime soon."

The time...it seemed to drag at him. She hadn't mentioned anything about leaving. Not once.

"I've had such a wonderful time meeting you this afternoon. Are you glad you decided to come?"

"I am," she said with a smile.

"I still don't see why you're not worth the trouble. If your intention was to convince me of that, you've failed. Miserably."

She held his gaze before bringing it back to the massive palace in front of them. "Oh, Seamus, you don't know the half of it."

"Well, I'd certainly like to, and then after, to get to know the other half."

She laughed and brought her eyes to his again. "You're so sweet. This would be much harder if you were rude or stupid or difficult to talk to."

"I can work on those things."

"I've enjoyed this afternoon so much, more than any in a long time. Shouldn't we just leave it at that? It'd be perfect. Forever. Nothing could change it."

"You want to go through life never getting to know anybody? I want to meet you again, Lisa."

"I knew this was a mistake."

Seamus knew then that she'd been telling the truth about why she was late. He imagined her standing in front of the mirror, trying to talk herself out of meeting him while getting ready. What was holding her back? What could be worse than what he told her?

"Did I say too much?" he asked.

"No, not at all. It's refreshing to speak to someone who's not trying to hide in the corner of every conversation." She reached over and took his hand from where it was resting on his lap. The touch of her skin on his felt wonderful.

"I'm not ..." She trailed off, seemingly unable to find the words.

"I have to get back to the factory now. My uncle told me to take my time but workers will be wondering where the new man is."

"Don't let them smell the beer on your breath. That could raise a few red flags."

"I'll keep my distance. How about we have dinner this weekend? I know you work most nights. How about Sunday, or even Monday?"

"Ok. I can do dinner."

He stood up and took her hand to help her to her feet. "It's settled then. I don't know anywhere, so you're going to have to tell me."

"How about the same café we met at today? You know that place."

"Perfect."

They walked back toward the tram, finalizing the arrangements for Monday night. She turned to him as they reached the tram stop.

"I have an appointment I need to get to," she said.

"And I should get back to the factory."

"Is your three hours up?" Her tram pulled up. "I need to get this."

He resisted the overwhelming desire to kiss her on the cheek. She smiled at him as she got on board.

"Until Monday," she said, and then was gone.

Seamus stood alone. A deep feeling of contentment washed through him. It was like nothing he'd known in years.

9

Lisa lay prone, her face pressed into the soft white pillow. The curtains were open, and she could see the light of the stars in the night sky. They looked like diamonds on a sheet of black velvet. She turned over and drew the sheet over her body, pulling it all the way up to her chin. She tried to close her eyes, to imagine herself somewhere else. It was hard to believe that she had that perfect time with Seamus just a few hours before. It seemed like a different world, and she a different person.

The sound of the radio came from the living room. It was easier to pretend to be asleep. She shut her eyes like a child, thinking about Seamus and their afternoon. He was the antithesis of everything about this situation. He was a gentleman. He hadn't even kissed her on the cheek yet. She drew a harsh breath that seemed to catch in her throat, forcing her to cough.

The faint sound of Debussy's "Clair de Lune" drifted in from the living room. She knew he was waiting for her. It was enough to deal with him in the bedroom without having to speak to him afterward. She brought her knees up to her chest, holding them there for a few minutes. Not moving, just listening. The sound she craved—him leaving—didn't come. The clock on the wall told her that she had to go to work soon. She couldn't wait him out.

She swung her legs around and onto the wooden floor. Her clothes were on the chair by the bed where she left them. She tried to make as little sound as possible, but knew he heard her. The footsteps she dreaded came across the wooden floor and he appeared at the bedroom door. He was in his military uniform, his graying hair slicked back over his head, and his salt-and-pepper mustache twitching above his mouth as he spoke.

"I thought you were never getting out of bed," Ernst said.

She didn't answer, just curled the sheet around herself to hide from his glare. It was more than she could bear to look at him. This had always been difficult, but after today, she didn't know if she could do it again. It was easier when every man was a leering pervert and all they wanted was to undress her. Knowing that men like Seamus existed made this so much harder. She got out of the bed. He didn't move, standing still in the doorway, watching her get dressed.

"The money for the kid is on the dresser," he said.

"Ok," she answered.

"Something wrong? You're quiet. Even more so than usual."

"It's nothing. I'm just tired." She finished dressing and stood up.

"Have a glass of brandy with me. I'm listening to some music."

The thought of sitting with him made her stomach turn, but what if she said no? How would he react? "I need to get to the nightclub." Her voice was dull and limp.

"Nonsense. I know you're not on stage for another hour at least, and your mother's at home with the child." He walked over and put a hand on her shoulder as if there were some kind of affection between them. "Come and have a drink with me. I'll drop you off at the club afterward. I have my car parked on the street outside."

"Shouldn't you get home to your wife and children?" she said.

He grabbed her by the face. His movement was so fast that she didn't have time to flinch or pull away. "Don't mention them here. Ever. You know the rules of our engagement."

He shoved her back and she stumbled a little before regaining her balance. He turned and walked around the bed, stopping to look back when he was in the doorway. His personality reverted back to what it had been thirty seconds before.

"Come and have a drink with me. It's been so long since we actually talked."

Lisa looked out at the night sky again before following him to the already-poured glass of brandy sitting on the table next to the bottle. He handed it to her and she took a seat beside him.

"How is the baby, anyway?"

"She's not a baby. It was her third birthday last week, and her name is Hannah."

"I know the child's name. I didn't ask that. How is she?"

"Flourishing somehow. My mother is a huge help." She took a sip of brandy. It burned her throat as she swallowed it. She put the glass down, wary of showing up for work drunk. Several girls had been fired for less. Ernst was looking straight out in front of him. His contentedness in this situation made her want to vomit. He picked a cigar off the table and lit it with a match. He shook out the flame and turned to her.

"You should think about moving out of that hovel. It's not good for the baby."

"I'm trying to save money. It hasn't been easy."

"It hasn't been an easy time for any of us."

Lisa somehow doubted times had been hard for Oberst Ernst Milch of the renowned Milch family. Joining the Army was a rite of passage for him—a method to prove himself to his father in a world where money didn't matter. Joining the Nazi Party allowed him to deny the defeat he and the rest of the military suffered in the Great War. It was a way to blame their own failings on politicians and Jews.

Ernst and the Nazis were a perfect fit, and he joined back in '22. He told her once that he was at the Beer Hall Putsch and marched with the rest of the mob that day until the authorities faced them down. He told the story like it was a badge of honor —that he was present at the dawn of a great new civilization that would propel Germany back to worldwide prominence. It was easier to pretend to be impressed.

She thought of Seamus again. He seemed a different species to the rat sitting beside her. They sat there a few more minutes as he droned on about the election and how the Nazis would ascend to power and drag the entire country back to greatness. She'd heard all his nonsense before.

"I need to get to work now," she said after a few minutes.

He put down his glass of brandy. "I'll drive you. We wouldn't want you to be late, now, would we?"

"I'd rather walk," she said.

"But I'm not giving you that choice," he said. "I'll drive you to work and that's the end of it. You can accept that or I'll take away the money I left you earlier. Your pride or food on your family's table. What's it to be?"

Lisa didn't answer. She felt like she was in a cage at the bottom of the ocean, the water crushing her. Milch went to get his jacket and slipped his arms into it. He turned around to her, holding his arms out.

"You should be able to afford to move out of that toilet soon enough, and you get to keep the child. I'd say coming here to meet me twice a month or so is a small price to pay for all of that. Now, let's go." He walked to the door and held it open.

Barbs of frustration rippled through her entire body, but she picked up her coat and paced past him through the door.

~

Wednesday, October 12, 1932

The children had no idea why he was so happy when he came home from work after meeting Lisa at the Romanisches Café. They didn't question his motives when he took them out for ice cream. They knew better. It felt like things were coming together and that they'd made the right move to this exciting, incredible, insane city. They came home well after bedtime, and he tucked the three younger children into bed.

Seamus and his oldest daughter sat in the lobby together. She was reading *Twenty-Four Hours in the Life of a Woman* by Stefan Zweig. She picked it up in the library that day, ostensibly to improve her German reading comprehension, but he knew she'd read Zweig's work before.

"How's the book?" he asked.

"Interesting," she replied without looking up.

He wanted to tell her about Lisa, but knew it was too soon. She was angry enough at him as it was. Meeting someone else and introducing her to the children was a delicate matter, not something he'd thought about before because he honestly didn't think it would happen. Marie was sick for a few months before she finally passed, but they never had a conversation about what he'd do after she went. They spoke about the children and what they'd become, but not about what the future might hold for him. He doubted he'd feel more at ease with being a single father with a long life left to live if she gave him her blessing to see other women after she was gone. But he did feel like a raft cast adrift on a strange ocean.

Perhaps Lisa was the star he could navigate home by. Perhaps not. Either way, she awakened him to a latent world he scarcely thought about or believed held a place for him. Could a man truly love two women in his lifetime? Could he fully give his heart not once, but twice? He was beginning to believe the time might have come to find out.

He knew he'd have to tread carefully with the children. No woman could ever replace their mother. Marie appeared in his mind and a pang of guilt stabbed at him when he thought of Lisa. The picture of his wife on her deathbed jumped from his memory into the forefront of his mind.

"Have you thought about Mom much since we arrived here?" he asked Maureen.

She closed the book. "Every day."

"I've been thinking about her myself."

"I try to keep her with me. That way it's like she's not gone, you know?"

"Do you talk to her?"

"I've tried. I thought I heard her at first until I realized it was just an echo of what I was saying myself—it wasn't her voice. So I stopped talking to her. I try to feel her. I know she's with me."

"I understand that. I remember the priest at her funeral told me that she wasn't gone forever, just waiting in the next room."

"I remember."

"I didn't draw any comfort from that. I couldn't talk to her from there. If she wasn't beside me, what did it matter where she was, whether that was in the next room or up with the stars, floating above?"

"He was only trying to console you."

"Yes, I know that. I don't hold anything against him. It's not his fault Marie died so young and left us alone. Nor hers either."

The clock on the wall sounded. They both looked up at it. Seamus took a sip from the beer on the table in front of him. He wanted to tell her about Lisa and all the hopes she ignited within him. He longed to share his dreams with Maureen, but knew it wasn't proper. He'd already said too much. She seemed a little taken aback by his candor.

"Are you ready for school next week?" he asked.

She shrugged. "Yes, I think so."

"Are you all right, Maureen?"

"I don't know."

"Is it Leo?"

"Yes, but it's more than that."

"What?"

"Some of the political goings on here are a little intimidating. The incident with those idiot boys on the train wasn't the best introduction."

"There are fools like them everywhere. Germany certainly doesn't have any monopoly on them. We have our fair share in America too."

"I know that. I think the thing that troubles me most, though, is how organized they are. It's like the hooligans all got together to form an army. I saw one of the Nazi speakers in the park the other day with Michael. We stopped to listen for a minute. Do you think the Soviets are going to invade?"

"No." He reached across and took her hand. "They won't. Their mission is to spread their ideology, not to conquer Germany. The Nazis have painted them as the giant evil in Europe to instill fear in people."

"Why?"

"Because fearful people will do anything they can to protect themselves. They'll vote for whoever they think will defend them. They're preying on people's innermost nightmares of hordes invading from the East."

"Clayton said the Nazis are going to be defeated in the next election."

"Let's hope he's right, but even if he's not, life will go on. People will still get up and go to work. The factory will still run, and you and your siblings will still go to school. They can't change all that."

~

It felt like they were going to a sporting event. The anticipation rippling through the crowd reminded him of going to football games or to see boxing matches in the city. But there was something eminently more sinister here than just that. The excitement on the faces of the people they were walking with was plain to see, but they weren't here to see their team play. They were here to see Adolf Hitler.

Seamus was walking with Helga and Clayton toward the stadium in Potsdam that the Nazis hired for their rally. The three were among a crowd of maybe 10,000, swallowed up on all sides by badge-wearing, armband-showing, flag-toting Nazi voters. Seamus tried to imagine himself among the fans of an opposition team, but knowing what they believed, it was hard not to feel bewilderment and some revulsion from being among these people. Many adolescents dressed in Hitler Youth uniforms walked among them. Girls and boys chatted with smiles on their faces about seeing the Führer, and how jealous their friends in school would be that they got to attend while others had to stay home. Some men in expensive suits walked arm in arm with their wives, but most people not in uniform were modestly dressed. They were the poor, the unwanted, the unemployed. They were the people the new Germany had left behind.

Many among the crowd were in military uniform. Several had eye patches or walked with wooden legs, or had arms missing. There were almost as many women as men. Seamus overheard one talking about how handsome Hitler was and had to stifle a laugh as he remembered what Lisa said.

Clayton was there as a journalist, and Seamus agreed to come to get a better understanding of his cousin, but Helga was a true believer. She spent much of the journey from the city griping about the ineffectiveness of the current government and how the National Socialists were the only ones who could deliver the change that Germany craved. Seamus bit his lip, commenting only on the journey and the situation back in America. Clayton didn't utter a word during her rants, only looking over at Seamus when he was sure she couldn't see him shaking his head.

"We're almost there," she said as the stadium came into view. She reached into her pocket and took out a small Nazi pin. They waited while she affixed it to her sweater. A few seconds later they were ready to go, and continued on.

Seamus wondered if this was a good idea, but kept his thoughts to himself. There was no privacy to share such notions among this crowd, enclosed by thousands of Nazi supporters. It all felt real now. Before this, National Socialism had seemed like an idea—a bunch of slogans shouted by teenage bullies in brown uniforms—but being here brought an end to any illusions he harbored. This was real. These people were committed to the cause and worshipped their Führer like a demigod sent down to Earth to rescue them from the horrors life had inflicted on them since the war.

They came to the stadium and showed their tickets at the gate to strapping young men with clean-shaven faces in SA uniforms. The stadium was more than half-full as they took their seats. Any places near the stage were already taken by people who apparently arrived there hours ago to be first in line to get to see their hero speak. A band dressed in the ubiquitous uniform of the SA played on stage, entertaining the crowd with rousing renditions of traditional German music of the type one might expect to hear in beer halls or country taverns.

Seamus sat in the middle of their group with Clayton on his left and Helga on his right. The journalist's countenance was a sharp contrast to hers. She was like a child on Christmas morning, while he looked as if he were trying to drink in everything he saw. He took out a notepad and started jotting down details of what he saw. Seamus wondered how the crowd would react to a foreign journalist in their midst. For himself, he decided to treat this like a sideshow and enjoy the spectacle. The words Clayton and others said to him about the Nazis being almost finished echoed through his mind, and he reassured himself that this time next year, the likes of this rally would be gone forever.

"How many people voted for the Nazis in the last election?" he said to Clayton, making sure to speak in German.

"More than 13 million," the younger man replied.

"Myself included," Helga said.

"But your father isn't a supporter?" Clayton asked.

"No, he's too old-fashioned to embrace the new wave sweeping Germany."

It was hard to say that Helga wasn't a kind person. She'd been welcoming and warm to him and his children. What drove her to believe in the Nazis and their promises? She was the only child of a wealthy industrialist. Many of the people in the crowd had likely been unemployed for most of the last 10 years. She seemed to have little in common with them.

"What first attracted you to the Nazi Party?" Seamus asked.

"Their clear vision for the future of our country. They offer a hope that no other party in the mess of German politics ever has. I'm sick of the idiotic corruption that has kept this country down since the war, and I think it's high time the people who betrayed Germany and lost the war for us were held responsible for that."

He was just about to ask her if she truly believed in the Nazi myth of the November Criminals—the idea that troops on the front could still have won the war but were betrayed by the politicians back home—when they heard a loud cheer as the young men of the Hitler Youth and their older counterparts in the SA entered the arena carrying Nazi flags. Scores of them marched in practiced step. They'd probably been training for this moment for months. They made their way around the track to the podium set up at the other end of the stadium. The rostrum was covered in the now-familiar Nazi flags. Pomp and circumstance seemed to be everything to these people.

"Everything is uniform, every rally is the same. It's part of the message that this is a movement. The Nazis are obsessed by symbolism," Clayton whispered to him.

"What's the importance of the swastika?" he asked. "Where does that come from?"

"It's an old Indian symbol that the Nazis appropriated for themselves. It's meant to represent Aryan purity and German national pride. Again, it's all about simple, consistent messaging."

The flag-toting SA and Hitler Youth, who must have numbered at least 100, made their way to the podium. A figure appeared. The crowd at the front rose to their feet, jutting their right arms into the air to cry out the Hitler salute. Then, they began singing in unison.

"What's that song?" Seamus asked his friend in a whisper.

"It's the Nazis' own version of the national anthem, written by a man murdered by Communists—a martyr to the National Socialist cause."

A great roar spread through the crowd like a virus as Hitler took to the stage. Seamus stood with the rest of the crowd, trying to make out the man they were all there to see. It was

surprising that he was on first. He thought there would be some
lesser speakers before him. But there he was: A pale, ordinary-
looking man with dark black hair. But even from this far back,
Seamus could detect an aura he'd never quite experienced
before.

These people wanted to please him. This was a major
reason Seamus had agreed to come. He wanted to see the
people react to the man they chose to be their savior. He
wanted to try to understand them. This rally, this whole movement, would be soon consigned to the trashcan of history.
Seamus knew this was different than anything he'd ever
contemplated going to before. He wanted to be able to say he
saw it, had breathed in the madness of it. Now he could.

Helga was enraptured. If the man on stage invited her up
and proposed marriage at that moment, she doubtless would
have accepted, but so would many other women in the
audience.

Hitler stood a few moments without speaking, saluting the
lines of SA and Hitler Youth approaching with Nazi flags. He
waited until they were all lined up in front of the stage to begin.
Hitler wiped a hand across his forehead. It was a fine day for
October, but he couldn't have been hot. The crowd took their
seats, and the cheering died down. There were no pleasantries.
The Führer leaned into the microphone and went straight in.

"In the November days of 1918 those in power promised to
bring our people, and particularly the German worker, into a
better and more productive future. Today, almost 14 years later,
who can bear witness to any improvements they made? The
German peasant has become impoverished. The middle class is
ruined. The hopes of millions have been destroyed. One third
of all German men and women find themselves unemployed,
without income. The Reich is indebted, and all the coffers are
empty."

The crowd was silent. His words were like weapons in his

mouth, and he seemed to spit them out like bullets. The effect he had on the crowd was startling. They seemed entranced.

Clayton was scribbling shorthand beside him. Seamus looked as much at the people sitting around them as the man on stage.

"Germany has slowly disintegrated," Hitler continued. "If the powers that be seriously want to save Germany, why haven't they done so already? If they wanted to do so then their policies must have been abysmal. If their policies were right, then they must have been insincere, or too ignorant or too weak."

He stood back from the microphone to let the crowd cheer for a few seconds before leaning in to resume his speech.

"Therefore, it is our duty to vanquish these parties. In order to secure their own existence, they must tear the country apart over and over again. Thirteen years ago, we National Socialists were mocked and derided. Today, our enemies' laughter has turned to tears." The crowd erupted in applause, and Hitler saluted. He waited a few more seconds for it all to die down.

"A faithful community of people has arisen that will overcome the prejudices of class madness and the arrogance of rank. Not because they are Catholics or Protestants, workers or civil servants, bourgeois or salaried workers—because they are Germans. We National Socialists march into every election with the knowledge that we are not merely fighting for ministerial posts, but for every German, who we will join together once more to share a single common destiny."

He spoke another 20 minutes or so, never mentioning the Jews and only referring to the perceived threat from the East in a few words. The message was clear—the National Socialists were the only ones who could return Germany to its former economic greatness. The other politicians were corrupt and must be removed.

Hitler held the crowd in thrall during his entire speech. No eyes wavered, no one stood up from their seat. Each person there seemed to believe that Germany was at a turning point. It was up to them to save the country they loved from falling into the abyss of liberalism and democracy and propel it back to its former greatness. They all felt the responsibility that Hitler had bestowed upon them. The very future of their country was dependent on them and what choices they made now. Nothing would ever be more important in their lives. Disaster awaited, and the only way to avert it was to vote for Hitler and his Nazi Party.

"The Almighty, who has allowed us to rise from seven men to 13 million in the space of just 13 years, will further grant us a new German Reich," Hitler said. His voice seemed to grow louder and more potent with each passing moment.

"It is in this new Reich we believe, and will fight for. And we are willing, as the thousands of comrades who went before us, to commit ourselves body and soul to building the dream of this new Reich for all Germans. If the nation does its duty, then the day will come which restores to us one Reich in the name of honor and freedom."

Hitler stood back from the microphone as the crowd exploded with cheering and applause. He leaned back in as the furor continued. "Work and bread!" he shouted and stood back to salute again.

The crowd joined him in holding their hands up in the salute made to honor him. They called out his name and began the song they were singing as the rally started. Everyone was on their feet now. It was hard not to be washed away by the tide of energy and emotion swirling through the stadium. Seamus fought it, but couldn't help the feelings rising within his chest. It was like nothing he'd ever known. Helga was euphoric.

Clayton was the only man in the arena scowling. He leaned over to whisper something, but his words were lost in the maelstrom of sound. Hitler stood at the podium, saluting, soaking in the adoration. But his face didn't change. He didn't smile. His face was the picture of concentration, hard as granite.

They stayed in their seats another hour or two. Some other speakers came out to parrot what their Führer alluded to in his speech. There was more mention of the Bolshevists and the threat from the East, but once more, the Jews were only mentioned in passing.

The sun was fading over the horizon as they left the stadium. The crowd around them was electrified by what they'd seen. Casual voters had become true believers, and the true believers seemed to have become fanatics. Helga's smile seemed tattooed on her face.

They only began to speak in earnest when they reached the car. Clayton climbed in the back. Helga drove. The streets were thick with people returning home from the rally, singing songs and waving Nazi flags. Helga waited until they were clear of Potsdam and on the road back to Berlin to ask the question.

"So, what did you think? Is Herr Hitler not the most impressive orator you've ever seen?"

"He's an excellent speaker," Clayton said.

Seamus waited a few seconds for his friend to say more, but he weighed in when he realized the journalist was finished. "It was an experience. I've never seen anything quite like it. The way he holds the crowd in the palm of his hand like that."

"Did you feel your spirit soar within you as the rest of us did?"

Seamus looked out the window. He didn't want to insult his cousin and was fully aware that he wasn't going to convert her. Her devotion to Hitler's cause seemed complete.

Clayton spoke up. "I just hope there's a place for all different viewpoints in whatever Germany becomes. I understand that this is a tumultuous time, and the people who've been left behind feel angry, but blocking out all other opinions but the ones you subscribe to is dangerous."

"I trust Hitler and his followers. They're true patriots who only want the best for Germany."

"Maybe so," Clayton said. "But the system of democracy gives the people a chance to take back any decisions they make."

"What about you, Seamus?" Helga said. "You were bereft before you received the letter from my father. What did the great democracy in American do for you? Not everyone is lucky enough to get a job from their uncle. The people you saw today are the same as you. They only want to work and get their fair share. They want to be able to feed their families. Why do you think Hitler ended with the slogan *Work and Bread*?"

She gave the men a couple of seconds to digest what she said before answering her own question. "It's because that's all the people want. The simple things they need to sustain them-selves have been denied them all these years, and they're sick of empty promises from incompetent politicians. Hitler is going to change all of that. That's why 13 million angry voices spoke up in the last election."

"What about the Jews?" Clayton said from the back seat.

"What about them?" she answered.

"The speakers tonight barely mentioned them, yet Hitler obsesses about them in his writings."

"There are many different policies to return Germany to greatness. There isn't time to discuss all of them. Tonight was about the many economic issues facing the nation."

"I understand that," Clayton said, "but what about the things Hitler writes about the Jews? Don't tell me the people in the crowd tonight were ignorant about him describing Jewish people as a disease, and repeating over and over that fighting the evil of the Jews is God's work. What do you think about those sentiments?"

"Not everything Hitler and the Nazis say is to be taken liter-ally," she said.

Seamus was surprised by the confidence in her voice. She didn't shrink at the question as he thought she would. He was wary of ganging up on her, so he kept quiet.

"You don't think the rhetoric he uses about the Jews is dangerous?" said Clayton.

"I think the concentration of power and wealth in Jewish hands is dangerous. I think they are to blame for the loss of the last war, and have much to answer for the economic situation that we find ourselves in right now."

"Is Herr Bernheim, the factory manager, Jewish?" Clayton said.

"Yes," Helga answered.

"Do you think he's part of some conspiracy to steal jobs and money from ordinary Germans? Do you think he and his family are a threat to the existing world order?"

"Of course not. There are always exceptions. Hitler is talking about the Jewish power complex that sets the rules for our society behind closed doors. He wants to free us from their power."

Seamus turned away to look out the window. A feeling of emptiness settled within him. He thought of Bernheim and all the others who Hitler tarred as enemies of the people. He hoped what he witnessed tonight was indeed only a sideshow and not some warning about what was to come in his new adopted home.

∾

Looking for a new house made it seem like things were finally beginning to come together. It had been so long since they had somewhere of their own. Maureen was tired of sharing with the boys, coping with their dirty socks on the floor and their snoring. She was weary of having to get changed in the bathroom and having to tiptoe into the room every night in an attempt not to wake the other children.

She hadn't had her own room since Fiona was a baby. It was difficult to remember those times, but the thought of having her own space was making her giddy. The car Helmut gave her father had already given them new freedom to explore the city and beyond. They went out to the countryside several times and saw the majesty of the forests and lakes just beyond the city. Berlin and the surrounding area seemed to offer the best of both worlds. It was as if one of the world's great cities was surrounded by an outdoor playground. The children loved it—they all did.

They had already looked at several houses, all near the factory. Each seemed like a palace to her after two years in Aunt Maeve's place, but her father wanted to see more. Helmut was in the front passenger seat. He insisted on coming along on their search—not that they would have wanted it any other way. She leaned forward as they drove into a neighborhood in Wilmersdorf, just south of where Helmut lived. They passed a large synagogue and turned down a leafy street with neatly painted eclectic houses, spaced just far enough apart to offer privacy. The front lawns were uniformly manicured. Nothing seemed out of place.

"Here we are," Helmut said. "Could this be your new home?"

Helmut said a lot of things to excite the children, and she couldn't help smiling either.

"I hope so," Conor said. "I'm sick of looking."

"It's an important decision," Maureen said. "We don't want to rush it."

"We're about 25 minutes from the factory here," Helmut said as he got out of the car. He held the door for Maureen and the other kids, and they spilled out onto the street.

"Wow, it's pretty," Fiona said. "You really think we could live here?"

"I don't see why not," Seamus said.

They ambled past the sign declaring the house was available for rent and met the real estate agent at the door. He was young, perhaps only four or five years older than Maureen. He looked her up and down like a dog at the butcher's shop window. Her father and Helmut didn't seem to notice, as they were already in the house. She stood away from him, focusing on the house instead. She pushed through the wooden door and into the foyer, which stretched into a large living area. The kitchen reminded her of Maeve's in Newark. She fought back the memories as she continued looking around. Michael flashed past, chasing Conor up the stairs, much to Helmut's amusement. She found Fiona hanging onto Father's hand in the dining room. The real estate agent was lurking beside them.

"Can you wait outside while we look around?" her father said to the real estate agent. Perhaps he had noticed him staring. "What do you think, Maureen?"

She took a few seconds to look around before answering. The house was empty, but still somehow full of life. It was easy to picture living here.

"I like it." She walked to the back window and peered out at the backyard. The lawn stretched back 50 yards, lined with trees, with a wooden fence to separate the area from the neighbors, and a garden shed.

"There's one more thing. Will we get our own bedrooms? Or at least one I could share with Fiona?"

"Yeah, Father. I don't want to share with those stinky boys anymore," Fiona said.

"Let's go upstairs and have a look, shall we?" her father said.

They climbed the wooden staircase, Fiona holding her father's hand all the way. Helmut was in the bathroom with the two boys, who were enjoying running the faucets for some reason. Their great-uncle seemed to be having as much fun as they were. Maureen walked into the nearest bedroom. Two more were located across the hall, and one at the end.

"This could be your room," her father said, standing at the door with a smile on his face. "I think a sixteen-year-old should have her own bedroom."

"I love it."

"We'll have to get furniture. It'll take a while to settle in," her father said.

"It's such a beautiful house," Fiona said. "Even better than Aunt Maeve's."

"And it will be ours. Just to rent, but I'll save up and we can buy a house of our own. Somewhere we can be a family for years to come."

Maureen turned to her father with a smile on her face. It seemed like he was keeping his promises after all. Anywhere they could be together would be home.

"It's wonderful. I love it."

A wide smile spread across her father's face, the likes of which she hadn't seen in years.

"Now let's see the rest of the house before we go down and talk to that real estate agent. If he looks at you like he did on the way in here again, I'll put him through the wall."

Maureen laughed and followed her father into the hallway.

10

Monday, November 14, 1932

Weeks had passed since she and Seamus first met, and Monday was their night. Hannah was sitting with her grandmother reading a book they borrowed from the library as Lisa prepared for her date with Seamus. He'd become the ointment to soothe her tortured mind, the utter antithesis of everything Ernst Milch stood for. Seamus was kind and gentle, handsome and funny. She didn't know where seeing him would lead, but she needed to know there were alternatives to the life of servitude Milch was forcing her to endure on an ongoing basis.

Her mother knew what she did. She was grateful for what Lisa was prepared to do to get the money she needed for the operation that ultimately saved her life. Her gratitude drowned out any criticisms of Lisa's methods, for she knew her daughter had no other choice than to take the opportunity that presented itself to her. They didn't talk about those times much.

There were enough problems in the present to deal with without rehashing the past.

Lisa brought two dresses over to the rocking chair her mother and daughter were sitting in.

"Which dress, girls?" She held up one, then another. "The red or the blue?"

"I like the red," Hannah said.

"You have such good taste," Lisa's mother, Ingrid, said. "I agree. Go with the red."

"You're such a clever girl," Lisa said and picked up Hannah, planting a massive kiss on the girl's cheek that made her giggle.

"Who are you going to meet?" Hannah asked.

"A nice person."

"I hope he's nice. You've been out with him how many times now? Five? Six?" her mother said. "It's about time you met someone with a heart in their chest."

"There are plenty out there that match that description."

"Why haven't you met any, then?" her mother said.

Lisa ignored the comment and rustled her daughter's sandy-brown hair before nuzzling into her cheek to kiss her again. "Will you help me get changed?"

"Of course," Hannah said and followed her mother into the bedroom all three shared. Lisa sat down in front of the mirror and placed Hannah on her lap.

"Can you help me?" Lisa handed her a brush. The little girl took it without another word and began running it through her mother's hair. "Oh, you're doing such a good job," Lisa said as she watched her daughter making a mess of her hair.

"Watch me do it now," Hannah said and began brushing her own hair. "I want to be just as pretty as you, Mommy."

"Oh, my love. You are the most beautiful thing I've ever seen. The most perfect little girl I could ever imagine."

Hannah smiled and kept on a few more seconds before putting the brush down on the vanity. The little girl examined her mother's hair in the mirror, seemingly happy with her efforts.

"Now for some lipstick," Lisa said. The little girl seemed about to explode with excitement. Hannah watched as her mother applied some before pressing her lips together. "You try it," she said and handed the tube to her daughter.

She held the red lipstick up to her mother's face, pressing it onto the skin around her mouth. It was hard not to laugh at the thought of showing up to meet Seamus looking like the monstrosity her daughter was turning her into. Hannah slipped and drew a red line across her mother's chin.

"Oh, I never thought to put it there. That looks lovely," Lisa said. "You're very good at this."

"I know. It's fun."

The clock on the wall reminded Lisa that the enjoyment had to end. Her daughter whined as she picked her up to put her on the floor. She led her back to her grandmother, who stifled a laugh as she saw the job the little girl had done.

"Wow, you did wonderfully. Your mommy looks even prettier than ever now."

"I just need to go in and make a few small adjustments, and then I'll be ready to go out. Thank you, my love."

Lisa went back into the bedroom and sat down at the vanity. Perhaps she would be late after all. Seamus wouldn't mind. It took a few minutes to undo her daughter's work. She started fresh and sat alone, listening to the sound of her mother and Hannah playing together.

Thoughts of Seamus's wife drifted into her mind. He never mentioned her and seemed determined to move on, but it was difficult not to feel her presence around him. He hinted at her meeting his children, but nothing more. It was coming—she knew that. Who would they see her as? Could they accept someone else? He hadn't told them about her yet—not even his older children. He told her he was dropping clues, alluding to the fact that he might bring another woman home someday. Their reactions were tepid, neither kicking up a fuss nor giving him their blessing.

Perhaps it would never happen. He knew nothing of Hannah and her father yet. She should have told him sooner, but the occasion never seemed right. She didn't want to contaminate the time they had with the sordid details of her arrangement with Milch. How would Seamus react? He'd probably drop her like a hot stone. She'd be alone again.

Her makeup done, she slipped the red dress over her head and walked out into the living area to have her mother zip up the back. She stood back, her arms out.

"How do I look?" she said.

"So pretty," Hannah said. "But what happened to your makeup?"

"I had to adjust it a little," she answered. "You did a terrific job, but I don't think my friend was ready for the new style you invented."

"You're a pioneer," Ingrid said and kissed the girl on the cheek. "Pushing back the barriers of makeup for women everywhere."

Lisa stood and looked at her mother for a few seconds. Life had been hard for her, and it showed. She wasn't yet sixty, but her face was lined and worn like that of a much older woman. The color had all but faded from her hair, and her brown eyes were glazed and dull. Lisa had the sudden urge to go to her and wrap her arms around her.

"What's gotten into you?" Ingrid said.

"I just wanted to say thank you."

Lisa drew back, smoothing down her dress with her palms. Affection had never been her mother's strong point. Ingrid was more of a survivor.

Lisa hugged her daughter one more time. "Be a good girl for Oma. You'll be all tucked up in bed by the time I get home."

"I don't want to go to bed," she replied.

Lisa smiled and stood up. She made her way to the door, taking a few seconds to look back before closing it behind her. Her dress and makeup brought a few comments from some young boys sitting at the bottom of the stairwell.

Most people in her building dressed in whatever they could throw together, often close to rags. It was different for her. She traded on her looks. She had to look good, whether in the club or going out. In a society that valued her beauty more than the brain in her head, she had to make the most of what she had. Going to college had never been an option for her. It was assumed she'd help out in the hotel while pursuing any girlish dreams she might have had on the side, such as dancing. Her brothers were meant to be the ones to inherit the family business. Her place was to get married and have children. Perhaps one day she could work as a secretary, or even a teacher. But the role of young mother wasn't for her.

Some good men, and also many others, tried to court her. She knew she could have married many of them, but she was waiting for the one who'd make her blood race and her heart jump. While anticipating the one who would intrigue her like no other, she ended up with Milch.

There had never been any kind of affection between them. It had only ever been a business arrangement. If her mother hadn't been sick, she never would have spent more than a few moments with him. But her mother *had* been sick. There didn't seem to be any other option at the time. Twice a month for an hour or two at a time seemed to be a small price to pay for her mother's life. So she accepted Milch's proposal, expecting their arrangement to end once her mother recovered. She got pregnant, and everything changed. Suddenly she needed more money to support the baby, as the pathetic wages she received at the club didn't cover their bills. Her mother required expensive medication now. Milch offered her a solution. Another small price to pay...

Her bimonthly liaisons with Milch choked the part of her that thirsted for love and beauty. His words seemed to wrap themselves around her like ivy on a tree. The touch of his hand made her cold to almost all others. Somehow Seamus was immune to the feelings inside her that had grown like weeds. There was something different about him. She tried to see other men these last few years, but Milch had poisoned the well inside her. She proposed ending their arrangement to Milch many times—he reacted like a charging bull.

His father was a wealthy industrialist and routinely rubbed shoulders with the decision makers in German society. Milch showed her a picture of him and his father posing with President von Hindenburg a few months ago to emphasize how powerful he was and how pathetic she was in comparison to him. Milch told her that he knew judges who would rule she was an unfit mother and have Hannah taken away. The thought of having her daughter put in a home struck such fear into her that compliance seemed the only option. What started out as a way to save her mother's life had become a prison of fear.

The abuse began after Hannah was born. She grew adept at using makeup to cover bruises and scratches so that no one noticed them, not even her mother. Lying to her was hard, but it was easier to tell her she fell at work. Telling her that Hannah's father had hit her wouldn't have served anyone.

The notion of telling Seamus something—or at least that Hannah existed—had been growing within her for weeks. He knew all about Lisa's childhood, her parents, and the hotel. He took to asking when he'd get a chance to meet her mother, but she always managed to deflect him with a mother-in-law joke. He hadn't offered for her to meet his children either, so she didn't push it.

Meeting Seamus was the flame to the tinderbox, and now

she thought about how she could escape almost every minute of the day. Milch was the jailer who held the key to the prison she was locked inside. If he didn't agree to release her, what could she do? Go to his wife? Was his line about taking Hannah away a bluff? It seemed like a massive risk to take. A life without her daughter would be torture beyond measure. How could she take that chance?

The restaurant was less than 15 minutes from the apartment, so she walked. A thousand thoughts swam around inside her mind as she went. The cold of the evening air bit at her cheeks, and she brought her scarf up to cover her face. Streetlights flicked on around her as the light of day began to give way to darkness.

The political posters that wallpapered the city were tattered and torn now. Another election had come and gone, and like many of the previous votes, it was more of a tie than a win for any particular ideology or party. The Nazis were still the biggest party in the Reichstag, but had lost seats. Hitler had not scored anything like the big win he expected to propel him to the power he craved. The Communist Party, his great nemesis, gained seats, while the centrist parties remained more or less the same. The mess of German politics would continue for the time being, at least. The chancellor would continue to rule by emergency decree, and Hitler remained on the outside.

Seamus was standing outside the restaurant waiting for her, tall and handsome in his hat and gray suit. He took the hat in his hand as she approached and a bright smile spread across his face. She wrapped her arms around him and kissed his mouth. The feel of him against her was intoxicating. He gave her a compliment on how she looked before they proceeded inside to their table. She held up a fork as they sat down.

"One of yours?"

"Probably not. We're not quite that upmarket."

"How is Helga after the election?"

"Better than I thought she'd be. She's not giving up on the Nazis—not by a long shot—but she's stopped complaining about the electoral process itself. That's progress."

"Does she recognize that her beloved Hitler is in trouble?"

"No, she's bullish as ever. Nothing can curb her belief in the coming National Socialist utopia."

"How is your new house? Are the children settling in?"

"They're happier than they've been in a long time. Maureen has her own room, so she's rid of the other kids at last. Michael and Conor got the short end of the stick as they have to share, but they're all pretty happy. It's amazing how much our lives have changed in such a short time. You'll have to come visit us sometime."

"Of course," she said.

The notion of visiting his house and meeting his children brought the moment into sharp focus. Thoughts of Hannah invaded her mind. How would he react? Was there any future in this or any other relationship? Milch owned her.

The waiter came to the table and they ordered. A dark mood was spreading through her, infecting her body like a plague. It was amazing she'd made it this far with Seamus. He didn't seem to notice—apparently her acting skills were better than she gave herself credit for. The truth was, she shouldn't have been here with this man. If Milch found out about him, they'd both suffer. Tonight had to be the last time they met. The thought of breaking both their hearts tore at her, but it was for the best.

She managed to get through dinner before he noticed. "Are you all right? You're more quiet than usual."

"I'm fine. Just a little tired, maybe."

He seemed to accept her explanation and ordered dessert. He finished his French-style ice cream and wiped off his mouth with a napkin. "I want you to meet my children."

The words hit her like a fist. She put down the cup of coffee in her hands. The moment had arrived, and she could feel Milch's hot breath on her neck. It made her skin crawl. Why did she have to give up Seamus for him? Surely there was some way out of this... It took her a few seconds to answer. She tried to cover her tracks by fumbling for the cigarettes in her bag, but the look on his face told her he knew she was stalling for time.

"You think that's a good idea?" she said after she lit a cigarette. "It's not an easy thing to introduce a new person..." She ran out of words.

"I've been thinking about it. We've only known each other a few weeks, but why waste time? My feelings for you are growing stronger by the day."

She stubbed out the cigarette, even though she'd only taken three drags off it. "I don't know, Seamus. I told you when we met that I was more trouble than I was worth."

"I remember. I'd been drinking, but I remember."

He was trying to make light of the situation, but his words were weak and the blood ran from his face. He knew what was coming. She hated what she was doing to him. The simple truth was that her toxicity poisoned every situation she touched. Her relationship with Seamus was no different.

The waiter came to the table. He managed to ignore the awkward air that had descended and made small talk for a few seconds about their meal. Seamus responded with a tight smile and paid the bill. He always insisted on paying. She gave up protesting a few weeks ago, but if now was to be their last time, she thought she should pay her way.

"Let me give you some money for that," she said.

"No, Lisa. This is on me. We've been through this—"

"I can pay my own way," she said. Her tone was sharper than she planned it to be, and it halted whatever he was about to say.

It took him a few seconds to respond. "I remember the warnings you gave me when we first met, and how I had to persuade you to meet me again. Nothing I've seen or heard has made me want to see you any less. The opposite."

"You don't know me."

"Well, then, tell me about yourself. I have more skeletons in my closet than an average haunted house. We all do."

"Can we go?"

She got out of the chair and made for the door. He followed two steps behind her. The street outside was as quiet as she expected it to be on a Monday night. He took her hand.

"Tell me what's going on inside your mind."

She didn't want to cry. She never cried—especially not in public. It was easier to walk away. She never told anyone about Milch. No one knew apart from her mother, and she hated burdening her with it. Seamus followed a few steps behind her. They walked in silence until the river came into view. The moonlight was shimmering on the surface, silver shards on deep black. She turned to him as they reached the concrete wall.

"I have a daughter."

"You never told me." He was smiling. "Why didn't you talk about her? How old is she? What's her name?"

"Her name is Hannah and she's three. She's at home in bed with my mother right now. I didn't tell you because of the mess my life has become. I didn't want to drag you into it. I thought we'd see each other a couple of times and you'd sense the poison inside me. That's what happens every time—I shut down and men leave. For some reason, you are different. I never meant for things to get to this point."

"Where you had to reveal yourself?"

"It's hard enough to deal with my own life without bringing someone else into it."

She leaned back against the wall, her arms folded over her chest. Another couple approached, in their fifties, walking hand in hand. They ambled by, greeting Lisa and Seamus as they went.

"I still don't see the mess," Seamus said when the other couple had passed. "You have a child. That's nothing to be ashamed of in my eyes."

"There's more to it than that."

"Tell me."

"What makes you think I want to tell you, or that you deserve to know? We've only known each other a few weeks and you think you can just reach inside me and pull out whatever you want? You're no better than the men leering over me and the other dancers at the club."

Her words seemed to knock the life out of him. He opened his mouth, but didn't speak for a few seconds. "That's not fair, and you know it. I still don't understand what's going on."

He reached out to her. "The father doesn't see the child?"

"I've already said too much."

"Tell me. I'm still here. I'm not running away."

His words were like spraying mist on the fire raging inside her. Why was she telling him? Why had she agreed to see him so many times? Why burden him with her pain when they'd never see each other again after this night? *Sometimes it's best to rip the bandage off in one fell swoop.*

"I can't do this. I have to go. I can't be the one to spoil your new life in the city with your family. You have so much to look forward to without me ruining it for you."

"Lisa, I'm not running away. He reached out to take her hand, but she pulled back.

"I've never told anyone about my life before, not in the detail that you deserve. The truth is, I was too scared. I've made such a mess of things."

She put her head in her hands, then brought her head back up with dewy eyes.

"My mother got sick about four years ago. It was cancer. We

noticed the lump early enough that the doctor said he was confident it hadn't spread. They could cut it out. All we had to do was bring her in and pay the bill for the surgery. We had nothing. If you saw the apartment we live in, where my daughter will sleep tonight—"

"I've known life like that. There's no shame in it."

"We couldn't afford the surgery. Not nearly. Without it my mother would die a slow agonizing death, over months and years." She reached into her bag for a pack of cigarettes. She offered one to Seamus. He refused, so she lit up her own.

"I was working in the club back then. Men hung around every night—they still do. I met one who was rich, and seemed charming enough. I knew he was married. Most of the men that hang around are—that's why I don't go within a country mile of them. But I needed someone to talk to, and he listened. I told him about my mother, and he offered me a deal." A tear ran down her cheek.

"He'd pay for my mother's surgery if I agreed to meet with him in an apartment he owned twice a month."

Lisa looked at him to gauge his reaction before continuing. His face dropped. "I'm listening," he said.

"He gave us the money and the operation was a success. My mother made a full recovery."

"Thank God."

"I thought it would end there, but he wanted more. I was just about to break it off with him when I found out I was pregnant. He told me he'd leave his wife—even though I never wanted that. I just needed someone to stick by me when I was pregnant. I had to leave the club before I started showing and suddenly, I had no income coming in. He supported me."

"Who is this person?" Seamus said, almost spitting each word. He looked like he wanted to destroy this man with his bare hands.

"His name is Ernst Milch," she answered.

"Like Milch Industries?"

"He's the son of Otto Milch."

Seamus shook his head. "One of our main competitors, although he's so much bigger than us he probably doesn't even know who we are."

"I had Hannah in September of '29."

"Just before the entire world went down the toilet."

"I was planning to go back to work—to find a better paying job before Christmas—but then the markets crashed and there was nothing."

"So, you had to keep your arrangement."

Lisa nodded, not making eye contact with him for a few seconds. "It went from money to support my mother to money for my daughter—the child I had with him. I went back to the club after a while, and realized I had to get away from him. He is never going to recognize our daughter as his own, and he's stopped the empty promises of leaving his wife for me. I didn't mind. I'd rather dig my eyes out with a rusty spoon than marry him. Time went on and I told him that I'd rather live on the streets than accept his money anymore, but he didn't accept that either. He changed his line of attack, saying that he'd have Hannah taken away from me if I stopped seeing him. He went to one of his friends—a judge. This person owed him a favor and said he'd rule that I was an unfit mother and have Hannah put in a home."

"You think he's telling the truth?"

"Would I be still seeing him if I didn't?"

Seamus tried not to take her harsh tone to heart. He closed his eyes.

"You remember what I said when we first met?" she said.

"I do, but I still think you're wrong. Have you tried talking to him? Reasoning with him?"

"That's all I've done since I met you. I want nothing more in this world than to be rid of him, but he won't let me go." She

stood up. "I've said too much. I'm sorry I came here. I just wanted..." The words faded in her mouth.

"You just wanted what?"

"To see you. I shouldn't have dragged you into this."

"What if I talk to him?" Seamus had received some money
from some orders but didn't have much. How much would be
enough to free her? Was she a commodity to be bought and
sold? It was all he could think of to do. "How about going to his
wife?"

"That's the ultimate threat. He said if I did, he'd have
Hannah taken away."

"Is there any way to test to see if he's bluffing?"

"I'm not risking her going into a home or being sent to
another family. I can't lose her. I'd rather die."

"Do you know who he fraternizes with? Who are the people
who were with him in the club the night you met? Do you
remember their names?"

"One of them was an Army officer—like Milch himself. I
remember another man was a lawyer or something. It was four
years ago, and I never saw them again."

"He never takes you out?"

"I haven't seen him in public since before Hannah was
born."

Seamus stood up and took her hand. "There's a way out of
this. I swear there is." He kissed her on the lips. "Try to find out
if his legal threat is real or not. Then we can figure out where to
go from there. If it's a bluff, then we're home free."

"We?"

"You didn't think I'd give up on you that easily, did you?"

"Actually, I did," she said with a rueful smile.

"Don't give up, Lisa. He might know a judge, or even several
judges, but that doesn't mean one is willing to call you an unfit
mother."

"I'm meeting him on Wednesday at eight."

"In two days? That doesn't give us much time."

"No, Seamus. There can't be an us now. I won't risk losing my daughter, or having some harm come to you."

"You can't just give up on what we have. Not for that gutter rat."

"I can't risk it." She shook her head and stepped back from him. "I won't. You don't know him. He's dangerous. I should never have started seeing you."

"I can't let you go," he said. His voice was weak. He reached out to her, but she didn't take his hand.

"I knew this was a mistake from the start. I should have gone with my first instincts and walked away. I'm sorry I did this to you, Seamus. You're a good man—one of the best I've ever known. I'm not right for you. I can't be the anchor that drags you down. I won't be. I can't risk losing Hannah."

He brought his hand back to his side, his face frozen. He reached into his pocket. "I wanted to give you this." He handed her a slip of paper. "It's my new address. If you ever want to come over and talk."

Telling him that wasn't going to happen would have been too cruel at that moment, so she just nodded and put the piece of paper into her coat pocket.

"Goodbye, Seamus."

"I'm serious, come and see me if you ever need someone to talk to."

"Thank you," she said.

She turned and walked away. It all felt like such a waste. She never hated Milch so much as in that moment.

11

Wednesday, November 16, 1932

Helmut was poring over some paperwork as Seamus knocked on the door. He looked up and motioned for his nephew to come inside. Seamus took a seat in front of the large mahogany desk, and the old man offered him a drink. Seamus declined. *Best to stay off that slippery slope.* Helmut didn't seem to care about drinking alone and walked to a table in the corner, took the top off a decanter, and poured himself a whiskey.

Part of the reason Seamus came in was to talk about his daughter, but now he questioned himself. What did he have to gain by expressing doubts over her political leanings to her father? Seamus wondered if she truly understood the depths of the vitriol the National Socialists preached. She never addressed the question of the Jews when they spoke about politics—a conversation they only had rarely now. It was tiresome to hear her parrot Hitler's lies over and over. Trying to dissuade her was pointless. Hitler and the Nazis were the only way forward—the only chance Germany had in her eyes.

Apart from her political views, she was a pleasant, even friendly person. The workers on the floor seemed to respect her, and she knew the business better than he did. For now, at least. He was stuck with her. She wasn't going anywhere. He'd have to tolerate her as much as Germany would have to tolerate the other 13 million people who voted for the Nazis.

"You were here late last night," Helmut said.

"Who told?"

"I have my sources. How are you settling in? Anything you need to talk to me about?"

"I'm enjoying myself, particularly with Herr Bernheim."

"Ah, yes. Bernheim is a gem. He's been a lynchpin of this operation since the day he arrived. I do fear for him after I...depart."

"You've got years yet. If there's one person who could prove the doctors wrong, it's you."

Helmut didn't smile like Seamus expected him to. He took a sip of his whiskey and stood up. He walked to the window overlooking the factory floor. Seamus got up and joined him.

"You'll look after them when I go, won't you?" He had tears in his eyes.

"Of course, Uncle."

"That's what I brought you here for." He pointed out a worker. "Armin Bruch has been with me since he was eighteen. Twenty years." He pointed at the man beside him. "Daniel Liefers has been working here 22 years. Irina Hess has been with me since I started the place back in '02. They're all kinds of people with different backgrounds and beliefs, but that shouldn't matter here. I need you to watch over them for me when I go. Helga is a good girl, but she's been swept away by all this nonsense about revolution and the evils of communism. She never married—never even seemed interested in the idea. I suppose she needed something to cling to in her life, and the National Socialists gave her that."

"She and Bernheim work well together."

"The Nazi voter and the Jew, eh? Miracles do happen. Apparently, she's able to leave the prejudices of her party behind when dealing with him—for now, at least. Bernheim is a professional and ignores her beliefs to get the job done. But I worry about what will happen when I'm not here to oversee the place. I don't want people pushed out because of what they believe."

"I'll make sure they aren't."

"That's why I'm going to leave the place to you and Helga to share."

"You're not going to die. You're healthy as a horse."

Helmut put his hand on the back of his nephew's neck. "I know you'll look after my people for me. I'm a happy man. Your father would be proud of the man you are today."

"Would he?"

"We all make mistakes. I've made enough for ten men. It's how we pick ourselves up off the floor when life beats us down that makes us who we are. It isn't how much adversity we face; it's how we react to it. I see how hard you're working here, and I know if your father saw that too, he'd be proud of you."

Seamus wanted to tell him that he wished he was his father, but just thanked him instead. It felt good to hear what he said. The thought of inheriting the factory with Helga was almost too much to process in that moment. Lisa, and what she said, was still lurking in his mind.

"What happened between you and my father? Why did he come home?"

"You knew him. He was a difficult person when he wanted to be. I bought him out and he moved back to America. Your mother never wanted to be here. That was more important to him than money."

They stood at the window another few minutes before Seamus told him he had to leave for lunch.

"I have an appointment with a lawyer friend of mine. I need to leave for an hour or two."

"You have legal trouble?"

"Not me. Lisa."

"The dancer you told me about?"

"Yes. She might be my ex-girlfriend. I'm not sure."

"Sounds like you need all the help you can get."

"Thanks, Helmut. I'll be back later. And don't worry. When you eventually retire, years from now, I'll be here to look after your factory and your people. I won't leave them in the lurch. You have my word on that."

"That's all I need to hear."

Seamus shook his uncle's hand and left him at the window, peering down at the staff.

Seamus made his way out to the parking lot and got into his car. Juggling work, the move from America, the kids, and the situation with Lisa was almost more than any reasonable person could handle, but perhaps they could find Milch's weakness, and it would be up to them to exploit it. Despite what Lisa believed, the business with Milch hadn't put him off the idea of being with her. In a strange way it solidified what he wanted, and he knew that was her. They would be together if Milch wasn't in the way.

He was confident that with a little prodding, she could convince him to let her go. Then the next step would be introducing her to Maureen and the children. Once they got to know her, they'd fall for her as hard as he had. He never thought he could feel like this again, and that his ability to feel this way had died with Marie. Lisa had resurrected a piece of him he believed was gone forever.

Seamus rode 10 minutes into the city center and parked on the street. A policeman on a horse rode past him, nodding a greeting, which he returned with a tip of his hat. He checked the numbers on the buildings and soon found the address. A staircase led him up to the second floor, where a young secretary with flaming red hair greeted him. He waited a few minutes in a comfortable leather chair before the door opened and Hans Litten, the lawyer who rattled Hitler so much that rumor had it no one could mention his name in front of him, shook Seamus's hand.

"Good to see you again," Hans said. "Come into my office."

The young lawyer held the door as Seamus took a seat opposite his large leather-topped desk. They made small talk about the last time they met—a week before in the lobby of a local hotel with the same group of journalists. Five minutes of conversation passed before Hans asked the question.

"I get the feeling you're not here on a social call. What can I help you with?"

"You're perceptive, Hans."

"It helps when you have someone on the stand."

"I need to speak to someone I can trust, and quickly. Am I right that nothing we share will leave this room?"

"Have you any cash on you? Any coins? Give me one. I'll retain your services as a client and you'll enjoy attorney-client privilege."

Seamus reached into his pocket and dug out a coin. He pressed it against the table with his finger and pushed it over to the lawyer.

"Excellent. I'll have my secretary write something up for you."

"I have a problem."

Hans listened without talking as Seamus told him every detail of the situation with Milch. The entire story took less than two minutes.

"This is the woman you met with Clayton in the Haus Vaterland?" Hans asked. Seamus nodded in reply. "That's quite the situation she's in. Do we know anything about this legal threat? The judge's name?"

"Nothing other than what I told you. We only have this man's word to go on."

"A judge would need some kind of evidence of a lack of care on behalf of the mother in order to rule against her, no matter how compromised he might be. Is there any evidence of such?"

"Not that I'm aware of."

"Let's say this man is telling the truth, and the judge does rule against your friend. The child would be taken into care, even on a temporary basis, while she lodges an appeal against the ruling. If someone was motivated to cause your friend maximum pain, they could gum up the workings of the legal system, and the child would be gone months before she got her back. It could be a difficult situation."

"Losing Hannah for that long would destroy Lisa."

"And that might be what this man is trying to achieve. The threat might not be taking her forever—I'm not sure he'd get away with that if the mother is as competent as you say. I'm not a family lawyer, but the wait could be six months, or even a year. It's hard to say exactly."

Seamus imagined the pain of losing a child for that long. He didn't see his own children for longer, but had the comfort of knowing they were safe with their aunt and cousins. Seeing her baby disappear into an orphanage could be enough to drive Lisa over the edge.

"What do you advise?"

Hans shifted in his seat. "The best solution would be to work it out with this man, one to one. Negotiating with him in good faith is the best way forward. You don't want to get the authorities involved until you've exhausted all possibilities of working this out. If you need any more advice, I'd be happy to help you, or even to recommend a friend of mine who specializes in this kind of case."

Seamus stood up and shook Hans's hand again. "Thanks for seeing me on such short notice."

"Of course. Anything for a friend."

The two men stood at the window to chat about the factory and when they might meet next before Seamus left. Lisa was due to meet Milch in five hours.

～

Lisa crossed the street and pushed the front door open. The stairwell was empty, as it always seemed to be. It was hard to remember a time when she saw anyone else in the small apartment block, let alone interacted with them. Perhaps Milch owned the entire building and didn't care to rent the units out. The rich could be so profligate with their resources. What difference would the pittance that rent might bring be when he had all the money he'd ever need?

Lisa reached the top of the stairwell and pressed her ear to the door—nothing. He was usually late, and she was thankful for that tonight. She pushed her key into the lock and walked into the apartment. She hung up her coat, put her bag down, and went to the kitchen for a glass of water. Her head was spinning a little from the schnapps she downed before arriving. The cool water from the faucet was some antidote to that. She went to the window and peered down at the street below for a few seconds. She put the glass down, took a seat, and waited.

A few minutes passed before she heard the sound she dreaded. Boots on the stairwell reverberated through the otherwise silent building. The door opened a few seconds later and Milch appeared, wearing a gray suit. He had the audacity to smile at her as he shut the door.

"No uniform tonight?" she said. It was all she could do to force herself to look him in the face.

"No. I'm thinking about leaving the Army. I might serve the country better as a civilian."

She was sure he wanted her to ask a follow-up question, but she had no interest in what his plans might amount to if they didn't concern her and Hannah. He took off his coat and hung it by the door. He stopped for a second, doubtless wondering why she wasn't making her way to the bedroom.

"I thought we could talk a moment first," she said.

"No. We can talk later."

"I'm not going in there."

He seemed surprised at the strength in her words. "You don't want the money I have for you?"

"Keep it." Her words were sharp. The pent-up anger in her was beginning to emerge.

"What's come over you? You spoiling for a fight tonight?" He flexed his fingers, balling them into fists and straightening them back again.

"Can you sit down and talk to me for a minute?" She'd seen that look in Milch's eyes before. She needed to be careful.

"I'll come and talk to you. How about a drink? Yes? Ok, let's have a drink first."

Milch went to the cabinet and took out a bottle. He poured two glasses of brandy. He left a glass of the brown liquor for her on the table in front of the sofa. Milch was already sipping the glass he poured for himself as she sat down. Her feet felt like concrete blocks. She thought of Hannah, of the future she, and maybe Seamus, could give her. She thought about never having to see Ernst Milch again.

"I might be getting a transfer to Bavaria, just for a year or so."

Her heart soared. Did this mean she could be free? Were things about to fall into place? She almost didn't dare say the words. "What does that mean?"

"Stupid girl. That means I would be stationed at a base—"

"I know that. What does that mean for us? For this?"

"It means you're coming with me. My wife will stay here. I'll need something more regular than we have now. You'll be given accommodation and a more generous amount for the child," he said. He took another sip of his drink.

"No. I'm not going."

"Wrong again. You're going, or you lose the little one. Imagine a child that age tossed into a girls' home? Tragic."

Lisa's brain shifted into gear. She couldn't leave Berlin. A life at Milch's disposal seemed like the worst thing she could ever imagine—except for losing Hannah. The mere act of sitting beside him was enough to make her skin crawl. Milch reached into his pocket for a cigar and lit it up.

"I can't leave the city."

"You have a choice. Leave with your daughter or stay here and lose her. I think you'll find coming with me a better option. If it even happens. I'm not sure yet."

"How much longer do you intend to keep this arrangement?" she said.

"You have some complaints?"

"I want to move on with my life. Coming here to see you every time you feel the need is stifling me."

"This again? Oh, come now," he said. He reached over and grabbed her thigh. "Are you talking about other men?" She didn't answer. "I'm not the jealous type, but do you really think any other man would want you? A ridiculous, washed-up demi-whore with a bastard child?"

Lisa whirled around and pointed a finger in his face. "Don't you ever talk about Hannah that way."

"You forget yourself," Milch said and swatted her hand away. "Where would you be without the money I give you for the child?"

"She's your daughter," Lisa shouted. "Your flesh and blood,

and you won't see her. You won't even be in the same room as her."

Milch was calm, and that irked her more. He took a puff on the cigar in his hand. Smoke rings hung in the air a few seconds before dissipating into nothing. "I have no idea if that kid is my daughter. How do I know?"

"Because I know. I wasn't with anyone—"

"So you've said 100 times. We've been over this before. I have a family. I have a daughter. She's at home with her mother, not in that hovel you live in with yours."

"You never answered the question: When does this end?"

"This ends when I say it ends," he said. His words were razor-sharp now. "This ends when I grow tired of seeing you, and that day has not come yet. Perhaps when your skin starts sagging and your hair turns gray, but until then you'd better keep our arrangement—if you want to keep that daughter of yours. One call from me to one of my friends in the judiciary and she'll be taken away. You'll never see her again." He grabbed her by the chin, digging his fingers into her flesh. She didn't cry or call out in pain. She wouldn't give him the satisfaction. "You remember that."

"I regret ever having laid eyes on you."

"Oh, now, that's not kind. You'd say that to the man who saved your mother's life?"

Lisa thought back to the night she met him in the club—him sitting at the table in his uniform with those other men. It was true—her mother would probably be dead now without the money he gave her for the operation. He preyed on her desperation. The money was nothing to him, just a matter of going to the bank, but to her mother, it was life. It was hard to regret what she did to save her, but now this had to stop. Enough was enough.

"Please, Ernst. I've done what you've asked all this time. I've given myself to you, I've never even thought of going to your wife—"

He slapped her across the face. The stinging pain brought tears to her eyes, and she bowed her head to hide them. "Don't you ever mention her. You don't deserve to kiss the soles of her feet."

He shoved her head and brought his hand back to the table to pick up the glass of brandy. "You know the rules of our engagement. Don't question them again or I might have to make a call to one of my friends about your daughter. It might be the best thing for the child. Some women aren't meant to be mothers."

She raised her hand to strike him back, but he caught it in the air, twisting her wrist back. It hurt far more than she let on. She stared into his gray eyes as he held her, not willing to give an inch. He let her go a few seconds later.

"I wanted nothing more than to have a pleasant drink, and you had to go and ruin the time we could have had together."

"I'd rather put my head in a lion's mouth than spend another minute with you."

"Get in the bedroom."

She didn't move. The frustration of years of abuse was boiling inside her.

"Get in there now. It's all you're good for."

"Never. I'll never do that again. You asked me if I had someone new? I do, and he's fifty times the man you'll ever be."

He slapped her across the face again. Without thinking, she took the glass in her hand and smashed it across the side of his head. It shattered as it connected, sending razor-sharp shards through his hair. He screamed and brought a hand to the side of his head. Droplets of blood came through his fingers. His eyes filled with rage.

He caught her by the arm as she tried to bolt, shouting obscenities at her. He grabbed her neck with one hand and punched her in the face with the other. Her head rocked back, and she fell onto the floor. The door was too far away. He reached up with his other hand to feel for blood on the side of his head. His palm came back colored red.

"You want it rough? Have it your way then."

A scream escaped as he dragged her across the floor. She was sure no one heard it. She yanked back against his grip, slippery with blood, and managed to get free. He stumbled backward as she raised herself to her feet. The door was ten steps away. She made it about four before he caught her and threw her down on the sofa. He was on her in seconds, his hands around her neck, the fires of hell burning in his eyes.

She brought her hands to his, trying to unclasp his fingers from around her throat, but he was too strong. She began to wheeze, gasping for breath. Trying to scream, she couldn't get the words out. A demonic rage had overtaken Milch. Her lungs were on fire, gasping for air. She reached out her hand to the table for something, anything.

She curled her fingers around the glass she broke against his skull and felt two long fingers of jagged shards jutting out from the base. Her vision dimming, she saw Hannah and her mother and Seamus. She seized the broken glass in her hand and used every sinew of strength she had left to drive it into the side of his neck. It sliced through his skin, embedding into his flesh. He brought his hands up to the wound and she rolled onto the floor, air rushing back into her lungs. Milch made a horrible gurgling sound, but she couldn't see him. Darkness overcame her.

It might have been ten seconds, or two minutes. It was impossible to say how long it took for her to open her eyes again. The immense pain in her neck was the first thing she felt. Then she saw blood on her hands and realized she had fallen between the couch and the table.

She listened. The only sound was that of the cars passing on the street below.

Garish crimson stains covered the brown leather couch. Apart from the pain in her face, her wrist, and neck, she didn't seem to be injured. Where was Milch? She dreaded to stand up, but knew she had to.

A gasp leaked from her lips as she rose to her feet. Milch was on the other side of the couch, lying in a pool of blood. His eyes stared into nothing. The glass she defended herself with was in his lifeless hand.

The instinct to run hit her like cold water. She fell back on the sofa, but then realized what she was sitting in and stood up again. *What have I done?*

12

Wednesday, November 16, 1932

It was dark as Seamus arrived home, a few raindrops falling on the windshield of the car his uncle had given him. He pulled up in front of their new house. Having the kids to come home to seemed like everything at that moment. Lisa came into his mind, but he didn't want to imagine her with Milch. Instead, he shifted his mind to his meeting with Andrei Salnikov, the man in the factory Helga warned him about. Contrary to what she said, he wasn't about to begin a left-wing insurrection. He was more concerned with feeding his wife and child. Seamus told him he wasn't interested in his political leanings as long as he got his work done. The Russian seemed happy with what he said and returned to his station.

Keeping so many people productive and happy was quite the juggling act. Seamus opened the car door and stepped out onto the driveway. He continued up to the door feeling like a rich man. He had everything he needed now—except Lisa, and he wasn't giving up on her.

A new house meant new routines, and Seamus was eager to establish them quickly. No matter what happened with work, he was determined to be there for dinner every night with his children. He pushed open the front door and announced he was home. Conor came running.

"How was school today?" Seamus said.

"Good! The teacher was sick," his youngest said.

"Sounds like a great day."

Seamus hung up his hat and coat and continued inside. The smell of chicken and vegetables hung in the air. Fiona and Michael were in the living room listening to the radio.

"Hello," Seamus said. "Homework done?"

"Yes," they said in perfect unison.

"You're just in time for dinner," Maureen said from the kitchen.

Maureen was the cook, and Michael set the table. Seamus sat with Fiona and Conor at the table, drinking a beer. Conor reached for the glass, pretending to take a sip before falling back in his chair in a faux drunken stupor. They all laughed. Maureen brought the food to the table. The children weren't talking about Maeve and their cousins as much as they had when they first arrived. Seamus wasn't sure if it was a good or bad thing. It was a fine line between letting go of the past and forgetting your roots.

"Any letters from America?" he asked as Maureen served the food.

"I got one," Maureen said.

"Who from?" Seamus asked.

"Leo."

"Ooh, your boyfriend," Conor said.

"I don't think I'll write back to him. What's the point?"

"You should. It's good to keep in touch. Especially when he took the time to write to you," Seamus said. He turned to the other kids now. "How about we send some postcards to your cousins after dinner?"

The children agreed before attacking the food their sister put down in front of them. They sat at the table until they were all finished before Seamus went to the kitchen with Conor and Fiona to tidy up. Michael and Maureen, their chores for the night done, were allowed to sit and listen to the new radio in the living room. The house wasn't quite what the children had dreamed of on the ship across the ocean, but it was comfortable and in a good neighborhood. Seamus thought back to the tent he lived in just three months before when the only work he could find was digging ditches.

The rain fell in earnest outside, and Seamus lifted Conor onto the counter once the dishes were done to watch the rivulets of water sliding down the glass. Conor made a game of it, choosing a stream of water as his own and racing it against one he assigned to his father. Conor was cheering his latest victory when they heard a knock at the front door. Seamus lifted his son off the counter and went to answer it.

He felt the breath stop in his lungs.

"Hello," Lisa said. She was dressed in her now-familiar blue coat and beret, both darkened by the rain. But there was something different about her. Her skin was almost translucent, and her lips were shaking. Her eyes were swollen and puffy.

"I wasn't expecting you. Is something wrong?"

"I need help."

His thoughts went to Milch. "What did he do to you?"

Her arms were crossed, and she was holding onto her coat as if it were a life raft on a raging sea. A tear ran down her face.

"Are you hurt?"

"I need help."

"Are you all right? Are you hurt?" he repeated.

"He was strangling me. I thought I was going to die. I had to," she whispered.

He stepped toward her. "You had to what?"

"I had to kill him."

The rage that had been building inside him gave way to horror. "Milch is dead?" he said so only they could hear. She nodded. "Have you called the police?"

"No, I can't go to prison. Ernst's father won't stand for it. They'll never believe me. I can't face the executioner for this."

Seamus ran a hand through his hair. A thousand thoughts were bombarding his mind. He tried to find some clarity in the madness of the moment, and found it in her eyes.

"Ok. My children are here. I can't leave while they're still awake. Give me a few minutes to get them off to bed. My car is unlocked. Sit in the passenger seat and wait for me. I'll be back as soon as I can. We'll talk this through."

"Thank you," she said.

Maureen's face appeared around the end of the hallway. Seamus cursed under his breath but recovered himself in seconds.

"Hello," his daughter said.

"Nice to meet you," Lisa said with a smile. Seamus was amazed at how she somehow managed to concoct one.

"Maureen, this is my good friend, Lisa."

The young girl stepped forward and looked at them, not knowing quite what to say. Lisa broke the awkward silence.

"Your father talks about you all the time. I was just passing by. I wanted to meet you all properly."

"Maybe soon," Seamus said.

"I hope so," his daughter said. "The kids are just about to go to bed." She stared at Lisa as if she couldn't believe she was real.

"Then tonight's not the time," Lisa said. "I'm sorry. I didn't mean to disturb you."

"No. That's fine," Seamus said. "You can meet the others soon. Very soon."

"That would be great," Maureen said.

"And Maureen, don't mention Lisa being here to the children quite yet, ok?"

"All right, Father."

"Until next time," Lisa said. Maureen smiled and disappeared back into the living room.

"I'll get the other kids to bed and be out as soon as I can."

He tried to hug her, but she didn't take her hands out of her pockets and hung onto her coat as he wrapped his arms around her. She stepped away and left, plodding toward his car. He watched her go before shutting the door behind him. The sound of the radio wafted in from the living room. Getting them to bed was paramount at this point. Every minute was vital. He walked back to where they were sitting.

"Fiona and Conor, time for bed. We'll have to write those postcards tomorrow."

"What?" Fiona said.

"Right now."

Michael and Maureen didn't move, as it wasn't even nine thirty. There was no way they were going to bed for another hour, at least. Forcing them to go would be more trouble than he had the energy to deal with right now.

He shepherded the younger children up the stairs, making sure they went to the bathroom before leaving them to get changed into their pajamas. He sat with the older children, pretending to read the newspaper. It may as well have been in Chinese. Neither seemed to notice.

"Maybe I'll go to bed too," Michael said. "I'm tired and I can't stand this radio show."

Seamus could hardly believe his luck. He remained taciturn as he could be as his oldest son got up and said good night. Maureen, reading a magazine on the couch, didn't move.

Ten minutes that felt like about a year ground past. Maureen was still sitting in the living room, reading a book.

"I think there's something wrong with the car. I'm going to go out and have a look. I might be a while," he said.

"Lisa's waiting for you outside, is she?" Maureen said without looking up.

"I'm going to take my coat. I think it might be still raining."

His daughter didn't answer, and he made his way out the front door. Lisa was sitting in the passenger seat of his car, staring out into the darkness. He opened the door and climbed in beside her, hoping somehow this moment wasn't real.

Her voice was still shaking as she spoke. "I'm so sorry. The last thing I wanted to do was to drag you into my mess. I should leave," she said. "This is nothing to do with you. You've got a family—"

"Stop it. You're not going anywhere. I'm going to help you through this no matter what we decide to do."

"I can't risk you getting in trouble because of me."

"You didn't do anything wrong," he said. He reached across and touched her cheek, which was cold as snow. "It was you or him, wasn't it? You did what you had to do to protect yourself."

"I can't believe this is happening. I can't go to jail. They'll take Hannah away. I'll never see her again."

"How did you get here?"

"I walked."

"How far?"

"Thirty minutes. I didn't want anyone to see me. I snuck out the back. I couldn't get on the tram." She opened her coat. Her sweater was covered in blood.

His mind snapped into gear. This was no time for indecision. "Where is Milch now?"

"Where I left him—on the floor of the apartment."

"We have to get him out of there and sanitize the place. No body, no crime. Before we do anything, tell me exactly what happened."

"He told me he might be transferred, and that if he was, I

would be coming with him to be his concubine. I told him I'd rather die. We fought and he hit me."

The swelling on her face was plain to see even in the dim light.

"I picked up a glass and smashed it over his head. He wrapped his hand around my neck and started choking me. I thought I was going to die... I picked up the broken glass and shoved it into his neck and he died. There's blood everywhere."

Seamus let out a breath, trying to think of what to do next. "And no one saw you? Or heard you fighting in the apartment?"

"I don't know. I don't think so. I was careful."

"Stay here a moment. I think there are some shovels in the shed. Do you know anywhere we could bury the body, somewhere no one would ever find it?"

"I don't know."

"Think."

"The forests outside the city? In the Spandauer, perhaps."

"Ok. We need to have somewhere in mind. Stay here. In fact, lie down in case someone sees you." She did as he asked and he got out of the car, making sure not to slam the door and alert his neighbors—or his own children. The side gate was unlocked, and he entered the darkness between his house and the neighbor's. The shed was at the back of the yard, and he fumbled around in the dark before finding two shovels. He took them in his hand, as well as a hacksaw—just in case. Lisa was still lying down as he arrived back at the car. He opened the back door and put the hacksaw and shovels on the seat.

"I have to check inside the house. I'll be back in two minutes," he said.

He pushed the front door open to the sound of the radio drifting through the air. He cursed under his breath. Maureen glanced up at him as he came into the living room. "Any luck with the car?"

"No. I'm going to have to keep at it. I might need to take it around the block a few times. You going to bed soon?"

"Soon enough," she said.

"Lisa's having some problems. She needs my help. I might be a while."

"I'm not your babysitter."

"I know that. You've done more than I ever could thank you for, but this is something I have to do. I will make it up to you. Name what you want in return."

"How about you buy me a car?"

"How about I let you take it out yourself this weekend."

"With dinner money?"

"Of course. But let's keep this between us, all right?"

"Fine. Good night, Father."

At the stand by the front door, he put on his coat and hat, and picked up two pairs of gloves almost as an afterthought. He'd read something in the newspaper about the Berlin Police being on the cutting edge of a new technology that could identify people with their fingerprints.

He went to the car and got in. Lisa didn't pop her head up as he started the car, instead waiting until they were clear of the house.

"I won't risk you losing your daughter, or even your life, for that piece of dirt, but this can never go any further than us, understand?" Seamus said. "Not your mother, not your best friend. No one."

"I'll never tell a soul as long as I live."

"Ok, it's settled. We keep this between us." Seamus took a second to breathe. "Lisa, you're covered in blood. You can't be seen on the street like that. Do you have any spare clothes with you?"

The sweater she was wearing was streaked with blood. The arms were stained red and looked like they'd been dipped in paint. Her skirt was almost clean, with just a few dots here and there.

"No, just my hat and coat."

"You were smart to keep it closed. We'll get by. Are there any cleaning products in the apartment? Soap for the floor, or the sofa?"

"Yes. Under the sink in the kitchen."

"Did anyone else use the place? Is there a cleaner who came in every week, or every month?"

"Yes. The cleaner comes twice a month. Next Monday, I think."

"Ok. Does anyone else know he was there?"

"No one. He was obsessed with his wife not finding out. He never drove there, only ever took the U-Bahn and walked two stops over in case anyone saw him. He usually wore a scarf over his face or pulled his hat down. He wore a long coat over his uniform to disguise himself."

She seemed to be regaining her senses. It was just as well, as she was going to need them if there was any chance of getting away with this.

"Did he ever boast about you to his friends, his fellow soldiers?"

"Never. He said it would be looked down upon, that he could never tell anyone."

"And you think he was telling you the truth?"

"I don't know. I think so."

"Does anyone at the club know about you and Milch? Anyone who met him when he came in?"

"A few from when he used to come in. But that I was still seeing him? No. I was too ashamed to tell. My mother would have died if anyone found out."

"Do they know where you got the money for your mother's operation? Did you tell anyone back then when it was going on?"

"No. I told my friends that Mother was sick, but never said where we got the money for the operation. My mother is a proud woman who'd rather starve on the street than have anyone know we were practically destitute."

"He owns the building?" he said. She nodded in reply before he continued. "His family is going to come looking for him sooner or later. We'll have to get him out and clean the place top to bottom...as if our lives depend on it.

"Getting him out of the middle of the city is going to be a problem. I can't park in front of the apartment on the street, and we're going to need to get the body down to the car without anybody seeing us...in the middle of the city."

"There's a back alley. The basement leads out to it."

"Perfect. We might just have some small chance of pulling this off."

They drove in silence for a few minutes before they arrived at the apartment building on Würzburger Strasse. Seamus pulled up on the corner to survey the quiet, deserted street. A light rain continued, which would be helpful to keep people indoors, but less advantageous when they had to bury Milch in the forest. The café opposite was closed. A man walked past, smoking a cigarette, seemingly oblivious to their presence. Had anyone seen her coming out of the apartment? He eyed the side street that must lead to the back alley Lisa mentioned.

"I'm going to have to go back inside to open the basement," Lisa said. "Pull the car down the alley."

Seamus nodded. "Good luck," he said as she got out of the car.

"Thanks. I love you."

"I love you too," he said.

She made for the front door of the apartment. He watched her as she went inside.

He was all she had, and the only thing standing in the way of Lisa losing her daughter forever, or maybe even facing the axman. If what Lisa said was true and Milch was obsessed with keeping their meetings secret, they might just have a chance of getting away with this...provided they could get the body down the stairs and into the back of the car without anyone noticing.

He started up the car and drove into the alley behind the apartment building, stopping outside the basement door. It was just after eleven o'clock, and there was no one around. Only a few lights through translucent windows reminded him there was anyone close by. Most of the buildings on the block were businesses and had closed their doors hours before. As long as they were gone by dawn, they had a good chance of getting him out. Then they'd have to bury him in the forest outside the city.

He turned off the car and waited for Lisa. What was he getting his kids into? They couldn't afford to lose him too. He blocked thoughts of getting caught out of his mind. Lisa had no choice in what she did. He wasn't going to lose another love.

Should he marry Lisa and take her and the kids back to America? Nothing awaited them there. They could barely afford the passage home. Helga would get the factory, and he wouldn't be able to keep his promise to Helmut. America offered nothing but poverty and failure. The notion of The Land of Opportunity held nothing but bitter irony for him. No, they'd deal with the situation and get on with their lives. With Milch gone, Lisa would be free of the noose around her neck all these years.

The basement door opened and Lisa's face appeared through the inky darkness. She beckoned him inside with a wordless gesture. He got out. His heart was thundering as he closed the car door behind him and followed her into the basement. The single bare lightbulb that lit it cast ghostly shadows on the walls. It was almost empty—nothing but a few boxes and an old bicycle that looked like it hadn't been ridden since the days of the Kaiser.

This would do. The distance from the door to the car wasn't

more than a few yards. Getting Milch from the basement into the trunk should only take a matter of seconds. Reinvigorated, Seamus followed her up the stairwell and extinguished the light Lisa left on for him. He steeled himself for what was to come: For what he was about to see and what they would have to do. Lisa's pace slowed as they reached the top of the stairs. She turned to him at the door.

"I know you don't want to go back in there, but the decisions we make in the next few minutes and hours are going to shape the rest of your life."

His words seemed to have the desired effect. She nodded her head. "You're right. Let's do this."

She took a key from her pocket and opened the door. He followed her through. The lights were off and she flicked them on. He had seen death many times during the war, but never like this. Milch was lying on his back beside the couch. His eyes were open, staring into nothing. His face was splattered with blood, his neck a gory mess. The crimson pool around him extended out two feet or more, saturating the rug. Seamus averted his eyes, trying to think, but Lisa already had the next move figured out.

"Help me get him onto the rug," Lisa said.

"Put these on," Seamus said and handed her a pair of gloves.

"Why?"

"So they can't trace us by our fingerprints. We'll have to clean every inch of this place to eliminate any trace we were ever here. Is the bed..."

"Used? No. I couldn't do that."

"Ok. Let's deal with him first."

Lisa took his arms and Seamus his legs and they heaved him onto the rug. Seamus took one end of it and rolled it up to cocoon Milch's corpse inside. It was some comfort not to have to see the man's eyes again. Seamus took the newspaper on the coffee table and laid it out on the floor by the door. Lisa helped him pick up the rolled-up rug with Milch's body inside and place it on the papers by the door.

She went to the kitchen and came back with washing powder, sponges, cloths, and several bars of soap.

They didn't talk much as they worked, cleaning every surface, every glass. They mopped the floor and tidied the kitchen, all while Milch lay enshrouded in the rolled-up rug on the hardwood floor. Seamus was thankful for the lack of carpeting in the apartment. That would have been near impossible to clean.

They scrubbed for hours. It was after three in the morning when they finished. They stood back to survey their work for a few moments without saying a word. Würzburger Strasse was still silent outside. The apartment was in showroom condition. All that remained to do was to dispose of Milch's body.

Seamus went to the car and opened the trunk. He left it and the basement door open as he made his way up the stairs to where Lisa was waiting for him. He felt like he should say something as they picked up the dead weight of Milch's body, but didn't. All he wanted was to get this nightmare behind them.

Lisa was struggling with the weight of Milch's corpse. Seamus moved his hands to bear more of the load. The rug they shrouded him in protected them from the now-almost-dried bloodstains, but he still felt his hands getting wet. They moved through the door and down the stairs, taking plenty of time to negotiate each step. Lisa went first, with Seamus behind her. They reached the bottom of the stairs when they heard a coarse voice in the dark.

"Do you want a hand with that?"

Lisa whirled around, only just managing to keep her hands on the carpet. Seamus felt his heart drop. He had to squint to make out the figure sitting in the darkness of the basement. Seeing him was difficult, but smelling him was not. The stench was almost overpowering. The man had a thick shaggy beard and seemed to be dressed in a soldier's over-coat, like most of the homeless that littered Berlin's streets who still wore the clothing they kept since the war. Many of them were hideously crippled. This man wore a patch over his right eye. The skin on his face was rippled and scarred, only partially obscured by his beard. The right sleeve of his coat was empty, his arm gone. Apparently, there was little sympathy or gratitude for those who had served the Kaiser's ambitions. The stairwell was dark. Seamus wondered if the beggar could make out the dark stains on the rug in the half-light.

"You shouldn't be here," Seamus said. His tone was friendly, but carried enough authority to get the man's attention.

"I've nowhere else to go. I'm just looking for somewhere to spend the night."

Thoughts crisscrossed Seamus's mind like flaming arrows. He and Lisa were stopped near the bottom of the stairs, and his arms were beginning to ache. How lucid was this man? Was he drunk right now? Seamus motioned for Lisa to negotiate the last two steps to the floor. How to get rid of this man? He didn't dare mention the threat of the police.

"You can't stay here," Lisa said. "This is private property."

Seamus set down the rug with Milch's body in it, hoping it wouldn't burst open. He reached into his pocket for his wallet. He held out a few banknotes. "Find yourself a hostel for tonight, and the next few."

The man reached forward for the money. He took it without a word. "It'd be nice to be able to afford breakfast tomorrow morning too."

"I need you to leave now," Seamus said. "I'll walk you out."

He shepherded the man out the door and toward the street. Neither said a word. Seamus waited a few minutes to make sure the homeless man wasn't coming back before returning to the basement.

"Is he gone?" Lisa asked. Seamus nodded his head. "Do you think he realized what we were doing?"

"I really don't know. It's dark down here, and he reeked of whiskey. I'm sure he sees things on the streets every night that would make our hair stand on end. We can't waste time worrying about him right now."

He went to the alley to make sure there were no other prying eyes. There was nothing and no one. He and Lisa brought Milch's body out to the car and loaded it into the trunk. Lisa went back upstairs to lock the apartment as Seamus waited.

A couple of anxious minutes passed before she returned. They departed the scene of the crime in silence. He didn't know the way so she directed him out of the city. The streets were all but empty. They didn't see more than ten cars in the time they drove. They didn't speak much. What was there to say?

They found a place in the forest about 20 minutes after they left the last of the city behind. The night was thick all around them as he pulled off the dirt road. They lifted the body out of the trunk and carried it deep into the thicket until all signs of humankind disappeared. The woods were deep and almost impenetrable around them when Seamus found the spot to dig the hole. They set up the flashlights on rocks and plunged the shovels into the soft ground. They worked in silence. It took them more than an hour to dig deep enough, and then they dropped Milch into it. Lisa threw in her blood-soaked sweater, covering herself with her coat as they worked to shovel the dirt on top of him.

"This wasn't the way I ever wanted it to be," Lisa said as they stood over the grave. "His wife and children will never know."

"They'll be better off without him. The world will be."

He sank his shovel into the pile of dirt they made and

emptied it on top of Ernst Milch's body. He was covered over in minutes, and they walked back to the car to drive back into the city.

"I'm quitting my job at the club," she said.

"No. Don't do anything out of the ordinary. We ride this out, together. Did Milch have any other women he used to see?"

"I don't know."

"I'll bet he did. They'll be pleased not to ever have to hear from him again. His wife will probably report him missing tomorrow. As long as no one can link him to that apartment, the police will be none the wiser, and without a body, the case will fade out and die."

He reached out and took her hand. It was cold as marble. "We'll get through this together." The woods faded into the darkness behind them. He understood that what they'd done, and that the secret they now shared would bind them closer than any marriage ceremony ever could.

13

Tuesday, November 28, 1932

Seamus was at work on a Tuesday morning, 13 days after they buried Milch, when the phone call came. A feeling of unease had settled within him since Milch's death. It sat in the pit of his stomach like a stone. Impending doom seemed to lurk in every dark corner. The only comfort he found was in distraction, whether that was work or the children.

Maureen and Michael must have noticed his nervous behavior, and certainly the fact that he arrived home at sunrise the morning after he and Lisa returned from the woods. They didn't mention anything about it, but the looks that Maureen gave him the next day hid nothing. She had heard him coming in. She and the others were up for school soon after. They knew something.

The visions of the blood-soaked rug haunted his nightmares and he woke up sweating several times since. Only Lisa beside him in his bed was comfort in those moments. Alone in the bed, he was defenseless. It was like the nights after the war, when Marie had been the one to hold him as he jolted awake.

There had been nothing from the police. Not yet. The story about the Army officer turned Nazi Party member who disappeared showed up in the paper three days after they buried him. Rumors abounded that the Communists were behind his disappearance, but no one other than the most ardent Nazis seriously believed them. The police certainly didn't. Clayton, at the house the previous night, referred to the rumors as nonsense. No evidence suggested that Communists or anyone else had taken Milch. The man had just upped and disappeared like smoke in the wind.

The sound of the phone on his desk jarred him from his thoughts. He was glad to have something else to focus on and reached for the receiver. Helga was crying, and Seamus, knowing something was wrong, felt his heart drop.

"It's Father," she said, struggling to get the words out. "He died."

Darkness seemed to cloud Seamus's vision, and grief choked him so he could hardly speak. "What? No. What happened?"

"I went to the house this morning to have breakfast with him before work, as we do every Tuesday. He was still in his bed. The doctors think it was a heart attack brought on by his condition."

"I'm so sorry about your father, Helga."

"I can't believe he's gone."

They spoke for another minute or so before he hung up. He went to Bernheim, who couldn't hold back his tears. Seamus gave him a few moments to compose himself before the two men went to the staff. They turned off the machines and stood below to listen. The men and women Helmut had made him promise to protect looked up at him as he began.

"I'm so sorry to tell you that Herr Ritter has died." A gasp rose from the crowd. Several women began to cry. A few men hugged each other. "Helga found him in his bed this morning."

Seamus felt Bernheim's hand on his shoulder as he continued. "I want to assure you that even in this saddest of times, you can be safe in the knowledge that your jobs are secure and that the factory will go on. My uncle brought me over from America for this very eventuality, and now that it's here, you have our word that we won't let you down. But for today, please leave the machines off. Go home and be with your families. Today we mourn a great man, to whom we all owe a massive debt."

~

The funeral was five days later. Seamus sat in the front row of the church with the children beside him. He held Fiona tight to him as she cried for most of the ceremony. Maureen, Michael, and Conor sat in their best clothes, glum-faced and mournful. They only knew him for a few weeks, but he illuminated their lives with his gregarious smile in that short time. He changed everything for them. No one would ever do more for their family.

Every worker from the factory came, their families in tow. Helmut would have reveled in the sounds of babies crying and calling out during his funeral. He was always more comfortable at a party. Helga sat beside Seamus, dressed head to toe in black. Seamus reached over to her and took her hand. She smiled back at him and then refocused her gaze on her father's casket. It was draped in flowers, with a bag of cards and letters from the workers on top of it, just as Helmut would have wanted.

The church was so packed that people were standing outside to pay their respects. Seamus remembered his promise to his uncle as he looked back at the workers in the pews behind him. Andrei Salnikov sat two rows back with his pretty wife and

three-year-old daughter. He nodded at Seamus, who returned
the gesture before turning around to face front once more.

~

Seamus and Helga went to Helmut's lawyer's office for the
reading of the will two days later. They hugged as they met
outside the office. Helga stopped him as he went to walk inside.
They stood on the street on Potsdamer Platz, people passing
them on each side.

"I already know what's in the will," she said. "Father went
through it with me when he updated it two weeks ago."

"He updated it that recently?"

"He wanted to see you at work in the factory before he
wrote you into it. I don't suppose he wanted to leave anything to
chance. He's going to split it between us fifty-fifty." Seamus
nodded. "He's going to leave his cash and other assets to me,
but he wanted you to have the house."

"He's leaving me the house?"

"He always wanted to fill it with children. This is the chance
he was waiting for."

"Are you ok with that?"

"I have my own house. I don't want that monstrosity."

Seamus shook his head, barely able to believe what he was
hearing. "I'm looking forward to being your partner." He shook
her hand. She smiled and they went inside.

~

Tuesday, December 6, 1932

A week passed. The feverish dreams Lisa had every night since
Milch's death began to subside to the point where some unin-

terrupted sleep was possible now. Her tormentor's name had disappeared from the headlines. The mystery of his disappearance was marked as unsolved, but she knew his family wasn't going to give up. She longed for the days she and Seamus could relax again, when they didn't feel the noose around their necks. Milch was dead, but she wasn't free. He still had a hold on her. Perhaps he always would.

She thought of the homeless veteran with the eye patch every day. What did he see? They had tried not to talk about it, for they knew it might drive them insane, but it was always there, simmering under the surface, threatening the life they were trying to build together.

The front pages were now focused on Hitler and his Nazi Party once more. There was even talk of Hindenburg appointing him as chancellor. Many business leaders had thrown their support behind him. It seemed like Lazarus was about to rise from the dead once more.

Lisa emerged from the kitchen in Seamus's new house—the mansion his uncle left him. There hadn't been much moving in to do as Seamus didn't have much furniture. The place was almost as Helmut had left it. Seamus had the idea to introduce her to the kids the day they moved in and it went wonderfully. She shared the joy of their dreams coming true in front of her eyes, and saw them each day since.

Maureen and Fiona were on the floor playing with Hannah, making her laugh by pulling silly faces. The two boys were outside playing soccer, and Seamus was in the bathroom when a knock on the door interrupted her thoughts. She went to get it. A small man, about 30 years old, greeted her. He was wearing a brown coat and holding a notepad. Her heart dropped. She tried to hide her feelings, to push them deep down into her belly.

"My name is Detective August Hecker. I got this address

from your mother when I called to your apartment earlier this evening. I have a few questions for you. May I come in?"

"Of course," she said.

He nodded thanks to her and stepped inside. She led him past the living room where the children were still playing and into the kitchen. Seamus arrived back as she was asking him if he wanted something to drink.

"This is Detective Hecker of the Berlin Police," Lisa said.

Seamus stepped forward to shake the man's hand.

"I have a few questions about the recent disappearance of Ernst Milch."

"I read about that in the newspaper," Lisa said. "I thought the Communists were to blame."

"We're still investigating. It's a missing persons case at the moment."

"Perhaps he ran away with his mistress?"

"We're not discounting anything," Hecker said. "I'll have a cup of coffee, please."

Lisa went to the sideboard and put the kettle on. Seamus offered Hecker a chair, and the two men sat down at the kitchen table.

"You mind if I smoke?" the young detective said.

"Only if I can join you," Seamus answered and placed a packet of cigarettes on the table. The policeman smiled and used the lighter Seamus gave him.

"What brings you here tonight, Detective Hecker?" Lisa asked as she poured the coffee. She turned her body so he couldn't see her hands shaking. Seamus seemed as relaxed as he would be sitting down with a friend to chat.

"I heard Herr Milch used to patronize the club where you work, and my inquiries there led me to you."

"I can't think why," Lisa said and brought cups of coffee for all three of them to the table. She sat down on the other side of the table from Hecker, concealing her hands underneath. She wished she could speak to Seamus, but they prepared for this. They had already agreed on what to say when this eventuality came to pass.

She wondered if the children were listening in. They knew nothing and never could. Seamus deflected their questions about why he'd been out all night until they stopped asking.

Hecker took a sip of his coffee. "What was your relationship with Herr Milch?" He reached into his jacket pocket for a brown envelope, which he left on the table.

"I barely knew him."

"Do you recall this night?" Hecker said and pushed a photograph he took from the envelope across the table.

The photo was of her and Milch at the club. She was dressed in full stage gear, sitting on his lap. Both were smiling for the camera.

"I met him a few times when he came to the club, but that was years ago. I haven't seen him in a long time."

Could he tell she was lying? This man was trained to spot liars. She reached down for her mug of coffee. It felt good in her hands.

"There were reports that you had a close relationship with Herr Milch."

Anger flared within her as she considered who might have told Hecker about her and Milch. How much had they said? How much could they have known? Milch was always discreet —the photograph on the table aside.

"We were friends for a while, but you must understand, Detective, that's my job. Men come to the club looking for friendship, and we're expected to provide them with that. We work the crowd every night. It's part of what we do. I've met hundreds of men like Herr Milch this year. To say I knew each one of them would be ridiculous."

"But you do remember Herr Milch?"

"He was a regular for a while, and as I'm sure you heard, he latched on to me. Some men get ideas of what we girls might do for them. They get above their station, so to speak."

"Do any of the girls provide other services for the men who come in?"

"Some. Not me."

"I hope you won't think me impertinent, but I need to follow every line of inquiry."

"Of course."

"Do you remember any of the other women at the club being close to Herr Milch?"

"No. I don't recall any being especially friendly with him."

"Would you say you knew him the best?"

"Perhaps, but as I said, he was one of hundreds."

"I'm sure you have your fair share of lecherous men in the nightclub," Hecker said.

"It isn't something I like to think of," Seamus said.

"Where did you two meet?" Hecker asked.

"The nightclub," Seamus said. All three smiled.

"Do you know anything about the disappearance of Ernst Milch?"

"Nothing," she said. Lying became easier with practice. "If I hear of anything, I'll be sure to let you know."

"Where were you on the night of November 15?"

"I was with Seamus, in his old house."

"All night?"

"Yes," Seamus said.

"My mother was home looking after Hannah. I returned to the apartment we share the next morning."

"Very well," Hecker said and stood up. "I'm sorry to have taken up your time. Thank you for your hospitality."

"You're welcome," Seamus said. "I hope Herr Milch shows up alive and well soon."

"We all do," Hecker said and shook their hands once more.

Lisa felt the muscles in her chest loosen. They were going to get through this. Hecker put his hat on as they strolled through the living room toward the front door.

"One more thing," he said. "May I have a word with your oldest daughter?"

Lisa's heart froze. Seamus tried to hide his panic, but she could see it in his eyes. "Is that really necessary?" Seamus said. "I don't want to bring the children into this."

"It'll only take a few seconds. We can do it here in the comfort of your own home, or I can take her down to the station. It's up to you."

"Ok, but I want to be there when you talk to her," Seamus said.

"That's fine. It's only going take a few seconds," Hecker said.

Seamus called Maureen into the hallway that led to the front door. She lifted her head from the book she was reading and pushed herself off the armchair. The three adults were standing waiting for her as she arrived. Seamus introduced the policeman to her.

"Pleased to meet you, young lady," he said.

She reciprocated, waiting for the questions she knew were to come.

"I'll keep this simple. I don't want to keep you from your book. Where were Lisa and your father the night of Wednesday, November 15th?"

"They were in our old house together," she said. "That was the first night I met her. I went to bed around nine thirty. That was the last I saw of them. I don't know how long they were up for after that." There was no hesitation in her voice. She looked him directly in the eye as she spoke.

"That's all I needed," the detective said. He thanked them for their time once more and let himself out the front door. Maureen turned and walked away without another word.

It took a few minutes for Seamus to calm Lisa down. He left her at the kitchen table, his assurances that they were going to be all right seemingly having the desired effect at last. He went to the living room. The other children were still playing as if they hadn't a care in the world. The boys had come in from the back yard. Maureen was nowhere to be found. Seamus went to her bedroom door and knocked.

"I don't want to see you," she said in English.

"Please. I need to talk to you."

A few seconds passed before he heard the sound of footsteps and then of the key turning in the lock. He pushed the door open. Maureen was standing there with her arms folded. Her eyes were red.

"The police, Father? You brought the police here? When is this going to end?"

"I'm sure that's the last we'll see of Detective Hecker. It was just a routine round of questioning."

He was doing it again—lying to her. But how could he tell her the truth? Lisa was defending herself. Better Milch was dead than her. There could be no stronger justification than that. He longed to tell Maureen. He wanted to tell her everything but knew he never could. Perhaps that was the true agony of being a parent—bearing the full weight of pain to protect the ones you love.

"You were out all that night. And Lisa showed up here out of nowhere."

"Yes. I wanted to thank you for what you said. It would have led to a nasty round of questioning—"

"And it's only coincidence you were gone the whole night that man disappeared?"

Seamus felt like he was in quicksand. "Of course it is, my sweet." The truth was on the tip of his tongue.

"I heard you talking to the detective in the kitchen and I said what I knew I had to. I didn't lie to that policeman for you.

I did it for the family, and for what we're trying to build. I haven't seen you the way you are with Lisa since Mother died. I haven't seen you happy. I lied to the detective to preserve what we have. I did it for Michael and Fiona and Conor, and Hannah."

"Thank you, Maureen," he said, holding in the tears. "Sometimes I feel like I don't deserve you."

"Earn this," she said. "And don't ever make me have to lie for you again."

The temptation to tell her everything passed. He was the father. He'd bear the brunt for her and the other children. He'd carry the weight of the secrets that could never be shared. He closed the door.

EPILOGUE

Thursday December 29, 1932

C hristmas came and went. Spending the time with his children, being there to see them open their gifts in their new house, was a joy beyond measure. He only hoped the new year would bring forgiveness from Maureen.

They hadn't heard from Detective Hecker or any of his colleagues since. Ernst Milch was forgotten. Even the rumors about his abduction by the Communists faded. Only the trauma of what they were forced to do remained. Seamus still saw Milch's bloody corpse most nights. He and Lisa talked about what had happened in private moments, more as a form of therapy than anything else.

She, Hannah, and her mother were living with them full-time now. Ingrid was kind to the children and helped out a lot. He knew that where Lisa went, she did also, so he accepted her as part of the package. Seeing Lisa every day awakened a happiness in him he thought he could never feel again. Their home was flawed, and in some ways dysfunctional, but crammed with love.

The children seemed settled in school and were making friends. Michael and Conor had taken to spending time in the woods nearby with the boys from the street and came back with dirty knees and smiles. Fiona adored Hannah and spent most of her free time fawning over her. Lisa taught Maureen how to do her makeup and took her shopping most weekends.

He looked at his watch. Maureen and Ingrid were watching the children. It was a far more fruitful combination than Lisa or Seamus ever thought it would be, as her mother seemed to revel in the family atmosphere. Lisa said she hadn't seen her so happy since before the boys went to the Western Front. Digging ditches in Ohio seemed like a lifetime ago.

Lisa had her arm in his as they strolled through the Christmas market, past tents and trees decorated with silver garlands and all manner of lights. They stopped to look at some toys—now cut-price as the season was coming to an end. They decided the children had enough and strolled on to the next stand, where they lined up to buy honey cake. Seamus finished his first, hoping that Lisa wouldn't want all of hers. He was disappointed when she ate every last crumb. She knew it and laughed. He threw his scarf around his face in faux anger and stormed forward a few steps, only turning around as he heard her laugh. She caught up to him and took his arm again.

"So, are you going to ask me to marry you or not?" she said.

He stopped walking and let go of her arm. "I was planning—"

"I'm ready for you to ask me now. I don't want to wait any longer."

"I don't have a ring."

"I don't care."

She was staring up at him with those beautiful brown eyes.

He took her hand. "Lisa, would you do me the honor of being my wife?"

"You already know the answer, don't you?"

"I want you to say it," he said with a beaming smile.

"I do. I mean, I will. Yes."

He took her in his arms and they kissed. His scarf fell to the ground. Someone in the crowd who heard the proposal called out and started to applaud. Several other passersby joined in, and soon they were surrounded by smiling faces. They broke their embrace to receive the congratulations of a dozen Berliners.

The clouds covering the night sky cleared to reveal a ghostly white moon. He watched it shimmer in her chestnut-brown eyes before embracing her once again. The crowd around them dissipated and moved on, smiles still fixed on their faces, but Lisa and Seamus stood still long after they left.

The End

The next installment in the Lion's Den Series— A NEW DAWN —is coming in January 2022.

I hope you enjoyed my book. Head over to www.eoindempseybooks.com to sign up for my readers' club. It's free and always will be. If you want to get in touch with me send an email to eoin@eoindempseybooks.com. I love hearing from readers so don't be a stranger!

Reviews are life-blood to authors these days. If you enjoyed the book and can spare a minute please leave a review on Amazon. My loyal and committed readers have put where I am today. Their honest reviews have brought my books to the attention of other readers. I'd be eternally grateful if you could leave a review. It can be short as you like.

ACKNOWLEDGMENTS

I'm incredibly grateful to my regular crew, my sister, Orla, my brother Brian, my mother, and especially to my brother Conor who went above and beyond. Thanks to my fantastic editors. Massive thanks to my beta readers, Kevin Hall, Vickie Martin, Karen Ott, Sabrina Hilpert, Frank Callahan, Lori Jones and so many others I don't have space to mention here. And as always, thanks to my beautiful wife, Jill and our three crazy little boys, Robbie, Sam and Jack.

ALSO BY EOIN DEMPSEY